DANCE TO YO

Gladys Maude Winifred Mitchell – or 'The Great Gladys' as Philip Larkin called her – was born in 1901, in Cowley in Oxfordshire. She graduated in history from University College London and in 1921 began her long career as a teacher. She studied the works of Sigmund Freud and attributed her interest in witchcraft to the influence of her friend, the detective novelist Helen Simpson.

Her first novel, *Speedy Death*, was published in 1929 and introduced readers to Beatrice Adela Lestrange Bradley, the heroine of a further sixty six crime novels. She wrote at least one novel a year throughout her career and was an early member of the Detection Club, alongside Agatha Christie, G.K Chesterton and Dorothy Sayers. In 1961 she retired from teaching and, from her home in Dorset, continued to write, receiving the Crime Writers' Association Silver Dagger in 1976. Gladys Mitchell died in 1983.

VINTAGE MURDER MYSTERIES

With the sign of a human skull upon its back and a melancholy shriek emitted when disturbed, the Death's Head Hawkmoth has for centuries been a bringer of doom and an omen of death - which is why we chose it as the emblem for our Vintage Murder Mysteries.

Some say that its appearance in King George III's bedchamber pushed him into madness. Others believe that should its wings extinguish a candle by night, those nearby will be cursed with blindness. Indeed its very name, *Acherontia atropos*, delves into the most sinister realms of Greek mythology: Acheron, the River of Pain in the underworld, and Atropos, the Fate charged with severing the thread of life.

The perfect companion, then, for our Vintage Murder Mysteries sleuths, for whom sinister occurrences are never far away and murder is always just around the corner …

GLADYS MITCHELL

Dance to your Daddy

VINTAGE BOOKS
London

First published in Great Britain by
Michael Joseph Ltd in 1969

Vintage
Random House, 20 Vauxhall Bridge Road,
London SW1V 2SA

www.vintage-books.co.uk

Addresses for companies within The Random House Group Limited
can be found at: www.randomhouse.co.uk/offices.htm

The Random House Group Limited Reg. No. 954009

A CIP catalogue record for this book
is available from the British Library

ISBN 9780099583875

The Random House Group Limited supports The Forest Stewardship
Council® (FSC®), the leading international forest-certification organisation.
Our books carrying the FSC label are printed on FSC®-certified paper.
FSC is the only forest-certification scheme supported by the leading
environmental organisations, including Greenpeace. Our
paper procurement policy can be found at
www.randomhouse.co.uk/environment

Printed and bound in Great Britain by Clays Ltd, St Ives plc

CHAPTER ONE

Galliarde—Heartless House

'...unmannerly modest as a measure, full of state
and ancientry.'

Measure for Measure.

---

(1)

Eiladh Beatrice Margaret Gavin, having put her fist in the
minister's eye, submitted with placid fatalism to the ceremony of
baptism. She was a happy baby and, since happiness has no
history, she passes, for the purposes of the chronicler, into almost
total obscurity.

'Well, that's that,' observed Laura, her mother, when the
cortège had returned to the Stone House in the village of
Wandles Parva, 'and now it's time I got back to work.'

'I may not need you yet,' said Dame Beatrice Adela Lestrange
Bradley, who employed her as secretary and treated her as a
favourite daughter. 'I am invited to pay a visit of indefinite length
to a certain Romilly Lestrange, who claims to be a distant
connection of mine by marriage. He lives, it seems, at a place
called Galliard Hall.'

'Romily? You haven't mentioned him before, have you?'

'For the sufficient reason that, until I received his letter, I was
unaware of his existence.'

'Funny he should suddenly pop up out of a trap. I'd give him a
two-eyed look, if I were you.'

'He has offered me a commission on top of the invitation. It
appears that he has been extremely worried lately by the strange
behaviour of his wife.'

'What does she do? – make spells and incantations? – dance
naked on the greensward by the lee light of the moon?'

'He says that she has contracted a habit of drowning
things.'

'*Drowning* things?'

'She began with a toy trumpet and followed this by consigning to the deep a transistor radio set and a dozen gramophone records.'

'Not a music lover, wouldn't you say?'

'I might leave it at that, if she had not continued by drowning, at intervals of nine months, a small cat, a pet monkey and a life-sized baby doll.'

'Well, there seems to be an obvious explanation. Either her husband won't give her a baby, or else she's had a miscarriage.'

'You mean she has aborted. Justice may miscarry; human beings do not.'

'Just as you say.'

'We must remember, however, that, in her journal, Marie Bashkirtseff informs us that on one occasion she felt impelled to throw the dining-room clock into the sea. I have the impression that, at the time, Marie was unmarried and, most probably, therefore, according to the fashion of the age, a virgin.'

'Oh, just an anti-mother complex, no doubt. I expect her action relieved her mind of all sorts of inhibitions and frustrations. Mrs Romilly has a different set of worries, that's all.'

'Worries – yes,' said Dame Beatrice thoughtfully.

'If this Romilly is a relative of yours,' said Laura, 'I think I had better write him our official letter before you go and see him. Relations always think they're entitled to get something for nothing.'

The so-called official letter was Laura's own invention and she was proud of it. It did nothing so crude as to give a scale of charges, or even to state, in unequivocal terms, that Dame Beatrice's services had to be paid for; nevertheless, people who received it, signed *L. Catriona Gavin, Secretary*, had no reason to be unaware that they were to expect a far from moderate bill. What was more, without reference to Dame Beatrice, Laura was always prepared to chase up any laggards. As she herself expressed it to her husband (although not to Dame Beatrice), 'There's always the State. If they're choosy, and want *us*, they've got to pay through the nose.'

'Oh,' said Laura's employer, on this occasion, 'there is no need for an official letter. I have accepted the invitation, and am off to Galliard Hall tomorrow afternoon.'

'Galliard Hall?' said Laura. 'Didn't somebody commit suicide there, or something, a few years back? The place was up for sale and the owner kept reducing the price, so I heard, because nobody would buy.'

'Because of the suicide?' asked Laura's husband, Assistant Commissioner Robert Gavin.

'I suppose so. Besides, it's an enormous old barracks of a place. I can't think who'd buy it.'

'My relative has either bought it or rented it, it seems,' said Dame Beatrice. 'Romilly? Romilly? It sounds the kind of name by which a male Lestrange would very likely be called, but I cannot say that it strikes any other chord. However, a family tree has many branches.'

'What was all that about the girl who chucked the dining-room clock into the sea?' asked Gavin.

'Clocks, so I understand,' said Laura's son Hamish, who was holding his baby sister in hickory-tough young arms, 'are thought, in morbid psychology, to symbolise the female cycle of . . .'

'Not in front of the child,' said his father, hastily. 'Chuck the brat over here. They talk about bouncing babies. Let's see if this one does.'

(2)

'Well,' said Laura, on the following afternoon, 'if Mrs. Romilly asks you to go swimming with her, find some cast-iron excuse.' They had finished lunch, the car had been ordered round to the front of the Stone House, and Dame Beatrice was about to set out for Galliard Hall.

'It is scarcely the right time of year for sea-bathing, and, in any case, I am not as fond of strenuous personal aquatics as you are,' she observed, 'so you may spare yourself all anxiety on my behalf.' She entered the car and waved her hand as it moved off down the drive; then she settled her small, spare elderly body comfortably against the upholstery, and as the car moved on to the New Forest road which linked Ringwood with Burley, she gazed out of the window at the passing scenery.

The vast stretches of Forest pasture on the common near her home gave way to woods and then to what seemed to be a limitless expanse of undulating country covered in brown bracken with a wayside edge of rough grass, broken by still and shining ponds and stretches of gorse and withered heather.

The road was a minor one until it merged, at Picket Post, with the highway between Ringwood and Romsey. The car swung off to the left, skirted most of the town and then, speeding up, made for Wimborne. Here a one-way street took a tour round the two-towered minster and then went left again at insignificant cross-roads and over an ancient bridge.

Up a long and winding hill and through a long, dull village ran the road, then it dipped past a farm and alongside a tree-bowered estate until, at a major roundabout, it dropped sharply south-west to Wareham.

After Wareham, with its defensive earthworks, its Saxon church-on-the-wall, its prominent priory church of Lady St Mary, its river and its flooded, riverside meadows (for the time was late February, a few days away from March), the scenery changed. The road wound on towards the Purbecks and across the moors of Slepe, Middlebere and Creech. Corfe Castle, a stark, defiant shell, reared itself, frowning, on the mound which bridged the only gap in the range. The road skirted skittishly round it.

One stone-built village followed another, once Corfe was passed, and then, at last, there was nothing to be seen but the clean and lovely lines of the rounded hills. Suddenly, from a valley which dropped to sea-level on the south, a magnificent headland shouldered into the sky and a flat, wide, sea-lapped moorland stretched away into the distance.

The road soon divided a large, partly-timbered estate into two unequal parks, and on the lesser of these, backed and sheltered by the hills, lay, at the end of a sloping drive, an impressive, intimidating mansion.

'I think we're here, madam,' said George. They had arrived at Galliard Hall.

The house belonged to the early years of the Stuart dynasty, having been built in about the year 1610. The front entrance faced north, and two gabled wings had Jacobean bay windows with the mullions and transomes of the period. It was clear that successive owners had done little to alter the original façade. It was equally obvious that this had begun to crumble, and the whole place, including the unweeded, untended drive and the cracked and broken steps which mounted in two flights to an ornate but battered front archway, gave an overall impression of poverty, neglect and decay.

George drew up in front of the terrace. At the top of the steps an elderly man, whom Dame Beatrice took to be her host, was waiting to receive her. Behind him, and a little to one side, were another elderly man wearing a green baize apron and, in the doorway itself, a couple of youthful maidservants.

The first elderly man seized Dame Beatrice by her thin shoulders and kissed her rapidly on both cheeks. The second elderly man went gingerly down the worn steps to help George with the luggage. The maidservants stood aside, curtsied, and followed their master and the visitor into the house. Dame Beatrice found herself in the great hall, a magnificent room with windows looking towards the drive, a heavy brass chandelier hanging from the middle of the ceiling and two carved figures, two-thirds life-size, standing at either end of the mantelpiece. There was a gilt-framed Corot on the chimney-breast between them. There were other pictures around the walls. Dame Beatrice thought she recognised a Lely and a Raeburn among them.

The floor was uncarpeted and was of black and white tiles, each a foot square. At some time the floor of the room above had been cut away and a balustered gallery substituted, giving the great hall height and light appropriate to its size. It was all extremely impressive and, after the dilapidated appearance of the exterior of the house, considerably surprising, for the interior seemed beautifully kept and maintained.

'You will like to go straight to your room,' said the host. 'Amabel will show you the way.' The older of the two girls took Dame Beatrice up a splendid, broad, oak staircase, which had finely-carved and pierced panels in place of the usual balusters, and three flights of nine treads each. These, with right-angle turns, led to the gallery which Dame Beatrice had seen from below. From this she was shown to her room, which opened off it.

Heavy plasterwork covered the ceiling with scrolls, cupids and flowers. The bed was a magnificent four-poster and the walls were hung with tapestries depicting young men and maidens of the eighteenth-century for ever (or until the tapestry fell to pieces) at dalliance in summer woodlands. Dame Beatrice murmured a line or two from Keats and received from the maid the information that there would be tea in the drawing-room as soon as she was ready for it, and that the bathroom was two doors along to the left.

'Would that be poertry loike, as ee was sayen, m'lady?' she concluded respectfully.*

'*Ode on a Grecian Urn*,' Dame Beatrice replied.

" 'Ah, happy, happy boughs! that cannot shed
   Your leaves, nor ever bid the Spring adieu.' "

'Oi loikes poertry. Tes a koind o' wetchcraft, Oi rackon.'

'How right you are, Amabel. It *is* Amabel, isn't it?'

'Yes, thank you, m'lady. Oi've put ee a can of hot water in the barthroom. There eddn't nothen laid on. You tells me what toime you warnts your barth and Oi sees to getten et for ee. Tes best in the marnen, ef that suit ee.'

'Excellent. How do I find the drawing-room, where I believe I am to have tea?'

'Down the stairs, through the hall, turn left into the doinen room and left again through the arch.'

In the drawing-room Dame Beatrice found a young woman of striking appearance, black-haired, red-cheeked and bold-eyed, in charge of two tea-pots. Of her elderly host there was no sign. The young woman gave her a brilliant smile and said, 'Hullo! In case you think I'm Trilby, well, I'm not. Do you prefer Ceylon or Indian tea?'

'Ceylon, thank you,' said Dame Beatrice, seating herself. 'I have to confess that, except as the title of a book which I have not read for many years, the name Trilby means nothing to me.'

'Uncle Romilly's wife. Isn't that the girl you've come to see?'

'I believe it is, but I was not told her Christian name.'

'Christian indeed! – Bread and butter or a toasted tea-cake? – A limb of Satan, if you ask *me!* The dance she's led poor Uncle Romilly these last few months!'

'Suitably so, perhaps, in a house named Galliard Hall.'

'It isn't any joke, believe you me! Poor Uncle Romilly is nearly off his head with worry. There's no piece of wickedness that Trilby can't think up when she's in the mood.'

'I understand that she has a habit of drowning things.'

'That's the *least* part of it. I suppose I shouldn't say such a

*No attempt made to reproduce the local dialect, but merely to suggest country speech. (*Author*)

thing, but the pity is that she hasn't, so far, poor idiot, drowned herself. And now she's invited all these mixed relations to the house, and, of course, as they *are* relations, Uncle Romilly can't exactly say he doesn't want them.'

'I wonder what you mean by "mixed" relations?'

'Oh, well, some are hers, you see, and some are his, and I can't *think* what will happen when they all get together.'

'May I ask why you say that?'

'Well, it would seem about as sensible to put the Montagues and the Capulets together in one house as the Lestrange family and the Provosts.'

'I seem to remember that the Montagues and Capulets were reconciled by virtue of the deaths of Romeo and Juliet.'

The young woman gave her a very sharp glance and continued:

'I wanted Uncle Romilly to let them know what is happening, and plan to have them at different times, but Trilby wants them all to come together, and, since she's been so difficult, Uncle Romilly gives in to her over everything. Well, if I'm not very much mistaken, this time there'll be murder done. They'll be at one another's throats from the word *Go*.'

'You do not, of course, speak literally, when you talk of murder being done?'

'Oh, don't I, just! You don't know them as well as I do.'

'I have relatives (of a sort) called Marshall-Provost, but the name Provost, of itself, is strange to me. However, as you probably know, I am a Lestrange myself by my first marriage.'

'Are you? Uncle Romilly didn't tell me that. He said your name was Bradley, but, if you are connected with the Lestrange family, I expect you know some of those who are coming. There are Hubert – he's a parson – Willoughby – he's a private secretary, I believe – the twins Corin and Corinna . . .'

'My late husband, of course, has been dead for many years, and these people would be of a younger generation. I doubt whether I have met any of them.'

'You might know Corin and Corinna. They changed their names when they became pop singers, I believe. As for the Provosts, well, there are Giles and Tancred – *he's* a poet – and, lastly, Humphrey and a girl named Binnie, Humphrey's wife, so she's only a Provost by marriage. I don't know what her maiden name was.'

'At all events, if it comes to a battle, the sides would appear to be well-matched,' suggested Dame Beatrice lightly.

'There is no "if" about it. It *will* come to a battle, if the Provosts run true to form. As it will also come to a matter of no holds barred, I'm not clear where to place my bets. Tancred, as you'd expect, is a *minor* poet – very minor – one slim volume published at his own expense – but he can be a menace, from what Uncle Romilly tells me. I don't know much about Giles, except that he's keen on horses. Humphrey is a master at a third-rate private day-school and Binnie is the original dumb blonde. Quite a nice child, if you don't worry about her having a vacuum where her brain ought to be, but completely moronic, poor dear. The Lestrange twins – you know, those I told you are in show business – take off her and Humphrey in their act. It's terribly funny – not that Humphrey cares much about it, of course. He hates Tancred, too.'

'All you tell me is most interesting. You refer to Romilly Lestrange as your uncle. Are you a Montague or a Capulet?'

'Oh, I've no connection with either the Lestranges or the Provosts. My name is Judith Dean, and I'm Romilly's house-keeper. He likes me to call him my uncle, but, between ourselves, my sugar-daddy would be more like it. After all, Trilby, in her present state, is hardly a wife, so Romilly brought me along to sort of fill the bill. You're not shocked, I hope?'

'Irregular unions are solely the business of the parties concerned, and are now too numerous to be interesting,' said Dame Beatrice. 'When am I to see Mrs. Romilly Lestrange, I wonder? You know, I gather, that she is to be my patient.'

'I shouldn't worry about being in a hurry to see her, if I were you. You'll have had a bucketful by the time you've finished with her,' said the black-haired siren coarsely. 'We've given you Romilly's old room; I hope you like it. Of course, he only rents the house, you know. I don't know how long he'll stay.'

(3)

Dame Beatrice did not see her nominal hostess that afternoon and did not mention her again. Dinner was a *ménage à trois*, with Romilly at the head of the table, Judith (barbarically regal in a flame-coloured dress with a neckline which plunged recklessly to her waist and barely contrived to cover her breasts), seated opposite him at the foot, and Dame Beatrice next to her host on his right-hand side. They were waited upon by the elderly man-servant. He had exchanged the green-baize apron, and the trousers and shirt which went with it, for the black and white livery of a butler. The meal was simple and good and the talk was of local affairs, in which, it appeared, Romilly took a land-owner's interest, however recent this was.

When dinner was over, the three retired to the drawing room to drink coffee, and then Judith played the piano and sang. She had a beautiful contralto voice and it had been well trained. It was dark by the time she began to sing, and candles had been brought in. They filled the room with shadows which flickered and moved, and more than once Dame Beatrice thought that a darker, more substantial shadow, had joined them. She wondered whether the nominal mistress of the house had crept in to enjoy the music.

At ten o'clock Dame Beatrice went to her room and by the light of her candle examined the only picture, apart from the tapestry, which was on the walls. It showed two young men, hardly out of their boyhood, dressed in mid-eighteenth century costume. They were evidently brothers, for they were much alike. She was about to turn from the picture and prepare for bed when there came a tap at the door. 'Come in!' she called. The door opened, and for a moment Dame Beatrice thought she was confronted by Joan of Arc. The figure which entered was clad in a suit of armour from the top of which emerged a flaxen head with page-boy haircut, wide-set eyes and a strangely gentle, expressive, beautifully-shaped mouth. 'You will be Mrs. Romilly Lestrange, no doubt. How do you do?' went on Dame Beatrice, recovering her self-possession.

The girl closed the door quietly and came forward.

'Don't tell them you've seen me,' she said. 'That's a treat they're keeping for tomorrow. I don't know who you are, but but they're up to something. Shine the candle on to your face. I want to see whether you're friend or foe.'

Dame Beatrice complied with this request. The mellow candle-light shone on her yellow skin, her sharp, black eyes, her scrawny, old-woman's throat and turned her diamond necklace into a thousand tiny pools of almost unbearable brilliance.

'Does it matter so much whether I am a Montagu or a Capulet, a Macdonald or a Campbell, a Guelph or a Ghibelline, a Round-head or a Cavalier?' she asked. The girl said solemnly and with conviction:

'It matters whether you're on my side or on theirs, that's all I know. They're as wicked as hell, and, although I try to show fight, I'm pretty helpless here. I don't know how they're going to kill me, but they will.'

'Indeed?' Dame Beatrice studied the speaker. The girl returned her gaze, and said:

'If you decide to help me, you do so at your own risk. It's only right that I should warn you. Who *are* you, anyway? I saw the car drive up, and Amabel told me which was your room, so I've come while they're still downstairs. You don't mind, do you?'

'Not at all,' Dame Beatrice replied. 'Why do you commit your *lares et penates* to the sea?'

The visitor looked perturbed.

'I know they say I drown things,' she said, 'but I don't, you know. I don't get much chance while they make me dress like this, do I? I mean, I can't leave the house. It would look so odd. People would think I was mad.'

'That is a point,' Dame Beatrice admitted. 'Why, though, should anybody want to kill you, or, for the matter of that, keep you confined to the house?'

'Oh, money. Always money. But I'm not going to give in, whatever they do or say. The money is mine when I'm twenty-five, and I'm not going to give it away.'

'Certainly not. One should never give in to bullying.'

'I know, but it takes a lot of courage to stand one's ground. They're having lots of people to come and stay, you know. They hope, that way, to frighten me. But I shall face them, all of them. Some of them might even help me. What do you think? They can't *all* be wicked, can they?' Her voice had risen to a note of panic. Her hearer wondered whether she was play-acting.

'I think I would go to bed, if I were you. We shall meet again in the morning,' said Dame Beatrice.

'Do you think we shall? I am not so sure. They don't like me to meet people from outside. Why did they ask you to come?'

'They thought I might be able to help you.'

'I don't think they meant it. You are in great danger, you know, if you help me in the way I need help.'

'I am accustomed to take care of myself.'

'Are you a relative of this family?'

'Mr Romilly tells me that I am. Let me see you back to your room.'

'Oh, no. I like to keep it to myself. Good night. I hope you will sleep well.'

'Thank you. Good night.'

The visitor did not depart immediately. There were two candles on the dressing-table. She walked across the room, picked up one of them and held it up to light the picture of the two young men.

'How do you like it?' Dame Beatrice asked.

'I'm wondering why they put it there, that's all. It wasn't there before you came. That makes me suspicious, you know.'

'Is your name really Trilby?' Dame Beatrice asked.

'Is that what they told you? You don't need to believe them. It's not a bad name to give me, all the same. Romilly is rather like Svengali, don't you think? Have you heard that song called *Puppet on a String*? Well, that's how I think of myself. Watch out for them. Good night.'

(4)

The maid who had shown Dame Beatrice to her room brought early tea and asked whether she would breakfast in bed.

'What is the household custom? Do visitors usually breakfast in bed?' Dame Beatrice enquired.

'Us don't have visitors, m'lady. Not they as stop the noight. Messus Judeth have hern in bed, but Master, he have hisn downstairs. Only ever had one house-party all the toime Oi been here.'

Thinking that an opportunity for a tête-à-tête with her host might be advisable after last night's visit from his wife, Dame Beatrice said that she would breakfast downstairs.

'In the small doinen-room, m'lady. Oi'll get your barth ready.'

'You should address me as Dame Beatrice. I am not the daughter of a hundred earls, you know, Amabel.'

'Yes, mum. Thank ee, Dame Beatrice. Oi'll tell our Voilert.'

Dame Beatrice found her host already at breakfast. He apologised for having no morning newspaper to offer her.

'I generally drive into one of the villages, or to Wareham or Swanage, to get one,' he said. 'Perhaps you'd care to come with me. There are things I ought to tell you about your patient which can be better said away from the house. Trilby is cunning and sly. It is part of her disability, poor creature, and cannot be helped, but it can be very disconcerting to find her listening to matters not intended for her ears, and watching happenings which do not concern her.'

'I should have thought that some of them *did* concern her,' Dame Beatrice midly remarked.

'Ah, you have been in conversation with Judith,' said Romilly, in a matter-of-fact tone. 'Trilby knows nothing of *that* relationship, I hope. To her, Judith is the housekeeper, nothing more.'

'Yesterday at tea-time your housekeeper mentioned that you are expecting a houseful of guests. I need not explain that I could hardly hope to do much for my patient in the midst of an exciting house-party.'

'Oh, the house-party won't be exciting and will have nothing to do with Trilby.'

'She can scarcely fail to be aware that the number of people here has been considerably increased.'

'Judith talks too much,' said Romilly. 'Well, while you are finishing your breakfast, I will go and get my car out of the garage and bring it round to the front of the house.'

'If you are going to tell me about your wife, it will be better if my man takes us in my own car. In that way you and I can give one another our undivided attention, and I am anxious to learn all I can about my patient.'

'Very well, then. Shall we say in half an hour from now? I have just remembered a letter I have to write. We can post it on our way.' He did not sound particularly pleased. Apparently he was not accustomed to having his plans sub-edited.

'Which way will that be?' asked Dame Beatrice.

'I suggest we go to Swanage. That will give me time to tell you everything about Trilby that I think you ought to know.' He left her and went out, humming a little tune. Dame Beatrice poured herself some coffee, and five minutes later she returned to her room. While she was there she wrote a short letter to Laura saying only that her surroundings were pleasant and her room comfortable and that she was hoping to begin the treatment of her patient later on that morning, and then she descended to the great hall and stepped out into the February sunshine to find that word had been conveyed to George and that he had the car at the foot of the steps.

'Good morning, George,' she said. 'Are they making you quite comfortable?'

'Oh, yes, madam, thank you, perfectly comfortable. One of the maids brought word you wanted the car this morning to go to Swanage, so I brought it round.'

'George,' said his employer, 'are you psychic?'

'I trust not, madam. It must make for fear and discomfort. All the same,' the stolid chauffeur added, opening the door of the car for her, 'I would not be surprised if I can guess why you asked the question. Something funny going on around these parts.'

'I wonder what makes you think that, George?'

'Talk in the servants' hall, madam, and talk which only takes place when the old man Luke isn't with us. Would you wish me to repeat what I have heard, madam?'

'I think it might help. We appear to have discovered a household which, in some respects, is out of the ordinary.'

'Sinister, madam, one might call it. It seems there is a lady living here who never goes outside the house at all, no further than an enclosed and overgrown bit of garden. Nobody acts unkind to her, but she always wears a suit of armour or other fancy dress, and, according to the maids, can't get at any ordinary clothes. The girls don't much like the set-up, but they get good wages and the work, they say, is easy, and the lady doesn't complain.'

'I have met the lady in question. She seems to be Mrs. Romilly Lestrange. She came to see me in my room last night. She appears to believe that her life is in danger. The whole atmosphere would tend to suggest that we find ourselves in the midst of Victorian melodrama, for me a unique experience. While I should not wish to betray too much interest in the gossip of the servants' hall, I feel that, for once, I am justified in asking you to keep your ears open and to report to me anything which you can learn concerning this somewhat extraordinary household. In short, George, I have been brought here to serve, I think, an infamous purpose, although *what* infamous purpose I have not yet worked out.'

CHAPTER TWO

Ritual Dance—Lamb to the Slaughter

> 'Or, like a nymph, with long, dishevelled hair,
> Dance on the sands, and yet no footing seen.'
> *Venus and Adonis.*

Romilly's behaviour on the drive to Swanage and back added nothing to George's conviction that there was 'something funny going on.' He spoke of the girl with affection and concern, and, at Dame Beatrice's invitation, agreed to give a detailed account of what he referred to as 'poor little Trilby's aberration.'

'Although whether you or anybody else can rid her of the obsession is more than I can hope for,' he concluded. 'It seems to be very deep-seated.'

'I should wish to have as complete an account of her behaviour as you can give me,' said Dame Beatrice. 'It will help me to make my diagnosis. Confine yourself, if you please, to those matters which have come to your own personal notice. I may be able to fill in the details from other sources.'

'Very well. I married Trilby nearly three years ago – my second marriage and, as I soon discovered, a mistake. Did you ever read a poem by Charlotte Mew . . . '

'*The Farmer's Bride?* Yes, indeed, As I have interrupted you, may I ask whether Trilby is your wife's real name?'

'No, it is not. She was married to me in the name of Rosamund. She chooses to call herself Trilby.'

Dame Beatrice had heard the girl's own version of this, but she made no comment except to say:

'Well, it is quite a pretty name, I suppose, if one dissociates it nowadays from men's hats.'

'It makes no odds what she calls herself, so far as I am concerned,' said Romilly. 'If you have read the poem, you will realise my difficulties. Here was I married to this girl who was more like a pixie than a creature of human kind. I soon found that she was terrified of the physical side of marriage, so I took her to a psychiatrist who uncovered the history of an unpleasant episode in her early life for which she was in no way to blame and which she had forgotten. After that, she seemed much improved, and consented to co-habit with me. A child was conceived, but, as I think I told you in my letter, it was still-born.

'No, you did not mention it. How disconcerting for you both! And this threw her off balance again?'

'Well, as a matter of fact, she behaved rather strangely while she was still carrying it. She took to wandering off alone, and if I attempted to accompany her, or went after her in the car, or even went to the length of locking her in her room (as I did on one occasion), she flew into such violent fits of rage that I was afraid she would do the child or herself, or both of them, some serious injury. I believe, in fact, that this is what must have happened. The doctor told me that she was perfectly healthy. There was no obvious reason why she should lose the baby.'

'But, *until* she lost the baby, she did not have this obsession about drowning things?'

'I did not recognise it at first as an obsession. When she flung gramophone records and a transister radio set into the sea, I regarded it as the slightly unbalanced reaction of a woman under emotional stress, and took little notice of it. It happened *before* she lost the child.'

'You mentioned in your letter a toy trumpet.'

'That was used at the séance.'

'Dear me! I had no idea that you and she dabbled in spiritual-ism.'

'My dear Beatrice!' Romilly's tone blended amusement and polite protestation. 'You surely don't think that, with the baby almost due, I would have assisted Trilby to play such a dangerous game as taking part in a séance? Of course I knew nothing about it, nothing whatever. For some three or four weeks previously, Trilby had been less than well, so I engaged a private nurse. It seems that this woman asked what we were going to call the baby, and when Trilby said she did not know, and did not want a baby anyway, the nurse said she knew of a medium and that it would be fun – *fun*, mark you! – to hold a séance and ask "those who had passed over" for suggestions, and for an assurance that both Trilby and the child would come through safely at the time of delivery.'

'How did you come to hear of this nurse?'

'My doctor recommended her to me, but, of course, when I dismissed her and explained to him why I had done so, he was appalled that she should have encouraged her patient (who was in a highly nervous state) to indulge in such a pastime.'

'You yourself were not in the house, I take it, when the séance was held?'

'No, of course I was not. The nurse must have known quite well that I should disapprove. I had to go to London for a couple of days, and it was while I was out of the house that this pernicious nonsense took place.'

'What appeared to be the effect on Rosamund?'

'She was in a state of semi-collapse when I reached home. The trumpet, as I said, had been used at the séance, and, after this was over, she seems to have taken the trumpet down to the coast near Dancing Ledge and hurled it into the sea.'

'How did you know?'

'When I found that she had gone out alone – she developed a streak of animal cunning just at that time, and evaded me whenever she could – I went to look for her, but I had no idea which way she had gone, and I did not catch up with her until she had thrown the thing over the cliffs. I am glad I did not know sooner where she had gone. I should have been mortally afraid that she would lose her balance and go over with it, but, thank goodness, she did not.'

'And this happened before she lost the baby, but her drowning of the cat and the monkey came later. Is that so?'

'And, of course, she also drowned the baby doll. That was the latest of all. I thought the baby doll was highly significant. It proved to me that, not only did she not want her baby, but that she might have murdered it if it had lived.'

Dame Beatrice offered no comment on this opinion. She said, 'And that was when you decided to consult me.'

'Just so. I thought things had gone far enough.'

'I shall be interested to hear her own explanation of these actions.'

'I doubt whether she will remember anything at all about

them. Besides, do you think that total recall is necessarily a good thing?'

'All things are relative, of course. Is it possible for you to set aside a room in the house solely for my use as a consulting-room?'

'That presents a slight difficulty. I have to find sleeping accom-modation for eight extra people, as I think Judith told you, and as only two of them can be asked to share, space is at a premium. I wonder whether you could use your own room? It is spacious, and I can supply you with a table on which to write your notes, and a couch on which Trilby could lie. I thought that, if you had your sessions with Trilby between tea and dinner, you could still take your afternoon walk, or your nap, or anything else you choose to do, between lunch and tea, and so have that time and your mornings and evenings to yourself or with us.'

'That would appear reasonable. Very well. I will see her at a quarter to six.'

'Excellent. Then we will dine at eight, if that will suit you. I don't know how long you will spend with her each day?'

'Not more than an hour, and it may be a good deal less.'

'I suppose you use the "stream of consciousness" method.'

Dame Beatrice did not reply to this. She said, as though she had not heard him, 'Or we could use Rosamund's own sanctum, I suppose. She might be more at ease there than in my bedroom.'

Romilly laughed.

'*She* might, but I do not think *you* would,' he said. 'She is the most untidy young creature in the world. The servants try to maintain some kind of law and order among her things, but I'm afraid it's a thankless task. However, they are quite devoted to her in their bucolic, country-bumpkin way. *Not* over-blessed with intelligence, I'm afraid, but there seems to be so much inbreeding in small villages that it is scarcely surprising to find the indigenous people not much better than morons.'

Dame Beatrice thought of the willing, kindly Amabel, who 'loiked poertry' and who, with her sister, had given George some information which he, a notably intelligent man, had certainly accepted at its face value, and she found herself by no means in agreement with Romilly's summing-up of his servants' mentality. However, she did not contradict him. She was interested to hear that she was expected to turn her bedroom into a consulting-room. She had not been shown the whole house, but it was a three-storey building and, even allowing for the long gallery which went from the front to the back of the house on the first floor, and the loss of the floor or floors over the great hall which had been demolished to leave the three-sided inside balcony from which her own and other rooms opened, Galliard Hall must contain at least twenty bedrooms, apart from those occupied by the servants.

The only conclusion she could come to was that possibly all the rooms on the second floor, except the servants' quarters, were unfurnished and out of use. With only two maids, a manservant, a cook (whom Dame Beatrice had not seen) and a housekeeper, it was probable that not nearly all the rooms in the mansion received attention.

She went up to her room when the trip to Swanage was over, taking with her the newspaper which Romilly had bought for her. It was almost time for lunch, so she tidied herself and listened for the sound of the gong. While she waited she walked over to the picture of the two young men and studied it afresh. For some reason, her thoughts turned to her secretary Laura, who displayed at times a vivid imagination and a sense of the dramatic. Laura she thought, having been apprised of the fact that the household was, in some respects, a strange one, and having encountered Rosamund, with her complaints, fears and suspicions, would have regarded the picture with a prejudiced and jaundiced eye. On impulse, she reached up and took it down. Behind it there was a neat, foot-square hole in the party wall, and the picture, which was on thin canvas with no protecting glass, had been put up to conceal this.

It was clear, she thought, why her own room had been chosen for her treatment of Rosamund Lestrange. Somebody – most likely the master of the house – must be determined to overhear all that passed between Dame Beatrice and her patient. She realised now why Rosamund had sought her out while Romilly was downstairs. Rosamund must also know that there was an opening in the wall behind the picture.

She was far too old and experienced to be surprised by the lengths to which human curiosity can go, but, in view of the facts in this particular case, so far as she knew them, the large, neat hole seemed to indicate something a little more reprehensible than

mere curiosity. She replaced the picture and, hearing the gong
sound for lunch, went thoughtfully down the stairs. Once again
there were only the three of them at table.

'Well,' said Judith brightly, 'how did you think Swanage was
looking?'

'I saw little of it,' Dame Beatrice replied. 'It is a pleasant town,
and I am thinking of taking my patient to visit it this afternoon.
It will help with the beginning of her treatment.'

'Oh, but, my dear Beatrice,' said Romilly, in the utmost dismay,
'surely that would be most unwise! The very thing we have to
watch most carefully is that she does not go near the sea!'

'That may be your opinion, but it is not mine, and, as I am
in charge of the case, I must be permitted to conduct it in my
own way. My theory is that we should give your wife every
opportunity to drown anything she pleases. It is the best way to
cure her of her obsession. I have decided to follow the principle
laid down by makers of cream cakes and sweetmeats, that of
allowing their workpeople to eat as much as they wish of the
product they are making. The novelty wears off and the appetite
is very soon satiated. In my opinion, the frustration which your
wife must feel in not being allowed to follow a course of conduct
which satisfies her ——— '

'But there is the risk that Trilby may drown, not merely trivial
objects and small mammals, but herself!' exclaimed Romilly.

'That risk, in any case, will be considerably less from a bathing-
beach, where I shall be in charge of her, than from the cliffs, for
instance, above Chapman's Pool, or – according to the photographs I have seen – I do not know the place – the rocks of
Dancing Ledge. As you yourself have told me, she has been able,
on occasion, to elude your vigilance and to reach that part of the
coast alone.'

'Well, *I* think it's a lot of nonsense!' Judith blurted out. 'Of
course she mustn't go near the water!'

'My dear girl!' said Romilly. 'You must not talk like that! My
cousin Beatrice, in her own field, is an expert. If,' he went on,
turning to her, 'you feel that to take poor Trilby to the seaside
will help her in any way, of course you must do as you wish. The
only thing is that either Judith or myself must come with you.
I could not permit you to take the risk of being alone there with
my poor, misguided little girl.'

'Even at this time of year, we should hardly be alone at Swanage. Besides, my chauffeur will be there if I need any help. The worst thing for Rosamund, in my opinion, would be for those nearest her to be eavesdroppers on our conversations,' said Dame Beatrice equably.

'Eavesdroppers?' cried Judith, indignantly.

'For want of a more euphemistic term, yes, eavesdroppers,' Dame Beatrice repeated firmly. 'That is how the patient would interpret your presence, I'm afraid.'

Judith rose from the table.

'I give up,' she said. 'The whole idea is crazy, and your reference to Uncle Romilly and myself is extremely offensive.'

'Sit down at once, Judith,' said Romilly, in a mild tone but with a clear command behind the softly-spoken words. 'We must allow Beatrice to act in the way she thinks best. After the first time, I doubt whether she herself will wish to continue the experiment alone.'

Dame Beatrice had no hope that she would be able to see her charge before the other two had spoken to her. She also wondered whether Rosamund would appear in the Joan of Arc costume. Before they rose from table – Judith having preserved a sulky silence after her last outburst, and Romilly having avoided the disputed subject and chatted with apparent amiability on trivial matters – Dame Beatrice said smoothly:

'Can Mrs Romilly be ready to join me at half-past two?'

Judith shrugged her shoulders. Romilly bowed and replied:

'Of course, of course, my dear Beatrice. I am afraid you'll find her incredibly costumed. She refuses to wear modern dress, and flies into a paroxysm if I suggest it.'

'Well, I'm often incredibly costumed myself,' said Dame Beatrice, accurately. 'At half-past two, then, I look forward to meeting her.'

'I wonder how she'll get herself up?' said Judith. 'Oh, well, it's her affair – and yours. Not that she hasn't plenty of sensible clothes if she chooses to wear them.' She turned to Romilly. 'Why don't you make her unlock that wardrobe and get out some respectable clothes and insist she put them on?'

'How does one insist, my dear? I can hardly threaten her, and, even if I did, I doubt whether she would take much notice.'

'You're far too soft with her, don't you think so, Dame Beatrice?'

'Oh, come, my dear girl! How can Beatrice answer such a question when, so far, she knows nothing whatever about Trilby?'

'I would not say I know nothing whatever about her,' objected Dame Beatrice. 'You yourself have been most informative. As for *insisting* on what a patient does or does not do, well, that depends either upon the patient's intelligent and friendly co-operation or, of course, her fear of death.'

'Fear of death?' echoed Romilly, forcing himself to laugh. 'Good heavens, there's no question of her fearing death! Why should there be?'

'Most people fear death to a greater or a lesser degree, and for a variety of reasons, do they not?'

'Oh, I see what you mean,' said Romilly. 'Yes, well, look here, Judith, my dear, if Beatrice is going to take Trilby out, it will be a convenient time for me to go over the household accounts with you.'

Judith pouted at this, and said that it was quite unnecessary.

Dame Beatrice went to her room to get ready for the outing, then she rang the bell.

'Oh, Amabel,' she said, 'will you ask my man to bring the car round? I am taking Mrs Romilly for an outing to Swanage.'

'Be rare and cold on the beach this toime of year, Dame Beatrice, mum. Swanage be bracen. Face east, that do, more nor south.'

'Yes, I had thought of that. We may need rugs. Will you tell George to get them out of the boot, and perhaps you or Violet will make sure that they are aired before he puts them ready for us on the back seat.' (If Rosamund's costume were a little too bizarre, she thought, the rugs would cover it up to some extent.)

'Oi'll do that, Dame Beatrice, mum. Be noice for poor Messus Trelby to go out proper. A fair old lettle hen en a pen her be, I do believe. Can't thenk how she aboide et, really Oi carn't.'

'She looks well enough on it,' said Dame Beatrice carelessly. Feeling herself dismissed, which was indeed the case, Amabel went downstairs to rout out George and the rugs. As soon as she was out of hearing, Dame Beatrice stepped out on to the gallery and turned the handle of the door next to her own. It was locked. This she found especially intriguing in view of the hole which had been made in the wall.

She went back to her own room, took down the picture and studied the hole again. It was not cut flush with the wall, which was of brick, but had been made in the form of one of those so-called squints in old churches which are cut obliquely through a wall or a pillar to give a view of the high altar from a side-chapel or a transept.

The purpose of the squint in her bedroom seemed to be to give a view of the head of the bed. Again she thought of the romantic-ally-minded Laura. Anybody pointing a gun through the squint from the room next door would stand a pretty fair chance, she decided, of putting a bullet through the head of anybody asleep in the four-poster. Although its frame-work, consisting of four tall posts and the tester they supported, was complete, there were no curtains to the bed.

'I wonder how many persons have been done to death in this room since the early days of the seventeenth century?' she asked herself pleasurably. Then she reflected that the squint might have been made for beneficent purposes – to watch over a sick person or to make certain that a beloved child was sleeping soundly. She replaced the picture once more and then went across to the bed and attempted to move it out of the line of fire. She realised that, apart from George and the two maids, there was nobody in the house whom she could trust. This included Rosamund, although why she felt so deeply suspicious of the apparently friendless and lonely girl she would have found difficult to explain.

She went over in her mind the last night's interview. 'I don't know how they're going to kill me, but they will . . . They're hav-ing lots of people to come and stay, you know. They hope in that way to frighten me.' Neither expression rang true. 'They don't like me to meet people from outside.' That remark was illogical, to say the least, considering that Dame Beatrice herself, and the number of people who were to come and stay, were all from outside. 'I like to keep my room to myself.' Why did she, Dame Beatrice wondered. Rosamund had noticed that the picture which hid the squint had not been there before the room was prepared for Dame Beatrice. If that were so, it seemed to indicate, even more clearly than her surreptitious visit had done, that she must have known of the squint. Yet, this being so, she had still chosen to come, in apparent secrecy, to the room, knowing all the while that anybody in the adjoining apartment could have heard her voice, known who she was and listened to the conversation between herself and Dame Beatrice.

Dame Beatrice could not move the bed. It appeared to be fastened to the floor, like a bed in a cabin at sea. Dame Beatrice borrowed another of her secretary's favourite quotations. 'Curiouser and curiouser,' she murmured, and, having studied the iron clamps, she straightened up, hearing footsteps on the wooden floor of the gallery.

CHAPTER THREE

Morris Dance—Beansetting

'. . . some to dance, some to make bonfires . . .'
Othello, the Moor of Venice.

---

(1)

Amabel had returned with a message.

'Mr Straker says O.K. about the rugs, Dame Beatrice, and well et be all roight ef he breng the car round to the soide door, as Mester have gev orders Messus Trelby ent to be seen front the house.'

'Oh, you all call her Mrs Trilby, not Mrs Lestrange, do you? She is still in fancy costume, then?'

'Never don't wear nawthen else nowadays, though there's a beg locked-up wardrobe in her room.'

'I see. Tell George that I will be at the side door in five minutes' time. Where do I find this door, by the way?'

'Roight through the hall, along the corridor off to the roight, through the arch as ee'll foind there, and there et be. Carn't mess et, ef you go loike Oi say.'

Dame Beatrice found Rosamund under guard, as it were, with George standing on one side of her, the elderly, sour-faced Luke on the other, and Amabel's younger sister hovering in the door-way just behind the other three. This time Rosamund was wearing a heavily-caped George III costume, with a tricorne on her head and buckled shoes on her feet. Her brown wig, Dame Beatrice noted, was not powdered, but was loosely tied at the back with a black, watered silk ribbon. She looked extremely attractive.

George opened the door of the car, saw his employer seated and then went round to the other side and helped Rosamund in.

'Swanage, George,' said Dame Beatrice, for Luke's benefit, in case he had been told to report back to his master. George saluted, shut the car door with the brisk click of a man who cares for his car's doors sufficiently not to slam them, and took his seat at the wheel. The gravel side-path up which he had backed the car (for there was no room to turn) was narrow and weed-grown, and, as he drove slowly towards the main drive, over-hanging branches struck the car on both sides. At each sharp crack Rosamuhd flinched and glanced quickly at Dame Beatrice. Over-acting again, her companion thought.

'Surely,' said the latter, 'they don't offer you violence, do they?'

'Not yet, but I feel it's only a matter of time,' the girl responded. 'It's the car. It makes me nervous. I haven't been in a car since Romilly brought me back from Dancing Ledge.'

'Where you drowned what?'

'I *don't* drown things. I *told* you I don't! That's just a story they put about. They try to convince *me*, too. They're trying to prey on my mind.'

'I see. What were you doing at Dancing Ledge, then?'

'I was running away.'

'When was that?'

'Just over a year ago. It was soon after Romilly became my guardian.'

'You mean your husband. And it was three years ago.'

The girl stared at her.

'Romilly isn't my husband. I'm his ward,' she said. 'I've only lived with him and Judith for about a year.'

'I see.' Dame Beatrice betrayed no surprise at receiving this information. 'Why did you want to run away?'

'Wouldn't *you* want to run away if you knew that they were after your money, and would get it, even if they had to kill you first?'

'You mentioned money and murder to me yesterday. What money would this be?'

The girl pulled off hat and wig, flung them down and kicked at them. As she did so, something heavy in the pocket of her long travelling-coat struck her companion on the knee.

'*My* money,' she replied. 'It was left me, but there are some silly, unfair conditions. You see, when I die, unless I have children, Romilly and Judith will have it all. That's why I'm so frightened. Of course, until I'm twenty-five, I can't have it, but neither can they, so I'm sure they want to keep me alive until then. After that, unless someone will help me, I think I'm doomed. Those two are capable of anything, and, alone and friendless, I'm helpless against them.'

'You say that until you reach the age of twenty-five you cannot claim your inheritance. That I can understand. Many families prefer the heir to be older than twenty-one before trusting him or her with a fortune. I also understand that the next heir, should you die without issue, is Romilly Lestrange. What I do *not* understand is why he cannot inherit if you die before you are twenty-five.'

'I don't understand it, either. It's something to do with my grandfather's will. It's all very unsatisfactory and puzzling. It seems, according to the lawyers, that if I die before the age of twenty-five, all the money goes to some old lady called Bradley. That's as much as I know. That's if Romilly has told me the truth, of course.'

'I thought you said that the lawyers had told you all this.'

'Oh, well, yes, so they did, but Romilly told me something more. According to him, if it could be proved that I was unfit to handle the money either before or after I inherit it, it would all be taken out of my hands and administered for me. I know what *that* would mean. In effect, Romilly would have it. He's my guardian.'

'Let me get this clear,' said Dame Beatrice, testing the girl. 'To inherit your grandfather's fortune, you must reach your twenty-fifth birthday. Should you die *before* that birthday, the money would go to an old woman named Bradley, whom you do not know. If you reach that birthday, and *then* either die or are considered incapable of managing your affairs, the fortune goes to Romilly Lestrange.'

'Or if I'm considered incapable *before* I'm twenty-five. Why did he ask you to come here?'

'I understand I am not to be the only guest,' said Dame Beatrice, side-stepping the question. 'Is there not to be quite a large house-party?'

'Oh, I believe so. Why should all these idiotic relations come to Galliard Hall?'

'Perhaps Romilly thinks that Miss Judith is in need of young society.'

'I think she's *Mrs* Judith. I think they're married. And do you

know what else I'm beginning to think? I think he dare not kill
me himself, and he's going to sound out these others, and find
which one can be bribed to do it for him. I suppose he's brought
you here as a second string to his bow, in case the killing doesn't
come off. You're a psychiatrist, he tells me, and your name is
Professor Beatrice Adler. Are you related to the *famous* Adler,
by any chance?'

'There are two famous Adlers,' · Dame Beatrice responded.
'There is Alfred Adler, the pupil of, and, later, the dissentient
from, Sigmund Freud, who, to my mind, was inestimably the
greater man, and there is also, of course, the musician Larry
Adler, of whom I hear good reports from my younger relatives.'

'Oh, yes, I adore him and his harmonica-playing. I think he's
wonderful,' said Rosamund.

'They allow you a radio-set, then,' said Dame Beatrice,
deciding to shelve the question of her name. In Romilly Lestrange,
she was beginning to think, she had hit what Laura would call
'a new high' in her catalogue of smooth villains. She was also
beginning to wonder whether Rosamund was quite what she
seemed.

'Well, they did, until they took it out of my room and threw it
away. From that time they haven't let me have any proper
clothes. That's to stop me running away again, of course,' said
the girl.

'And you did not throw the radio set into the sea?'

'Of course I didn't! I wanted it. I miss it terribly.'

'Nor did you drown the gramophone records, the cat, and the
monkey?'

'Of course I didn't. They made it all up. They've also got some
silly story about a baby doll. It's all such a lot of nonsense – but
it's very wicked, all the same. I'm in a trap, and I'm dreadfully
frightened.'

'Were you ever pregnant?'

'How could I be? Surely they didn't tell you *that!* I'm not even
married.'

'That, of course, is not necessarily an obstacle to a pregnancy.'

'You're not on their side, are you? I thought you were my
friend! Have you brought me out here to kill me? I've got a
pistol in my pocket, you know!'

George spoke for the first time since the car had moved away from the house.

'Don't be silly, miss,' he said, in a severely avuncular tone. 'I beg your pardon, madam. I ought to tell you, though, that ever since we turned off B3351 I've had an idea I was being followed, and now I'm sure I am. Would there be any instructions?'

'No, George. Just carry on to Swanage, as planned.' She turned to her charge. 'What was your grandfather's name?'

'Felix Napoleon Lestrange. He died in April, 1966.'

'So you are a Lestrange by birth? Most interesting.'

As they passed the obelisk on Ballard Down, George reported that the other car had turned off to the left for Studland.

'Was it Romilly's car?' asked Rosamund.

'To the best of my knowledge and belief, miss, it was the old Standard I've seen in the garage. The colour was the same, but they've been keeping far enough away – I've lost them now and again on the bends – for me not to be able to read the number plate, so, of course, I couldn't take my oath on it.'

(2)

'Do we dare to ask how you got on this afternoon, my dear Beatrice?' asked Romilly, when they were gathered ready for tea.

'Certainly. We spent a short time – twenty minutes, perhaps – gazing at the sea. We also had our first session.'

'Were other people there?' asked Judith. 'If so, didn't they stare?'

'Why should they stare?'

'Oh, well, surely they would think Trilby's get-up rather unusual.'

'Have you been in London recently?'

'No, I haven't. Why?'

'If you had, you would see nothing unusual in the way Mrs Romilly was dressed. The latest fashions for the young are so bizarre that even a Georgian costume, complete with *jabot*, lace ruffles, knee-breeches and buckled shoes, would be considered rather unenterprising, and, in any case, Rosamund had covered her finery with a heavy, caped coat.' She thought it unnecessary to mention that she and Rosamund had not left the car. They had lowered the windows and sat warmly wrapped up in the car rugs.

'Really!' said Judith. 'I wonder how Trilby has learnt about the London fashions, then?'

'Oh, they are pictured in the newspapers, no doubt,' said Dame Beatrice. 'I suppose you allow her to see a newspaper from time to time?'

'Never mind the fashions,' said Romilly. 'How did she behave?'

'She was no trouble, if that is what you mean. Of course, I have yet to gain her full confidence.'

'But you have already had an effect on her?'

'Very possibly. I should have even more effect on her if I could remove her from this house for a time.'

'She made no attempt to throw anything into the sea?' pursued Romilly, completely ignoring the suggestion.

'Certainly not; neither did we make any attempt to drown one another.'

'You are being facetious, my dear·Beatrice.'

'In my opinion, you yourself have been treating matters all too seriously. There is nothing more debilitating for any invalid than to allow her to think she is worse than is really the case.'

'Well,' said Judith, 'I hardly see how Trilby could be worse than we think her. To change the subject, Uncle Romilly, our guests begin to arrive tomorrow. I wonder, Dame Beatrice, whether you would care to see what arrangements I have made for them? I imagine that you will not take the after-tea session Uncle Romilly had arranged, as you have been with Trilby all the afternoon?'

'No, I shall not need to see her again today.'

'While you are showing Beatrice over the house, I think I would like to talk to Trilby myself,' said Romilly. 'I am interested to find out what she thought of her afternoon out.'

'Not if you wish me to continue the treatment. Any interference at present would set her back, I'm afraid,' said Dame Beatrice. 'I do beg of you not to question her.'

'I *am* her husband.'

Dame Beatrice shrugged her thin shoulders.

'I have no desire, of course, to make an issue of it,' she said, 'but, after all, you may be her husband in name, yet you neither have her at your table nor in your bed.'

'Plain speaking!' Romilly looked surprised and amused.

'There are times in every doctor's life when there is nothing else for it. The professional, not the individual, speaks, so you must bear with me and allow me to give the orders where my patient is concerned.'

'Very well.' They were seated in front of one of the two fire-places in the great hall. 'Shall we go into the drawing-room?'

'No, let's have tea in here,' said Judith. 'I'm warm and comfort-able by this beautiful log fire. It seems a pity to move. Ring the bell, Uncle.' Romilly did this, but the bell was not answered quickly enough to please Judith, who spoke sharply when Amabel's sister, at the end of five minutes, appeared from the corridor which Dame Beatrice had traversed twice that afternoon. 'You've been a long time coming, Violet!'

'Sorry, Messus Judeth, Oi'm sure. Us ben looken after Messus Trelby. Such a lovely tea her've etten, ee'd hardly credet, her haven such a poor appetoite as a rule.'

'Really!' said Romilly. 'That is excellent news, Violet. She's found an appetite, has she? I'm delighted.'

'Tea in here, and at once,' said Judith. 'Bring that small table forward, and we may need another one. You and Amabel can carry it here from the drawing-room.'

'Ee can have Messus Trelby's trolley. That ud be best, Oi reckon.'

Violet, having proved her independence, retired to bring in the tea.'

'You'll have to speak severely to that girl,' said Judith, flushing until her face looked as round and as red as an apple. 'She is becoming quite impossible.'

'It is only her country manner,' said Romilly soothingly, yet with a note of warning in his voice. 'I think we must overlook it, especially as maids are difficult to obtain. We don't want her giving notice. If *she* goes, I'm pretty sure that Amabel will go with her, and they're very clean, good workers. You've said as much yourself.'

'That girl is on the verge of insolence!'

'Oh, no, I think not, my dear. And if she brings the things in on a trolley, there really is no need for a second table.'

'She'll have to do as she's told when our visitors come. I won't have her insolent to *them*. I'm sure Dame Beatrice doesn't take insolence from *her* servants. I've noticed how very respectful her chauffeur is.'

'George has been with me for many years,' said Dame Beatrice, 'and my other servants, except for the kitchenmaid, who is a country girl from Warwickshire, are French.'

'That might account for it,' said Judith. She looked balefully at Romilly. 'Uncle can't manage servants, anyway. He's much too soft with them.'

Romilly traced a pattern on the handsome rug with the toe of his shoe. Without looking up, he said:

'You are right, of course, my dear, but, if you can understand a syllogism, think of this: all housekeepers are servants. You are a housekeeper, therefore you are a servant.'

'How can you talk like that, when you have me call you Uncle?'

'Wait. I have not finished. I cannot manage servants, therefore I cannot manage you. And, of course, I cannot, but, at any rate, I can continue to try. I forbid you, utterly and absolutely, to attempt to take Violet to task for what she said about the tea-trolley. Think, my dear girl, *think!* How could you run a house this size without the help of the maids?' He raised his eyes and looked her straight in the face. There was an awkward moment of silence before Judith said sullenly:

'All right. You're only storing up trouble for yourself, but I suppose you must have your own way.' She made an attempt to smile, and added, in a light and playful tone, 'You're a very wicked old man!'

Dame Beatrice, who had been casually working at an indeterminate piece of knitting, dropped it on the rug as the tea-trolley made its noisy approach to them across the tiled floor.

'How nice to have a cup of tea,' she said. What she thought was a different matter. It was that, in this particular household, even impudent servants had to be conciliated.

(3)

Dame Beatrice that night wrote to Laura.

'The situation here is fascinating, macabre and in many ways incredible. I am living in a world of Sheridan Le Fanu, Edgar Allan Poe, Wilkie Collins and the Brontës. Imagine – a simple matter for a romantic such as yourself – a house inhabited by a smiling villain, a light-of-love who calls him her uncle, a sinister manservant, two country maidens of unblemished character, and an heiress who is permitted to wear nothing but fancy dress for fear she will elude the villain and his paramour and make her escape from their clutches!

'Of course, I do not know how much I should believe of the victim's story, but I have so little liking for her (alleged) persecutors that, when you have leisure to spare from attendance upon Eiladh, I wish you would make a few enquiries for me.

'I want to know details of the Will of a certain Felix Napoleon Lestrange, who died in April, 1966. I do not know where he lived, but, with that sufficiently unusual name, identification should be a reasonably simple matter.

'You will wish to know what has befallen me since my arrival in this house. I was made welcome with an effusiveness which aroused my suspicions. My bedroom, which, I have been informed, must also be my consulting-room, has had an interior wall breached so that a foot-square hole communicates with the adjoining room. Any conversations I may have with my patient, therefore, can be overheard. I have circumvented this invasion of our privacy, so far, by taking the patient out in my car and holding a conversation with her during the drive. We went to Swanage, and were followed. This added to the general impression of what I feel sure you would refer to as Rosamund being trapped in the Den of the Secret Nine. I feel that my move to talk with my patient in private has scarcely found favour with her captors, who were most anxious to accompany us on our outing, a policy with which I found myself unable to agree. Their attempt to follow us was indicative, I thought, of their state of mind.

'I have also discovered why I was sent for at this particular time when, according to Romilly's own statement, it would have been better, from the patient's point of view, to have called me in a year or more ago, but, when I have mastered the contents of the Will, I shall know whether my interpretation of the evidence is justified and what is the best course to pursue. My patient appears to have no idea of my identity. I have been recommended to her, it seems, under the name of Professor Beatrice Adler. I mention this because, if what she has told me is correct, something in the terms of Felix Napoleon's bequest may surprise you.

'I would not trouble you so soon did I not think (as she herself does) that my patient is in extreme danger either of death or (which appears to be my rôle) found incapable of managing her affairs and so losing all control of her fortune. I hasten to assure you that I myself am in no danger whatsoever. I am thought far too valuable to be liquidated, and George, the good, reliable fellow, is alive to the *nuances* (if I may put it in that way) of the situation as they strike both of us at present, and is prepared to cope with anything untoward which may crop up.'

Having closed and stamped her letter, Dame Beatrice descended to the great hall with the intention of walking to the end of the drive and putting it into Galliard Hall's own post office collecting box, a neat affair affixed to the outside of the wall which abutted on to the road. She had reached the hall door when she was intercepted by Romilly.

'You are surely not thinking of taking a walk in the dark, my dear Beatrice?' he said.

'A walk? No, that is an exaggeration,' she replied. 'I am going as far as the postbox at your gate.'

'A letter? Oh, I see. You had better give it to me. We let the dogs loose at night.'

'You are nervous of being burgled?'

'Well, you will admit that this house is in a lonely situation and there are valuables. These pictures, for example' – he waved his hand towards those which Dame Beatrice had noticed upon her arrival at Galliard Hall – 'I am told are probably worth several thousand pounds, and I have treasures of my own. Then there are some quite valuable trinkets which, from time to time, I have given Judith. They, like the pictures, are insured, of course, but I should be loth to lose them, and so would she.'

'I am not in the least afraid of dogs,' said Dame Beatrice, 'but as you will not wish me to run the risk of being attacked, you will not be averse to accompanying me as far as the gate.'

'Oh, nonsense! Give the letter to me. I could not dream of allowing you to run your own errands when I can so easily do them for you.'

Dame Beatrice had not the slightest intention of delivering her letter into his hands. She smiled her reptilian smile and said:

'My only object was to study the stars. It is a singularly clear and beautiful night, but, as late as this, there will be no collection of letters. It will do equally well in the morning. It is only a note to my secretary about some work I want her to do while I am away. Rosamund tells me that she has a birthday coming along. When would that be? I should wish to give her a present.'

'She didn't tell you when it was?'

'She merely mentioned that she would be twenty-five years old.'

'Oh? Well, it's on the twenty-ninth of May.'

'I must remember to wear an oak-apple in my hat,' said Dame Beatrice genially.

'I hope she has not been stuffing you up with any nonsense?'

'What kind of nonsense?'

'Well, she expects to come into this money of hers when she is twenty-five, and she seems to have some manifestly absurd idea that other people are after it, and will stick at very little in order to get hold of it. All part of her aberration, of course, but I just thought I'd warn you not to take her accusations seriously, particularly if they refer to Judith and myself.'

'Of course I shall not pay attention to her fears unless they are well-founded. The twenty-ninth of May? How interesting!' She gave him a little nod and went upstairs to her room, her letter still in her hand.

CHAPTER FOUR

Pieds-en-l'Air—Family Gathering

'Oh, master, if you did but hear the pedlar at the door,
you would never dance again after a pipe and tabor.'
The Winter's Tale.

---

(1)

The first of the guests arrived on the following day. The morning
was damp and misty. Dame Beatrice, returning from dropping
her letter into the pillar-box, saw that the hills behind the house
were shrouded in grey and that the clouds promised rain before
noon.

She joined Romilly, as before, for breakfast, and remarked
that it looked like becoming a wet day. She wondered, she added,
whether he was going into Swanage for a morning paper.

'No,' he replied. 'I'm expecting Tancred and some others. No
telling when they're likely to turn up, so I had better stay in, and
there's nobody I can send, unless your man would like to go.'

'Tancred?'

'Yes. He's a ruddy poet. I can't stand him, but he had to be
asked, you know. Can't leave anybody out. Matter of fact, I can't
stand any of them. Hubert might be all right, but I don't know
him as well as I know the others. In any case, I have very little
use for clergymen.'

Tancred Provost turned up in a taxi which he had shared with
his presumed cousins Humphrey and Binnie. Humphrey, as
Judith had indicated, was a somewhat seedy schoolmaster and
(Romilly explained to Dame Beatrice when the visitors had been
shown to their rooms) must have married Binnie in a fit of
scholarly absent-mindedness or in a state of mental aberration,
for they were, in all respects, a notably ill-assorted couple, he
thought.

Dame Beatrice herself thought it far more likely that the
shabby, ineffectual, unprepossessing man had been tempted into
marriage by his partner's flaxen head, characterless, innocent,

43

half-open mouth and babyish blue eyes which she widened, as though in surprise, in response to every remark which was made to her.

Tancred was an attractive young man, and it was clear that he was prepared to champion Binnie against her husband's weak spitefulness, for Humphrey, like most of his kind, compensated for his own shortcomings by making a butt of his dim-witted spouse. What appeared to be a typical exchange between them occurred as soon as they appeared downstairs again.

'Well, Binnie, my dear,' said Romilly, 'I expect you are ready for your lunch.'

'I'm dieting, Uncle Romilly. What are we having?'

'Well, really!' exploded Humphrey. 'What a question to ask your host!'

'A perfectly proper question, if she's dieting,' said Tancred. 'What *are* we having for lunch, Uncle Romilly?'

Humphrey glared at him. Romilly replied, 'I've really no idea. It's Judith's pigeon.'

'I wish it *could* be pigeon,' said Binnie wistfully. 'Oh, boy! How I love pigeon pie!'

'I'm afraid it won't be that. How charming you look, my dear,' said Romilly. 'If that's the result of dieting, I must admit that the sacrifice is worth it.'

'Oh, do you like my legs? These minis do something for legs, don't they? I mean, if you've *got* nice legs, why shouldn't you show them off? And a mini does show them off.'

'At twenty-three that might, possibly, be desirable,' said Humphrey. 'At thirty-three, no! You seem to forget that you are almost middle-aged, my dear. I've told you before, and I tell you again . . . "

' "He said it very loud and clear; he went and shouted in her ear," ' said Tancred. 'Oh, come off it, Humphrey!' He turned to Binnie, rolled his dark eyes and declaimed:

'Ah, shall I have you only in my dreams,
And long for sleep, and loathe to be awake?'

'What are you babbling about?' snarled Humphrey.

'I am quoting the first two lines of a little thing of my own,' said Tancred. 'If you talked poetry to the poor girl instead of criticising her legs . . . '

'I'm *not* criticising her legs, damn your impudence! I merely stated . . . '

'We are none of us criticising her legs. We are admiring those, and talking about her diet,' said Romilly. 'Ah, here comes Judith. Judith, my dear, Binnie is on a diet. What are we having for lunch?'

'A diet? Oh, dear!' said Judith. 'I'm afraid it's not diet-y food. We're having Scotch broth, turbot and a saddle of mutton. Binnie could have the turbot, I suppose, but . . . '

'I shall have it all,' said Binnie. 'Heavenly, heavenly lunch! We never get a lunch like that at home, not even on Sundays. I suppose Humphrey doesn't earn enough money. Perhaps, if they made him a housemaster in a big public school—'

Humphrey's snort of fury at this remark was taken by Binnie as agreement, and she seemed about to enlarge upon her theme when Tancred took her by the arm.

'What you want,' he said, 'is to hear the rest of that smashing sonnet of mine. It's all about *you*. Come along into the hall. The acoustics are better in there. They suit my voice.'

During lunch the wrangling between the married couple went on. Dame Beatrice could not believe that Binnie's capacity for exasperating her husband was not the result of a careful study of his vanities and his weaknesses. On the other hand, when Binnie interpolated one of her banal and meaningless remarks, Humphrey contested it with a blunt cruelty which left her, more often than not, in tears, but which induced in Dame Beatrice some sympathy for both partners in such a mésalliance. Matters were not helped by Tancred, who, as though moved by a disposition of kindness towards Binnie, invariably criticised Humphrey's arguments and, having the better brain and a poniard of wit against which Humphrey's bludgeonings seemed always to come off second best, reduced his opponent to teeth-grinding fury. At this the imbecile Binnie would leap into the arena with, 'Oh, Tancred, you beast! Oh, leave him alone! He can't help it if he isn't rich and clever!'

Dame Beatrice wondered which of them Humphrey would murder first. She extricated herself from the unseemly exchanges as soon as she could, stating that she was ready for a session with her patient.

'But it isn't the right time,' said Romilly. 'It's after tea you are to have her, isn't it? I thought you said . . . '

'What's this about a patient?' asked Binnie, interrupting him. 'Can I help with the nursing? I love sick-beds.'

'Yes, you may help,' said Dame Beatrice, neatly circumventing Humphrey's comments. 'Come along up to my room.'

'Oh, but, really, Beatrice!' protested Romilly. 'I thought all your sessions were to be held in secret.'

'Yes, so did I,' she replied. 'Since, however, a certain picture in my room has indicated that they are not to be so held, I see no reason to refuse Mrs Provost's reasonable and helpful request.'

'Will you call me Binnie?' the dumb blonde asked, as they went side by side up the splendid stair.

'With pleasure, my dear.'

'What's the matter with the patient? Why is she in your room? What did Uncle Romilly mean about secrets? Do you think I could get a divorce? Of course, it would ruin Humphrey's career, and I love him really, and I haven't any money of my own, so perhaps I'd better not try.'

'The patient is suffering from slight melancholia brought about by the circumstances in which she finds herself. She is not in my room, but I shall send for her. Your Uncle Romilly thinks her condition is worse than it is, and so he wishes my work here to be kept secret except, of course, from himself and his house-keeper. I do not know whether you could get a divorce, although, if you did, you could claim alimony from your husband, if you had right on your side.'

'Do you mean I could get money without having to work for it? That would be very nice, wouldn't it? I'd like to model clothes, but you need brains for that, and Humphrey is always telling me I haven't any.'

'There is no need for you to believe him, is there?'

'Do you know why we've come?'

'I thought it was to join in a family gathering.'

'No, not quite. Uncle Romilly has made all sorts of promises to make sure we came along. He has promised Humphrey a headship. There's an interview. But what would Humphrey do with a wife like me? I wouldn't know what to say to the parents, and, of course, I'd have to have better clothes. Humphrey is dreadfully mean about clothes. Just look at the rags I'm wearing!'

'I think you look very nice, and, of course, as you pointed out to us, his salary may not be large.'

'I don't know what it is. He never tells me.'

Dame Beatrice opened the door of her room to find that Rosamund had already installed herself in it. She gravely introduced the two girls.

'Oh, we've met once before,' said Binnie. 'You're not the patient, are you? I'm prettier than you, but I expect you've more brains than I have. How oddly you dress! Do you like dressing up? *I* did, when I was a little girl.'

'So you do now,' said Dame Beatrice. 'Didn't you tell me you wanted to model clothes?'

'I wish you'd show me your clothes, and let me try them on,' said Rosamund quickly to Binnie. She was wearing Joan of Arc's armour again. 'Could we go to your room?'

'No, you cannot go now,' said Dame Beatrice. 'We are to have our session at once, instead of after tea.'

'I love my tea,' said Binnie, 'and I can see that Rosamund is quite as well as I am. I think I'll go downstairs.'

She left them. Rosamund said:

'Is she quite all there?'

Dame Beatrice did not reply. She scribbled a few words in her notebook and handed it over. Rosamund read the sentences she had written and nodded intelligently.

'War,' said Dame Beatrice, loudly.

'And peace,' said Rosamund automatically.

'Peace-makers.'

'Pace-makers. People who help people to win races.'

'Race-antagonism.'

'There was a young lady named Starkey . . . '

'That, surely, was fusion, not antagonism. Let us begin again.'

They played out the farce until the sound of a door being shut told Dame Beatrice what she wanted to know.

'I'll go now,' said Rosamund, who had heard it, too.

'Do not attempt to do what you had thought of, even if Binnie lends you some clothes,' said Dame Beatrice.

'Very well. I see you know what it was.'

'It was obvious, of course. But that is not the way.'

'You mean I should be found and brought back?'

'I could not prevent it, at this stage. Have a little patience. Why has Romilly invited all these people here?'

There was a tap at the door.

'So sorry to intrude,' said Romilly. He went over to Rosamund, who shrank back as he approached her. 'I think you had better do as you suggested just now, my dear,' he said. 'Make yourself scarce. You may join the others downstairs, if you wish to do so, but you must behave yourself, mind. No nonsense and no tantrums, and you are to pay no attention to anything Tancred may say to you. You know which one is Tancred. You met him the last time he came. He will flatter you, maybe, and talk all kinds of nonsense about his poetry, but it is all meaningless. Do you understand me?'

'Yes,' said Rosamund sullenly, 'but I don't want to go down-stairs. I like it here with Professor Adler.'

'Yes, my dear, I am sure you do, but I wish to speak with her in private, so run along, there's a good child. If you ask Amabel, she will give you some lemon drops. You like lemon drops, don't you?'

With obvious unwillingness, Rosamund left them. There was silence until she had closed the door. Then Dame Beatrice said:

'This is an intrusion, you know. I do not care to have my sessions interrupted.'

'I am sorry about the interruption, but, with all these people in the house, I had to find a way of seeing you alone.'

'For any particular reason?'

'For one thing, I need to know why you dislike me. I suppose there is a connection with Trilby. I ought to have stressed that she is a pathological liar, but I am certain you have far too much experience of these cases to be taken in by her. She was planning to run away again, was she?'

'How did you know that?'

'I did not know it. I made a guess that it would be the first thing over which she would attempt to enlist your aid.'

'Did you also guess that I should refuse it?'

'I gave you credit, of course, for ordinary common sense.'

'I think you have been eavesdropping, you know. You over-heard our conversation, did you not?'

'My dear Beatrice!'

'It would be rather naïve of you to deny it. I have found the hole in the wall, as I thought I had sufficiently indicated.'

'I simply do not understand you!'

'Do you not?'

'The hole in the wall? Whatever can you mean?'

'If you will take the trouble to remove the picture of those two young men, you will see for yourself what I mean, and then perhaps we shall both know where we stand.'

'Remove the picture?' He stepped across the room. 'You mean there is a hole in the wall which is being covered by it?'

'You may satisfy yourself that that is so.'

Romilly studied the picture before he took it down. His surprise, when he did so, was either genuine or remarkably well simulated. He put the picture on the floor with its face against the wall and stared at the foot-wide squint. He ejaculated, as he turned and met the sharp black eyes of his guest:

'Good gracious me! Who would ever think of such a thing!'

'Most people would recognise this as a house of secrets, I think. Perhaps the hole was there when it was built.'

'I see that you have a suspicious mind.'

'It is a feature of my profession.'

'Ah, yes, of course. Of *both* your professions, perhaps. Beatrice, I did not only bring you here to examine Trilby. My life is threatened.'

'By whom?'

'I don't know. The would-be murderer may be one of my guests. I want you to spot the guilty party. That is one reason why I invited you.'

'Since your demise has not yet been accomplished, there can be no guilty party.'

'Guilty by intent, I mean, of course. You will be wondering how I know that I am in danger. I will tell you. One of these visitors must, I think, be my own child. Which one I do not know, but, whichever it is, that one will attempt to kill me.'

'What makes you think so?'

'A gipsy warned me.'

'Really, now!'

'Oh, I take it seriously, I assure you.'

'Well, I am sorry, but I have not the slightest intention of following that example. If you mean what you say, why have you invited them here?'

'To get the matter settled once and for all, and I need your expert help. As a psychiatrist . . . '

'I decline to be a party to such nonsense.'

'Even if I accede to your request?'

'What request would that be?'

'To allow Trilby to be treated in your own home or at your clinic.'

'I think you must have read my mind.'

'In what respect?'

'If you had not been willing to release her, I should have laid an information against you for detaining the girl here by force and for refusing her the rights of liberty and the pursuit of happiness.'

'You must be joking! Trilby is my wife.'

'I am in expectation of being able to prove that she is nothing of the kind.'

'You've gone behind my back?'

'Certainly, if you choose to put it like that. I will go further. Rosamund is completely *compos mentis*, and you know it. What your object has been in keeping her here without modern clothing, so that she cannot escape, and why you have seen fit to pass her off as your wife, I have no idea. However, there must be an end to it. I shall take her with me tomorrow morning.'

'Not just yet, Beatrice. At least allow her to stay until my house-party is assembled.'

'I see no reason for that. Binnie, who seems reasonably well-disposed, will lend Rosamund some clothes which will do for a day or two, until I can get her properly fitted out. As for your own troubles, whether they be real or imaginary, I suggest that you contact the police.'

'But what should I tell them?'

'What you have told me.'

'They might not believe me.'

'Well, *I* don't believe you, either.'

'Beatrice, if you leave me in the power of these monsters, my blood will be upon your head.'

'I have borne greater responsibilities than that.'

'I won't *let* you go!'

'No?' said Dame Beatrice. 'Well, well!' She seated herself composedly in an armchair. 'You can scarcely guard that door for the rest of the day. You have guests arriving at this very moment.' She had heard a car drive up.

'I can lock you in!' said Romilly, with an attempt at playfulness.

'You could, perhaps, if you had the key. I took the liberty of removing it from the door almost as soon as I arrived here, and have been carrying it about with me ever since.'

'Well, I shall not think of attempting to gain possession of it by force,' said Romilly, laughing. 'But, my very dear Beatrice, *please* do not think of leaving me at present, whether you believe or not that my life is in danger. At least allow Trilby to meet her guests and enjoy their company for a day or two. Oh, and another thing! You must not think that I keep her shut up in this house. She has a wardrobe full of women's clothes, but she keeps it locked. When you have won her confidence you may be able to persuade her to attire herself normally.'

'We shall see,' said Dame Beatrice. 'Meanwhile, your visitors continue to arrive.'

'Yes, we had better go down and meet them.' He hung up the picture he had taken down, and then shook his head at it. 'Very strange,' he said. '*Most* strange. This used to be *my* room, you know, but I certainly did not realise that there was a hole in the wall. I wonder what other secrets this fine old house contains?'

Dame Beatrice made no attempt to guess, and Romilly led the way downstairs. In the hall they found Judith and Rosamund in conversation with a long-haired youth and a crop-headed girl who, it was easy to see, were the twins, Corin and Corinna.

'It's too terribly good of you to put us up for a whole week,' said Corinna to Romilly.

'Too terribly good,' echoed her brother. 'Saves the expense of digs, and seaside digs are ghastly, anyway. Hullo, Great-aunt,' he added to Dame Beatrice. 'I don't suppose you remember us, because you haven't seen us since we were babies. How are you? This quiet chap beside me is Giles. Tancred I expect you've already met, likewise Humphrey and Binnie, who are having a row in the parlour. Well, now that we all know one another, I'm bound to inform you that my twin is dying on her feet for a cup of tea. I know it isn't tea-time, but if you want to save a life . . .'

'It is quite time for tea,' said Judith, 'but we were hoping that Hubert and Willoughby would have joined us. It doesn't matter, though. They can have theirs later.'

'Well, we can't very well have our meeting until they arrive,' said Romilly.

'What meeting would that be, Uncle Romilly?' asked Tancred.

'I want to acquaint you all with the provisions of my will.'

'Oh, goody! exclaimed Binnie. 'Is your fortune big enough to go round?'

'If it isn't, you shall have my share, Binnie,' said Tancred, 'and this evening, in the twilight, I'll read my poems to you. You'd like that, wouldn't you?'

'I like money, but I don't understand poetry very much.'

'You don't need to understand mine.'

'I suppose it's quite incomprehensible, anyway,' said Humphrey, sneering, 'as well as being thoroughly poor stuff.'

'An usher wouldn't know whether it is or whether it isn't,' said Tancred. 'What do you dish out to your pupils? Longfellow, or Mrs Hemans?'

Tea was brought in, dinner followed at seven and, after dinner, Judith played and sang. At half-past ten a move was made towards bed.

'We can't expect Hubert and Willoughby tonight, it seems,' said Romilly. On gaining her room, Dame Beatrice rearranged her bedding so that she was sleeping head-to-foot in the big four-poster. She left the picture leaning against the foot of the wall, although what whim had caused her to take it down again she hardly knew, any more than she knew what instinct had made her change her bedcoverings round. She did know that, in spite of his laughter, which had sounded spontaneous and unforced, she had made an enemy of Romilly. There was also the slight mystery as to which member of the household had actually invited the guests, and there was Romilly's anxiety, which had been apparent during the whole of the evening, because two of the guests, Hubert, the clergyman and Willoughby, the secretary, had neither put in an appearance nor sent a letter of excuse. Romilly had fumed and fidgeted and made several references to their absence, so much so that Judith, who did not seem to share his feeling of unease, had at last chided him sharply.

'For heaven's sake,' she had exclaimed, 'stop worrying over the wretched pair! What does it matter whether they're here or not? You didn't have them last time, anyway.'

'I don't want to hold my meeting without them,' Romilly had pettishly replied. 'It will spoil everything if we're two people short.'

Dame Beatrice was glad that the evening was over. What with the bickering of Humphrey and Tancred, Binnie's tears, which started up readily when her husband was more than usually unkind, Romilly's fretting and a certain restlessness which all this not unnaturally induced in the quiet and inoffensive Giles, together with the vapid and (she thought) nervous chatter of the twins, the hours between tea and dinner and then between dinner and bedtime, had been anything but pleasant.

She got ready for bed in a leisurely manner, for it was very much earlier than her usual time for retiring. On the other hand, there was no point in staying up, for she had too much respect for her aging eyesight to strain it by attempting to read by candlelight, which was the only form of lighting in her vast and shadowy room. Neither, at that hour, did she expect to fall asleep, and she was lying contentedly in the huge, comfortable bed, glad of her own company after the uneasy and boring hours downstairs, when she was aware of slight sounds coming from the direction of the hole in the wall. The next moment there was a startling report from a firearm. Dead silence followed for a moment and then came the sound of a door closing. Dame Beatrice had locked her own door. She slipped out of bed, made her way to the locked door and listened, but even her keen hearing could detect no further sound.

The silence, however, was not prolonged. There were footsteps on the stairs and in the gallery, and voices raised excitedly. Then came a hammering on the door of her room and a shouted question from Romilly.

"Beatrice! Beatrice! Are you all right?'

'Perfectly all right,' she replied. 'I thought I heard the sound of a shot, though. Could it be so?'

'Well, I certainly heard something,' said Corin's voice. 'Hullo! Talk about a gathering of the clan!'

There were excited exclamations in various tones. It was clear that most, if not all, of the household, were gathered on the landing outside. Dame Beatrice lit a candle, put on dressing-gown and slippers, hung the picture up again and opened the door.

'Where did the sound seem to come from?' she mildly enquired.

'Certainly from this part of the house,' said Romilly, shading his candle against a draught from the staircase. Dame Beatrice glanced around her. The absentees were the servants and also Binnie, Rosamund and Tancred. The others wore dressing-gowns, except for Giles, who had pulled his trousers on over his pyjamas, and Humphrey, who was wearing an overcoat over his nightshirt.

'It *sounded* like a shot,' said Romilly, 'but it could hardly have been that. What did you think it was, Beatrice?'

'I thought it was a shot,' she replied. 'But, as you say, it seems unlikely.'

'You don't suppose,' said Giles, 'that Hubert and Willoughby have arrived, and what we heard was their car back-firing?'

'That seems possible,' said Judith, who was looking particularly handsome in a scarlet dressing-gown embroidered with gold thread. 'Perhaps somebody had better go downstairs and find out.'

'An excellent idea,' said Romilly. 'You girls get back to bed, and you, too, Beatrice. Giles and I will investigate.'

The crowd dispersed. Dame Beatrice closed her door and locked it. Then she found the powerful electric torch which always accompanied her and made an inspection of what had become the foot of her bed. She was interested but not surprised to find that the marksman, whoever he or she might have been, had not tailored the shot. As nearly as she could judge, the bullet would have travelled in a direct line to her pillow, had her bedding not been rearranged. She would probably find the bullet embedded in the mattress, she thought. She returned to bed and slept lightly but soundly until six.

At breakfast there was some speculation, but not as much as might have been expected, as to the origin of the noise. Dame Beatrice, who, after rising, had rearranged her bed so that the pillows were at the right end of it, contributed little to the pointless discussion, and it very soon changed to a peevish monologue from Romilly concerning the non-arrival of Hubert and Willoughby. Since she knew neither of them, for her any real interest was lacking. However, as she had found not only the bullet hole in the bedclothes, but the bullet itself (which she decided had come from a ·22 rifle), her interest lay in wondering who had fired it, and whether the would-be murderer had expected to kill not herself but Romilly, as the room she occupied had at one time been his own. In view of the fears he had expressed to her, and which, at the time, she had treated lightly, she thought that he might have been the intended victim. It was clear, later in the day, that he himself thought so. He said to her, when they chanced to find themselves alone:

'I suppose it *was* a shot?'

'Oh, yes,' she replied. 'It was a shot. It came from the direction of the hole in the wall in my room.'

'It was intended for me, no doubt. What a lucky escape you have had.'

'I have no idea for whom it was intended.'

'I should imagine it has substantially reduced the value of the picture.'

'No, no. I had taken the picture down.'

He stared at her, but asked for no explanation, and in this unsatisfactory state the matter rested, except that when she next visited her room it was to find that a kind of rough wooden shutter had been affixed to the hole in the wall, and that the painting of the two boys had disappeared.

CHAPTER FIVE

Danse Macabre—The Wicked Uncle

'If my tongue cannot entreat you to acquit me, will you
command me to use my legs? And yet that were light
payment – to dance out of your debt.'

King Henry IV, Part 2.

---

(1)

Laura was delighted with the letter she had received from Dame
Beatrice, her emotion tempered merely by regret to think that,
so far, she was excluded from the fun. She would have been even
more regretful had she known about the mysterious shot in the
night. However, leaving the baby Eiladh in the capable and willing
hands of Zena the kitchenmaid, she drove to London in her own
small car, parked it on the outskirts and took a taxi to Somerset
House.

The provisions of Felix Napoleon's will were straightforward
enough, and Laura had no difficulty in memorising them. There
was no doubt that Rosamund, subject to the conditions of which
Dame Beatrice had been made aware, was the principal beneficiary. The money was left to 'my granddaughter, Rosamund Mary
Lestrange,' when she should have attained the age of twenty-five
years. Until that time, the estate was to be held in trust by the
old man's lawyers, and the interest on the money allowed to
accumulate. Laura read the rest of the provisions and stipulations
with great interest, for there was no doubt that if Romilly was an
unscrupulous and criminally-minded man, the girl's fears for her
own safety were not imaginary, and Laura admitted as much in
her return letter.

Dame Beatrice received this letter at a quarter to ten on the
morning following the shooting. There had been some more
speculation as to the cause of the noise which had roused the
household, but as, apparently, nothing had resulted from the
shot except the somewhat curious circumstance that none of the
servants seemed to have heard it – a circumstance confirmed by
George and Amabel when Dame Beatrice off-handedly mentioned

the matter to them separately – speculation died down in favour of a general discussion, when Romilly had left the breakfast table, as to the reason for his having arranged the house-party.

Dame Beatrice, who did not contribute to the discussion, but who listened with interest to it, realised that one thing which she had been told was, on the face of things, completely untrue. There was no family feud between the Lestranges and the Provosts. There was a running skirmish between Humphrey and Tancred, but it was a private fight, not a family matter. She wondered whether the appearance of the brothers Hubert and Willoughby would prove to be the match which might be applied to the gunpowder, but she could not, at that point, detect any presence of explosives. In the early afternoon, however, more drama, this time of a rather ridiculous sort, was suddenly introduced by Rosamund.

Lunch was over. The last two of the guests, Willoughby and Hubert Lestrange, still had not put in an appearance. The others, with Romilly, Judith and Dame Beatrice, were taking coffee in the drawing-room when Rosamund put in this dramatic and disordered appearance. She was wearing a white nylon nightdress and had a cock-eyed wreath of dripping wet hazel-catkins on her hair. She said:

'Look! I'm Ophelia, all wet from the river.' Then, in a tuneless voice, she began to sing.

'My God!' exclaimed Humphrey. 'What on earth is this?'

'And will he not come again?' mouthed Rosamund, continuing her caterwauling.

'Who?' interpolated Binnie, obviously interested.

> 'No, no he is dead,
> Go to thy death-bed,
> He never will come again,' sang Rosamund.

'Who won't?' demanded Binnie, in a louder tone.

> 'So excellent a king; that was, to this,
> Hyperion to a satyr,' replied Rosamund obligingly,

in a clear, elocutionist voice.

'Beatrice!' cried Romilly, putting down his cup. 'For God's sake help me out with her!' But it was Tancred who rose from his seat on the settee where he was partnering Binnie.

'Come on, girl,' he said. 'You can tell me all about it upstairs, and, if you're good, I'll read you my poems.'

'Don't believe it,' said Rosamund sulkily. 'You don't want me to sing, that's all.'

'There's one poem I know you'll like,' said Tancred persuasively. 'It's all about *you*. Come along.'

'I want one about *me*,' said Binnie. 'You promised one about *me*. And that's my nightie she's got on!'

Tancred took Rosamund by an unresisting arm, and led her from the room. Dame Beatrice rose in leisurely fashion, placed her empty cup on a small table, and followed them out. After a moment, Binnie followed, too.

'Don't see why she should pinch my nightie,' she said. 'I'm going to get it back. It's not that I grudge it her, but she can't just go about sneaking things. It's not right.'

'She's worse than you told us in your letter, then,' said Humphrey to his uncle. Romilly looked gloomy. Dame Beatrice, who had not gone upstairs in the wake of Rosamund and Tancred, but who had stepped aside to allow Binnie to pass her, noticed this from her vantage point at the side of the archway which did duty for a door. She heard Romilly answer:

'Well, it's bound to be progressive, I suppose, although she's been a little calmer of late.' Dame Beatrice came back into the room.

'She will be calmer again in a minute or two,' she said. 'I warned you that this influx of guests might excite her.' She settled herself composedly in the chair she had previously occupied and looked across at him.

'I can't help that,' he said. 'I had to call the family together for a very good reason, and, as you are an interested party, I had to get you to come along, too. There is nothing you can do for Trilby. She's naughty, not deranged. I expect you have found that out by now. Well, now seems as good a time as any for me to hold the business meeting which is the prime reason for this pleasant little get-together.'

'I don't see how you can,' said Corin. 'We're short of four members of the group. Don't we wait until Binnie and Tancred come down, and Hubert and Willoughby get here?'

'I don't know why all the rest of us should wait,' said his twin sister. 'Those other two can hear all about it later on. Don't forget we've got a rehearsal at ten tomorrow morning, and we *must* run over our programme before dinner tonight.'

'The meeting need not take long,' Romilly insisted. 'I have enticed you here on various pretexts. None of my offers was genuine. I had better confess that at once. You, my dear Humphrey, were led to believe that I could obtain for you a House at a minor public school. I am not in a position to do so. Tancred has been told that a publisher is prepared to put out his poems and guarantee him a respectable advance and a scale of royalties. This is untrue. Binnie – I wrote to her separately, Humphrey, and had the letter delivered by special messenger at a time when I knew you would be at school – thinks that I can get her a job modelling clothes. Giles has been promised . . . '

'Oh, cut it out!' said Giles. The belligerent words were expressed in a quiet voice, but with a degree of menace which encouraged Humphrey, who, so far, had responded only with a red face and a bristling attitude, to put his face almost into Romilly's and exclaim:

'You rotten, lying, oily swine!'

'Just a moment, Humphrey,' said Judith. 'Let Uncle Romilly finish what he has to say.'

'I had to find the means to get you all together,' went on Romilly, 'and to pretend to offer each of you something to his advantage seemed by far the best way. Hubert expects me to get him ecclesiastical preferment, and Willoughby wants to . . . '

'Knock your block off, I should think,' said Giles. 'Have you forgotten that he has been out of a job for months?'

'I have forgotten nothing,' said Romilly. 'Hear me out. Having gathered you together under these false pretences and lying promises, I propose to acquaint you with the terms of my Will.'

'So you told us,' said Binnie, appearing in the archway. 'I think Trilby and Tancred have gone to bed together. What Will? Do we all share, or have you left everything to Corin and Corinna?'

'Why us, Binnie?' asked Corin, pushing back his shoulder-length, unkempt hair.

'Because – yes, I've been in the next room, listening; so convenient, not having proper doors – because it seems to me that

Corin and Corinna are the only people who haven't been promised things.' She advanced into the room. 'You two got your own booking at the Winter Garden, didn't you?' she asked.

'Sure,' said Corin, 'but Romilly offered us free board and lodging and the use of a car while we were down here.'

'The estate which I propose to buy later on, and all my money,' said Romilly deliberately, '*might* be willed to whichever one of you murders me, and I am not disclosing the terms of my bequests at this stage. Therefore, as a murderer cannot gain financially by the death of his victim, I have a feeling that I shall remain alive for a good long time, you know. Just my idea of a little bit of fun. That's all. Enjoy yourselves.'

'The murderer could gain financially so long as he wasn't caught,' said Giles grimly.

'He *will* be caught,' said Romilly, with a significant glance at Dame Beatrice. 'One of you has taken what he thought was a shot at me. I advise him not to try again. Well, I'll leave you to think things over.'

(2)

'But it doesn't make sense,' said Binnie, for the fourth time since the discussion had broken out, which it did upon Romilly's departure.

'It *must* make sense to one of us,' said Corin. 'As *I* see it, it's a warning. The old man's got a hunch that one of us intends to do him in. That means it really *was* a shot we heard last night.'

Binnie squeaked in dismay. Her husband said morosely:

'All that nonsense aside, the fact remains that he's got us all down here by making lying promises to us. If you ask *me*, he deserves to be shot.'

'Well, I advise you not to have a second go,' said Tancred, coming suddenly into the room. 'I've left Rosamund with Judith, by the way. I suppose their absence is to be desired, rather than deplored, under the present circumstances. Incidentally, Cousin Humphrey, why *do* you want to liquidate our host and close relative?'

'You'd want to do it yourself, if you had the guts of a flea,' said Humphrey violently. 'Didn't he promise you that he'd got hold of a publisher who would pay for those rhymes of yours? Well, he hasn't, and he won't. He's been leading us all up the garden.'

'Meaning you won't get that better job to which your talents as usher do not entitle you?'

'Look here,' said Giles, 'our quarrel is with Romilly, not with one another. He promised to lend me the money for a part-share in some racing-stables, and the promise is just as worthless as those he made to the rest of you. Don't let's bicker.'

'The promise he made to *us* isn't worthless,' said Corin.

'Isn't it?' asked his sister. 'What if he doesn't lay on the transport he promised us? Have you realised what it's going to cost if we have to pay for a car to get us to Bournemouth and back each day? The money we're paid for our show is going to look pretty silly with about fifty pounds knocked off it.'

'I hadn't thought of that. He wouldn't be such a swine, would he?' asked her twin.

'I don't know. He's made fools of Humphrey and Tancred and Giles. Why should *we* escape his morbid little sense of humour? After all, how much do we know about him, anyway? We've been out of touch with him since we were babies, except for that silly house-warming he chose to give, and he doesn't own this place, anyway; he only rents it. I'm not at all sure we were born, in fact, before he went out to Kenya or wherever it was. What I can't understand is what his game is. I mean, why on earth bring us all together like this, on the strength of some lying promises?'

'I wonder what he promised Hubert and Willoughby?' said Giles. 'Perhaps it wasn't enough to make it seem worthwhile for them to show up. Anyway, I don't know about the rest of you, but I'm off. I wouldn't stay a minute longer under his beastly roof if you paid me!'

'Isn't there a New Forest meet in the morning?' asked Tancred, with apparent innocence. 'Pity to miss that, as you're here.'

(3)

When Dame Beatrice came down to breakfast on the following morning it was to find her host alone at the table. The remainder of the previous day had been strange and, to everyone but herself

and Tancred, who both enjoyed bizarre situations, very un-
comfortable.

Judith had come down to face the glum and grim silence which
followed Tancred's last words and observed, with false brightness,
that 'poor little Trilby' had been soothed and put to bed and was
being watched over by one of the maids, and that Romilly had
been called out unexpectedly, but would be back in time for
dinner.

'I should think it would choke him,' muttered Humphrey.
Aloud he said: 'I suppose you and he have taken it for granted
that Binnie and I will be leaving first thing in the morning?'

'Oh, must you go so soon?' asked Judith. 'I must arrange
about the car, then.'

'We're all going,' said Tancred. 'At least' – he glanced at Giles –
'most of us, I think.'

Dame Beatrice had also decided to leave, provided that Romilly
kept his promise about allowing her to take Rosamund with her.
Laura's letter, confirming her own and the girl's own fears, had
clinched her determination to remove the prospective heiress
from Romilly's clutches and make provision for her safety. After
all, the child was related to her, even if somewhat obscurely, and
Dame Beatrice had never attempted to shake off the sense of
responsibility which was the glory and the curse of her generation.
What she was to do with Rosamund ultimately she had no idea.
Marriage would be the best solution if matters arranged themselves that way, although whether the possible husband was to be
envied, Dame Beatrice had begun to be doubtful.

Romilly stood up as she came to the breakfast-table and placed
a chair for her.

'Is anybody else up?' she asked.

'Humphrey and Binnie have breakfasted and are packing.'
Romilly laughed as he spoke. 'Humphrey has taken my little
jokes rather badly, I'm afraid.'

'Your little jokes?'

'Why, yes. All that clap-trap about the murderer, and so forth.
I merely wanted to amuse them all, you know. One thing, Corin
and Corinna knew better than to take me seriously.'

'They are staying on, then?'

'Oh, yes. So is Giles. There's a meet of the New Forest hounds this
morning. He was up and away an hour ago. I've lent him a horse.'

'What about Mr Tancred?'

'Not up yet. Don't suppose he'll be down before ten. I'm expecting to hear from Hubert and Willoughby by this morning's post. Wonder what they've got to say for themselves? Dashed uncivil to accept an invitation and not turn up. Post doesn't get here until the middle of the morning. That's the worst of living in the wilds. Ah, here's your fresh toast. What are you thinking of doing with yourself today?'

'I thought I would take my patient to the Stone House.'

'You're not throwing me to these wolves?'

'You spoke a minute ago of your little jokes.'

'That, yes. But I still believe my life may be in danger. You must stay and see me through. Humphrey is very angry with me. He believed I could get him that public school place.'

'I shall not stay. Rosamund will be better away from this house, and I decline to be a party to your little jokes.'

'Well, before you go, would you get your man to run Humphrey and Binnie in to Wareham? They want to catch a train to Water- loo. My own car is needed for Tancred, who, for some reason, wishes to go to Shaftesbury.'

Dame Beatrice wondered how he knew this, as nothing, so far as she was aware, had been said about such an expedition on the previous evening. However, she made no demur. She said:

'That means, then, that Rosamund and I will be leaving a little later than I had anticipated.'

'Oh, you must certainly stay to lunch. Judith would never forgive me if you left without saying goodbye to her. Besides, you must be here when the post comes. I am anxious to show you the letters from Hubert and Willoughby. I cannot think why they have not written sooner to tell me they could not come along. I shall accompany Humphrey and Binnie to Wareham to see them off, so I may not be here to receive the letters.'

'You surely will not want to miss the postman when he comes. And if Humphrey is as angry as you say——'

'The letters will still be here when I get back, for surely those two boys will write? The point is, you see, that I want to make quite sure Humphrey and Binnie really *do* catch that train. Humphrey is in a very unpleasant mood, as I indicated, and I should not wish him to do me the mischief which I am sure he did not contemplate when he came down here.'

'You do not wish him to forestall the murderer?' Dame Beatrice facetiously enquired. Romilly took her seriously.

'Oh, Humphrey would not dare to go so far, but he might resort to fisticuffs, and I have a horror of unthinking violence,' he said.

'There are other kinds of violence, of course. Very well, I will accompany you to Wareham and George will protect you. Humphrey will not care to resort to violence in our presence.'

It was clear that her company was the last thing Romilly wanted, and it gave her inward amusement to watch his struggle with himself before he said:

'Well, that would be very nice, of course, but your man will be sufficient protection. Besides, would it not be better if you spent the time with your patient? With myself out of the house and the others upstairs out of the way, I should have thought . . . '

'We'll take Rosamund with us,' said Dame Beatrice. 'She will enjoy an outing, and since she and Binnie are of a fashionable slimness, they can sit in front in my car with George, and then there will be plenty of room for the rest of us on the back seat. I can sit between you and Humphrey and keep you apart. That way, you will feel perfectly safe.'

'Well, if you think it a good idea to take Trilby,' said Romilly, with the utmost unwillingness, 'I suppose it's all right.'

'By the way,' said Dame Beatrice, as though struck by a sudden thought, 'if you are going to Wareham in my car, who is to drive Tancred to Shaftesbury? – or is he, perhaps, to drive himself and return here later?'

'Oh, no, he does not propose to return. Luke can take him there and bring my car back.'

'Then I think perhaps I will change my mind. It is a much longer drive to Shaftesbury than to Wareham, and will be more of a treat for Rosamund, as she seems to go out so little. You had better take Humphrey and Binnie to Wareham in your own car, with Luke to protect you, and I will transport Tancred and Rosamund in mine. How will that be?'

(4)

Binnie, whose boneheadedness was almost equalled by her kindness of heart, had left Rosamund a slip, a woollen frock and a cardigan. She informed Dame Beatrice of this loan during the few moments they had together before Romilly took the married couple to Wareham to catch their train.

'Too bad she shouldn't have proper clothes,' said Binnie. 'Humphrey doesn't know I've lent them to her, so you won't say anything, will you? He's always saying I'm stupid, and so I am. If he finds out about the dress and things, I shall say I did it to spite Uncle Romilly. He hates him, you see. If anybody *does* murder Uncle Romilly, it's almost sure to be Humphrey. I shouldn't really mind if Humphrey went to prison for a good long time. Could you get me a job as a model? I would prefer clothes, but artists or photographers would be all right. If it was an artist, I might be his mistress, mightn't I? I'd like to be some-body's mistress. I wouldn't mind if he beat me and we had to live on bread and cheese and beer. I'd like him to be tempestuous, like some of those people in the Wednesday plays. And we'd make love all night and scratch each other's eyes out all day (except when he'd be painting, of course), and my picture would be in all the picture galleries and the Academy, and all that, and everybody would say, "Isn't she wonderful?" I'd love it, wouldn't I?'

'Yes, it would be very nice,' said Dame Beatrice. 'I think I hear them calling to you that the car is at the door. Thank you very much for lending Rosamund the clothes. It is most kind and thoughtful of you. If you'd care to give me your address, I will keep in touch with you.' Kitty Trevelyan, Laura's friend, she reflected, had her own *salon* (the foster-child, inciden-tally, of a prosperous hair-dressing establishment) and might be willing to give Binnie a trial. 'What are your – let me see now . . .'

'My statistics?' prompted Binnie. 'I'm classical.'

'By that you infer?'

'I don't infer. I know, Thirty-five, twenty-three, thirty-five – but Humphrey wouldn't like me to give you our address. He's ashamed of our little semi-detached.'

Dame Beatrice made a note.

'I will keep those figures in mind,' she said, 'but, of course, I make no promises. Goodbye, Mrs Provost.'

'Goodbye. I *do* like you,' said Binnie.

'Your kind words are reciprocated,' Dame Beatrice replied.

*   *   *

C

(5)

Once clear of Galliard Hall, Dame Beatrice stopped at a public telephone kiosk and rang up the Stone House in her own village of Wandles Parva. Laura answered, and was warned to expect her employer and a companion at some time during the afternoon, probably later rather than earlier.

The Wareham road took them past Sleeping Green and Winterborne Zelston to Blandford Forum, bland indeed in its eighteenth century elegance. This was the result of a fire which, in 1731, had destroyed most of the old town and caused it to be rebuilt in a fortunate style of architecture and with a unity of design unsurpassed except, perhaps, in parts of Dublin and Bath.

From Blandford the road ran due north, and a string of villages with their delightful Dorset names – Steepleton Iwerne, Iwerne Courtney, Iwerne Minster, Fontmell Magna, Melbury Abbas – came and went, along a road almost free of traffic.

The journey had begun with Tancred seated in front beside George, and Dame Beatrice beside Rosamund at the back, but after Dame Beatrice had made her telephone call she suggested that Rosamund might care to have Tancred beside her .

'Would he,' asked Rosamund, 'recite to me some more of his poetry?' So the change-over was effected and from time to time the poet's voice broke in on Dame Beatrice's thoughts. His work, she thought, was largely derivative. It was not difficult to pick out what he had been reading at the time of each short composition, and this, in so young a man, and one who fell short of posessing any very striking talent, did not surprise her. What she did find interesting was his obvious lack of interest in anything much later than the 1930's.

> 'Oh, were my love the sleeping fields,
>   And I the all-embracing snow,' intoned Tancred in
the snuffing voice of a man reciting his own poetry,

> 'I would enfold her dreaming peace
> And veil her lovely brow.'

There was rhyme, rhythm and a certain artlessness about the stuff which had its own attraction, Dame Beatrice decided. She listened to the rest of the short lyric. Later on – with Rosamund saying never a word of praise or criticism – one of the poems showed an even clearer derivation.

'Greatest Lover, ere my youth be gone,
Give me lovely things to muse upon—
Poets' griefs and songs, and lovers' joys,
Girls and sleeping babes and laughing boys;
Pools where the lazy fish serenely lie,
And ploughland furrows mounting to the sky;
Rounded hills where dream the older gods;
Goatfoot prints of Pan on country roads.'

The sestet which followed, to complete the sonnet, was less derivative and therefore less successful, Dame Beatrice thought. Tancred was seated directly behind her, so that it was easy enough – although she did it only once – to turn her head and glance at Rosamund, leaning back in her corner behind George with closed eyes and a slight smile. Rosamund, there could be no doubt of it, was thoroughly happy. There was a pause – dramatic effect, no doubt – and then Tancred began again. This was meant to be the words of a song, he explained.

'Twine your lovely head with flowers,
For their beauty is your own . . . '

Poets, even the least gifted of them, have extraordinary advantages, thought Dame Beatrice, when it comes to expressing their love – often, she reflected, insincerely.

Laura voiced these thoughts that same evening after Rosamund had been put to bed in the Stone House.

'The patient,' she stated, 'is rapt and starry-eyed. What have you been a-doin' of?'

'Allowing her to make the journey to Shaftesbury in company with a young poet, so-called,' Dame Beatrice replied. 'I fear she may have interpreted some of his words as personal compliments with erotic overtones, but, then, I believe they slept together last night.'

'Glad it's your responsibility, not mine. Incidentally, I don't notice any signs of nervous instability of the kind that I had envisaged.'

'There are none. The child needs a change of environment, that is all.'

'What was Cousin Romilly's object, then, in representing her as a candidate for the bin?'

'Oh, that was made clear. Go to bed. In the morning I will tell you all. How is Eiladh?'

'Flourishing, and no trouble to anybody. Liable to be ruined by spoiling, I'm afraid. I'm hardly allowed to do anything for her myself. Celestine and Zena have taken her over completely, and Hamish writes his weekly letter from school with extraordinary zest. He keeps begging me to put in for special week-end leave for him, so that he can come home and see her again, but, of course, I shall do nothing of the kind. The holidays come quite soon enough as it is, and he gets five weeks at Easter. I've tried to hound him into going with the school party to Brussels, but he's adamant. He's absolutely hooked on the baby.'

'I told you how it would be.'

'Yes, I know you did. I don't understand Hamish, and I never shall.'

CHAPTER SIX

Sarabande—Dancing Ledge

'. . . when you dance, I wish you
A wave o' the sea . . .'

The Winter's Tale.

---

(1)

Dame Beatrice had anticipated that repercussions would follow the abortive family gathering to which, for reasons which still seemed obscure, Romilly Lestrange had elected to invite his relatives. The repercussions which did follow, however, were not what she would have expected. They began in the morning succeeding the day on which she had introduced Rosamund into the Stone House, a move of which Laura did not altogether approve.

'She may be in fear of her life, and an escaped prisoner and all those things,' she said to Dame Beatrice when Rosamund, who seemed to favour plenty of sleep, was not up by a quarter to ten, 'but there's something all wrong about her.'

'Yes,' Dame Beatrice agreed, 'mixed up with all my sympathy for her orphan state, and the really great danger I believe her to be in, I have the feeling to which you allude. I will now tell you something interesting, trusting to your native sense of fair play to read nothing into the information which is not contained in the very slight evidence which is all I am able to give you.'

'All right,' said Laura. 'As a former student of history, I will try to keep an open mind. Does this (whatever it is) concern Rosamund?'

'That is where we have to keep an open mind. I simply do not know. However, this is the story, for what it is worth. I think I told you in my letter about the hole in the wall. This was a kind of squint intended not, as in a church, to give a view of the altar, but (as, thinking of you, I soon realised) to give a fair chance to a marksman in the adjoining room of putting a bullet into the head of anybody lying in the bed.'

69

'I don't understand why thinking of me should give you such an idea.'

'Do you not? I think our dear Robert would. Anyhow, when I also discovered that the bed was clamped to the floor so that it could not be moved, I thought that there was really no point in taking chances. I moved my pillows around so that my head was where whoever had arranged the bed had intended my feet to be, and prepared to sleep soundly.'

'Neat and practical. Don't tell me that, after these precautions, nothing happened?'

'Nothing of any consequence. However, I continued to exercise vigilance during the rest of my stay.'

'You stayed there another night, after finding out a thing like that?'

'For more than one reason. I was not quite ready to leave; also it did not seem likely that any bullet would be intended for me. The master of the house has not only designs (I believe) upon Rosamund's life, but he also fears for his own. As the room used to be his (if what he told me was true), he may have been the intended victim. To conclude, he now has had the hole screened off, not with the canvas-backed picture which had covered it when I was first shown into the room, but with a stout screen which proved to be a fixture.'

'You do see life when I'm not with you! Did you have a quiet night after all that?'

'Certainly, once the household had settled down.'

'Settled down? Then something *did* happen?'

'There was a certain amount of disturbance. Somebody thought he had heard the sound of a shot, but somebody else – Judith, I think it was – suggested that it might have been a car backfiring, and that the noise might have heralded the appearance of the two brothers Hubert and Willoughby Lestrange. Romilly went to investigate, but with no result.'

'Nobody had been hurt, then, if it *was* a shot?'

'Nobody.'

'You talked about my native sense of fair play before you told me this Wild West story, but, at the thought of it, beneath a flippant line of talk I am concealing a sensation of horror at the danger you may have been in. By "fair play" I take you to mean that there is the possibility that Rosamund could have taken a pop at you had she wished to do so. After all, she knew Romilly had moved out of that room and that it had been given over to you, didn't she?'

'She did, of course, and I do not lose sight of the fact that she may believe she has a motive for wishing me out of the way.'

'You mean because of the way the will of her grandfather is worded. But does she know who you are? Anyway, it's a bit of an outside chance that you'd ever inherit, the way I read the provisions.'

'She may have reached the stage when *anybody* named in the will seems a potential threat to her inheritance. I do not imagine that she is particularly well-versed in these matters.'

'And the next, or equal, subject is Romilly himself, I suppose?'

'Well, not necessarily. It is true that he, Rosamund and Judith – not forgetting Romilly's sinister and dour manservant Luke, who may also have known that Romilly's room had been changed and that I had been given it – all knew where I was sleeping, but there are other considerations. I did not feel it would be fitting to tell you, in front of Rosamund, of Romilly's extraordinary treatment of his guests, but it turned out that he had brought them to his house under false pretences by promising them benefits which he was unable to bestow. The details do not matter at the moment – although I have some plans which I may be able to carry out later on – but the point is that, as some of them had visited Galliard Hall at some previous time, they might have thought that Romilly was still in occupation of the same room ... '

'And could have taken a pop at showing that they were displeased with him,' said Laura. 'That sounds much the likeliest theory, I should say. Well, thank goodness they didn't do it – at least, not through the hole in your wall.'

'Of course, it was not until the day *after* this disturbance that Romilly told his relatives of his April Fool jesting.'

'That does rather knock my theory on the head, then.'

'Therefore we may shelve it, and read our letters,' said Dame Beatrice, reflecting upon how relatively simple it is to use truthful words to give an entirely wrong impression of the truth.

(2)

It was one of Laura's tasks, as secretary, to deal with the

morning's correspondence. She collected it from the table in the
hall and left there any letters which were addressed to the servants.
The rest she sorted at the breakfast table, for most of Dame
Beatrice's official correspondence was sent direct to her London
clinic and dealt with there. For the rest, Laura sorted out her
own letters and passed on, unopened, anything of a personal
nature sent to Dame Beatrice. A telegram came addressed to her
employer that morning so she handed it over without comment.
Dame Beatrice read it and handed it back.

'Hubert and Willoughby were not at the gathering,' she said.
'The inference to be drawn from this telegram is that Hubert
has been murdered, but who would want to murder an inoffensive
clergyman?'

'Do you intend to go along.'

'I was not particularly attracted to Judith, but she may be in
need of help.'

'May I come with you? I mean, Eiladh doesn't really need me
and *I* need a little diversion. Babies are all very well, but, having
pleased my husband and my son by giving up nine plus eight
months of my rapidly-vanishing life to the procreation and
maintenance of one that I didn't particularly want, I *do* now want
some fun. Please let me come.'

'Of course you must come. I will telegraph Judith to expect
us this afternoon.'

'What about the girl Rosamund?'

'Celestine can take charge of her for a few hours, I think. I
will warn her not to allow her to wander away.'

They arrived at Galliard Hall at half-past three. This time
there was nobody on the terrace. Luke, in his butler's garb,
answered the door, his customary hang-dog glumness replaced
by an equally hang-dog expression of fear and anxiety.

'The master's in the small drawing-room, madam, if you'd
come this way,' he said.

'Is he alone? Dame Beatrice asked.

'Except for Mrs Judith, yes, madam. The police have gone.'

Judith was lying on a settee with the drop-end down. Romilly
rose from an armchair when the visitors were announced and
managed to smile, although he looked haggard and appeared not
to have shaved. The high colour had gone from Judith's cheeks,
her eyes were lustreless and she looked extremely ill. She raised

herself on one elbow and then lowered her feet to the ground, sat up and held out both hands to Dame Beatrice.

'How good of you to come,' she said simply. 'We're in the most dreadful mess.'

Dame Beatrice introduced Laura, to whom she then gave a small notebook.

'Now,' she said, when they were seated and Laura had produced a ball-point pen, 'to business. What's it all about?'

(3)

'Uncle Romilly and I found the body,' said Judith. 'After you had taken Trilby away yesterday he was very restless and . . . '

'I was worried about her,' put in Romilly. 'I wondered whether, after all, I'd done the right thing in letting her go. In her condition I thought she might be better in an environment she knew, than among comparative strangers and in unfamiliar surroundings. By the way, did Tancred get to Shaftesbury all right?'

'Oh, yes, and on the way he entertained Rosamund by reciting his poems to her. Are Corin and Corinna still here?'

'They will be returning this evening. They know nothing, so far, about Hubert's death. They went off to rehearsal as soon as they had breakfasted. Luke and I had returned from depositing Humphrey and Binnie at the railway station. The twins, as you are aware, are not early risers, so we were back in time for Luke to take them to Wareham to catch the Bournemouth train. They were to lunch there, and their act – whatever it is – is timed for three o'clock in the afternoon and eight o'clock each evening. They will have to find their own way back. I cannot keep on providing transport. As it is, I am saving them a good deal of money by entertaining them here for the week.'

'The police will want to question them,' said Judith. 'We were asked whether anyone else was staying in the house.'

'Where is Giles?'

'He hasn't come back from the New Forest yet. I expect his friends who were members of the Hunt have asked him to stay. We had to mention him, too, of course, and we had to tell the police that you, Tancred and Trilby, and also Humphrey and Binnie, had been staying here.'

'How did Giles get to the meet?'

'Oh, a friend with a horse-box picked him up and will bring him back – a young man who lives at Lyndhurst and is a follower of the Hunt. I suppose we shall have to ask Giles to stay for dinner, but I do hope he won't expect to be put up for the night again. Perhaps he could stay with the people he stayed with last night, instead of with us. It's no time to have casual visitors in the house,' said Judith. She had regained something of her usual colour and animation.

'Suppose we begin at the beginning,' suggested Dame Beatrice. 'Having disposed of the rest of us, you two were left here alone, except for the servants. Please go on from there.'

'We had lunch at half-past one,' said Judith, 'and then, as it was a fine day and Uncle Romilly seemed restless, as I said, I thought it might be a good idea to go out for a short drive, leave the car at a convenient spot and take a stroll. I drove, and it was left to me to choose the route, so we went to Lulworth Cove and parked the car on the grassy common there, where everybody parks in the summer, but, of course, at this time of year, it's too early for visitors, so we had the parking space pretty much to ourselves.'

'Judith wanted to walk over Dungy Head to Durdle Door,' said Romilly, 'but it is a steep climb and I thought the path might be slippery, so I suggested going down to the Cove and then returning to the car and continuing our drive. We did this, and from Lulworth we took the road to Steeple and then it occurred to me to show Judith where I had found Trilby when she drowned the cat and the monkey . . . '

'And the life-sized baby doll,' put in Dame Beatrice, who, after her sessions with the girl, no longer believed a word of this story.

'Exactly,' agreed Romilly, with suspicious alacrity. 'And the life-sized baby doll. Well, as you probably know, there is no very direct route from Steeple to Dancing Ledge. We had to go through Church Knowle to Corfe Castle and then branch off for Kingston and go a good part of the way towards Langton Matravers. We left the car at the nearest possible point and took a path to make the rest of the way on foot. Dancing Ledge is not entirely a natural formation. The cliffs have been ridded (as it is called in these parts) by blasting, in order to quarry the stone, and then galleries have been driven into the rocks. Long platforms of stone have been left, and on these, at this particular spot, the waves do appear to dance, and on the Ledge itself a bathing place was blasted out for the use of schoolboys at the end of last century.'

'Uncle Romilly has a poor head for heights,' said Judith, taking up the tale, 'so he did not linger long on the nearby cliff-top, only long enough to say to me, "I can't stay here, my dear, I must retreat. But your eyes are younger than mine. Isn't there a man lying out on Dancing Ledge?" I looked as he pointed, before he walked away, and, of course, it was as he had said.'

'I went to the coastguard station as soon as we got back to the car,' said Romilly, 'and told them I feared someone had fallen over the cliff, but, of course, we never dreamed it was Hubert. The police obtained my address from the coastguards and they've been here since yesterday harassing and harrying us.'

'Has anything been heard of Willoughby, the brother?'

'Not a thing. He has not written and he has not come. I wondered whether I should mention to the police that he seems to have disappeared, but it is somewhat early days to suggest that.'

'*Disappeared?*'

'Well, I would not think of using such an expression had it not been for this dreadful business about Hubert.'

'You had no difficulty in identifying the body, then?'

'Well, the head and face were greatly disfigured, I suppose through contact with the rocky ledge, but I had little doubt.'

'Why should the police have thought that you might know who the dead man was?'

'I have myself to thank for that. I was greatly upset when I first spotted the body on the ledge, and I blurted out something at the coastguard station about Hubert and Willoughby having failed to turn up at my house, and, of course, that got passed on to the police. It's the most terrible thing! They seem prepared to treat Hubert's death as a case of murder!'

'So I gathered from Judith's telegram. Have they anything to go on?'

'I have no idea. They tell one nothing; they merely put interminable and very searching questions. I suppose they are inclined to rule out suicide, as Hubert was in holy orders, but I think they have ruled out the possibility of accident, too. Their questions suggest as much. Now you, my dear Beatrice, have had a wide experience in these matters. I told you that I had fears for my

own life, and now I am beginning to wonder whether Hubert
could possibly have been mistaken for me. What do you think
about that?'

'Well, I can hardly say, but it seems to me very unlikely. How
old would Hubert have been?'

'Yes, I see what you mean. Nobody knowing me can have
thought that so young a man – yes, yes, I take your point, of
course. But it seems inexplicable. Besides, what was he doing in
the neighbourhood of Dancing Ledge? It really is nowhere near
this house. He could not have been on his way to us, could he,
if he made so stupid a détour as that?'

'When is the murder supposed to have taken place?'

'Oh, if the police know that – as, I suppose, they must do, near
enough – they are keeping it to themselves. You know what they
are! They never tell you anything if they can possibly help it.

(4)

"I could bear to go and take a look at Dancing Ledge,' said
Laura, when they had thoroughly discussed this latest visit to
Galliard Hall. 'Is there any reason why I shouldn't?'

'I do not suppose so. The police will have completed their
on-the-spot investigations by the time we go, I should imagine,
and the place ordinarily must be open to the public, or Romilly
and Judith could not have gone there. Get out the Ordnance
maps and let us decide upon the best way to get to the Ledge
from here.'

Laura did as she was told. Dancing Ledge was clearly marked.
Behind it the hills rose steeply for about a quarter of a mile, and
after that the slope was more gentle. Working inland from the
cliffs, nothing but a footpath was marked until the map showed
the secondary road which ran between Kingston and Langton
Matravers and finished at Swanage.

'Bournemouth and Sandbanks for us,' said Laura, 'and then
over the ferry, don't you think? Looks a bit of a scramble to
get down to the Ledge. Is Romilly capable of it?'

'I shall know better when we have explored the terrain for ourselves. I wonder whether Rosamund would care to come with
us? The invitation would come better from you than from me, I
think.'

'Is that an order?'

'Yes,' said Dame Beatrice thoughtfully, 'I think it is. I should like to know how she reacts to the suggestion. Approach the matter bluntly. Simply tell her we are going to Dancing Ledge, and ask her whether she would like to accompany us.'

'Does she know about the body?'

Dame Beatrice favoured her secretary with a crocodile grin.

'Oh, I'm sure she does,' she replied. 'There is an account of it in the newspaper which arrived this morning and I am perfectly sure that she has read it.'

Laura found Rosamund in the library and issued the invitation in the forthright manner advised by Dame Beatrice.

'Dancing Ledge?' said Rosamund, turning away from the bookshelf she had been studying. 'Why should I want to go there?'

'For the sake of an outing, that's all.'

'Oh, no, thank you, I'd rather stay here. Henri is going to teach me to cook. I am to help get tonight's dinner ready.'

'Oh, well, keep the arsenic well away from the soup,' said Laura lightly, glad that they were not to have Rosamund's company on the expedition. She reported the brief exchange to her employer.

'Didn't turn a hair at the mention of Dancing Ledge,' she said. 'Just said she'd rather stay here because Henri was going to teach her to cook. Do you suppose her childlike appearance and innocent air have bewitched the staff?'

'I think they feel sorry for her. I gave them an account of her orphaned condition – that was for Zena's benefit – and dropped a hint to Henri that she was a patient of mine who was suffering from melancholia and must be taken out of herself as much as possible. I took Celestine more fully into my confidence, for she is intelligent enough to realise that there is nothing melancholic about Rosamund. Well, let us be off. The days still draw in very early, and we have to allow ourselves time to cover the ground after we have reached our objective. Tell Henri to put us up some sandwiches, and perhaps it would be best for us to use your car, and for you to drive it.'

'Fine! I suppose you want to leave George at home to help keep an eye on Rosamund.'

'I want George to stay behind to keep an eye on the other car. If he were to drive us in mine, there is just the chance that

Rosamund, if she can drive, might take it into her head to go off in your car and then she might run into some sort of danger. As I have taken her out of Romilly's sphere of influence, an accident to her might place me in an invidious position.'

'You do think she's irresponsible, then?'

'I did not care much about the Ophelia exhibition. It was most extravagant and unnecessary. Irresponsible, however, is not the word I would have chosen. The point is that, having, one might almost say, abducted her, I must exercise the greatest care to see that she comes to no harm and that Romilly has no opportunity to contact her.'

'There's something you're not telling me,' said Laura.

'My suspicions are possibly unfounded, unkind, and unworthy of me,' Dame Beatrice replied, 'so we had better leave it at that.'

(5)

The trackway to Dancing Ledge, indicated by an unofficial signpost easily missed unless one was looking out for it, was a roughly-made little road much too narrow to allow two cars to pass. It led to a large house with outbuildings, and for a short distance the road was better surfaced, presumably by the owners of the house, for it deteriorated again beyond it. So far it had been bordered by trees and ragged hedges, but suddenly it ended on open pasture and some farm buildings came in sight, together with a notice which forbade parking on the verges but offered facilities for this at the farm.

Laura had driven with extreme caution over the very rough parts of the road, and, in any case, she had to pull up when she reached the farm gate. A comely young woman emerged from the building, smiled, asked a shilling for a parking fee, and indicated where they might leave the car.

After that, it was country walking. There were gates to be opened and shut, fixed wooden barriers to duck under, and a stile, consisting of two iron bars, to be climbed. Dame Beatrice, thin and wiry, and still remarkably agile considering her years, made nothing of these obstacles, and needed no assistance from Laura. On the far side of the last barrier they had to begin the steep descent which they had seen indicated by the contour lines on the map. It was rough and difficult in places, and they took their time.

'Better keep on the grass,' suggested Laura. 'The path is on chalk, and is bound to be slippery this time of year.'

From the top of the slope they had already seen the sea. The countryside was gloriously open, but stone walls and wire fences marked off the various pastures. To the right was Saint Aldhelm's Head, and beneath their feet, when at last they reached the grassy top of the cliff, lay Dancing Ledge, a long, flat platform of rock parallel with the almost straight line of the coast.

'I suppose the body was found out there on the Ledge itself,' said Laura, pointing to where the sea, in the calm air (for it was an almost windless day, unusual on that coast at that early time of the year), lapped lazily in tiny cream-topped ripples. 'How about if I beetled down and took a closer look?'

Knowing that she wanted to do this, Dame Beatrice agreed, and watched her as she made the scrambling descent. The cliff, at this point, was not high, and, in spite of the fact that the way down, worn smooth by the shoes of summer visitors, was very slippery, Laura negotiated it without difficulty and was soon standing on the broken ground where the cliff face, in former times, had been quarried away.

She soon returned, and announced that there was nothing more to be seen than could be descried, perhaps better, from where Dame Beatrice was standing. Then they began the steep climb back to the farm.

'Don't know what *you're* thinking,' said Laura, as they halted, half-way up, to take breath and look back at the misty view, 'but whoever got poor Hubert down this way had his work cut out.'

'There are two ways in which it could most easily be done,' said Dame Beatrice. 'Either the corpse was *not* a corpse when the descent was made, but was killed on the sea-shore itself and then pushed on to the Ledge, or else it was brought round by boat. This was a known spot for smugglers, and it was perfectly possible, so I read, to get a boat up to the Ledge in calm weather to land contraband cargo. I think the first theory is the more likely one, but that is for the police to decide.'

'What, then, is *our* next move?'

'I think it might be interesting to take tea with Romilly and give him an account of our excursion. His last question to me was whether I thought that Hubert could possibly have been mistaken for Romilly himself. I would say that it seems to me extremely unlikely. As to theorising about the means of bringing the body to the Ledge, I am sure I am right. Even if it had been transported as far as the farm by car, it is clear that it would have had to be manhandled from the farm onwards. This could scarcely have been done by daylight, or by one person, and I cannot see that it would be possible after dark, especially at this time of year and on such a rough and slippery path.'

'Besides, there are those over-and-under barriers, put up, I suppose, by the farm people, to stop the passage of cars over their land. I don't suppose there were any barriers at all when the smugglers were operating, but even *they* must have had their work cut out, even if they parked the contraband at the farm, as I suppose they did. Up to the farmhouse it must be the best part of a mile from the Ledge, and some of it is horribly rough and steep, and going down is as bad as coming up.'

'Oh, yes, I think we must rule out the possibility that the corpse was carried by the way we have come. The police will have come to the same conclusion. Even if more than one person was involved, the operation would be so hazardous that I cannot think anybody would conceive of it.'

'Of course, we don't know yet – and I suppose we shan't, until we hear the medical evidence at the inquest – the cause of the death, do we?'

They found Romilly and Judith in the same state of alarm and despondency as that in which Dame Beatrice had left them. Romilly, however, cheered up at the sight of them, and Judith rang for tea with an alacrity which suggested that she also welcomed their visit.

'So you have been occupying yourself on my behalf,' said Romilly, when the tea-things had been cleared away. 'I had so much hoped you would. It is extremely good of you, Beatrice. The police have not troubled us again, but, as I think I told you yesterday, they want to question everybody who was staying here. I'm afraid my little jokes have had a most unfortunate aftermath. What do you propose to do now? Dare I hope that you and this charming young lady, your secretary, will stay here for a few days and see us through our ordeal? I am sure we have not seen the last of the police, and I should welcome your advice and support.'

CHAPTER SEVEN

Sword Dance—Kirkby Malzeard

'Creaking my shoes on the plain masonry,
    Till honour be bought up, and no sword worn
    But one to dance with.'

The Taming of the Shrew.

---

(1)

'My first duty, as I see it,' said Dame Beatrice, 'is to return home
to be with Rosamund. If, as you say, the police wish to question
everyone who was staying at Galliard Hall at the time (so far as
this is known) of Hubert's death, then my place is with the child.'

'But you'll come back?' urged Romilly. 'I need you here. I am
not accustomed to have dealings with the police.'

'I hope to come back, in due course. Meanwhile, there is
always your lawyer if you need advice. I assume you have already
made contact with him.'

'Well, no, but I suppose I had better do so. The police seem
to think it odd that Judith and I should have chanced upon the
spot where the body was lying. I was compelled to protect myself
by explaining what had taken us there.'

'I see that Rosamund undoubtedly will need me to safeguard
her interests when the police call at my house.'

'I wish you were staying here, at least for today and tomorrow.
I quite anticipated that you would be on hand when the police
pay us their next visit. It may even be this afternoon. If not, it is
certain to be tomorrow. Could you not stay to dinner and spend
the night here? It will be no trouble to Judith to provide a bed
for Mrs Gavin.'

'She can have Tancred's room,' said Judith at once. 'The
maids have put it to rights.'

'It is very kind of you, but I feel we must get back to Rosamund.
I take it that you have given the police my address.'

'We had no choice. We had to account for the whereabouts of
all of you. I could be certain of where you and Trilby would be,
and equally so in the case of Humphrey and Binnie, but I could

give no exact address for Tancred, for, beyond mentioning that he was staying in Shaftesbury, he added no details, and the address to which I wrote when I invited him was a London one. However, they have their way of tracking people down.'

Amabel came out to the car when the visitors had taken their leave. She said, when the window was let down, 'Please, Dame Beatrice, mum, could I speak to you? It's the police, mum. Voilert and Oi, us don't fancy stoppen in a place where the police keeps comen.'

'No, mum,' said Violet, who had followed her out.

'Keep coming? Why, how many times have they called?'

'Twoice a'ready, and comen again tonoight or tomorrow, so Mester warned us. Fritten us, they do.'

'There is no need for you to feel frightened. You certainly cannot leave in the middle of their enquiries. They might think that you had something to hide. In any case, I am quite sure they wouldn't allow you to go.'

'But us don't know nothen about what happened to the poor gentleman, mum, and what us don't know us can't say, can us now?'

'Do you think Amabel was telling the whole truth?' asked Laura, as the car approached the great gates.

'I am convinced she was not. I saw, as you did, her sister's tug on her apron. There is something they both know, and it is the knowledge which frightens them, not the police as such.'

'You didn't try to get it out of them, I noticed.'

'At such an early stage I doubt whether it would have been worth the effort. Besides, I do not think they would have answered a direct question. There are other means to the same end.'

'Have you any idea what it is they know?'

'I have as many theories as there were guests, servants and residents at Galliard Hall last week. The most likely one, so far as I can see at present (which, I may add, is almost no distance at all), is something to do with the non-appearance of Hubert and Willoughby at Galliard Hall at the time for which they were invited.'

'But that might be fearfully important!'

'It might. Time will show. Meanwhile, I shall be very glad indeed to get back to Rosamund.'

They were met at the front door by Celestine, who was quivering with righteous wrath.

'Figure to yourself, madame, the police have come here!'

'Oh, yes? I will see them as soon as I have removed my outdoor things.'

'But they are no longer here, madame. I sent them away. "Never," I said, "do I admit intruders when madame and Madame Gavin are both out of the house. How do I ascertain," I asked them, "that you are not thieves and assassins?" They show me little cards. I pouf at their little cards. "Forgeries," I say. "If not, madame will know, when she comes in. I have heard," I say, "of warrants to search. Have you such warrants?" They say there will be no search, but only a few little questions to the *jeune fille* madame brings home with her. "There is also a little baby in the house," I tell them. "Shall I have a little baby wake up *parmi le bruit de pas, le bruit de pas, comme les chevaux de charrette*, made by your big, ugly boots? *Non*," I say, "but certainly not, messieurs." '

'You'll get us all arrested one of these days,' said Laura.

'You did rightly, Celestine,' said Dame Beatrice. 'The *jeune fille* I brought with me is in a highly nervous state and in no condition to stand up to police questioning when I am not here.'

'There has been, as usual, an assassination, then,' said Celestine, in a resigned tone, 'and madame will once more be toiling to assist the police to arrest a monster.'

Laura followed Dame Beatrice into the library where they had left Rosamund on their departure for Galliard Hall. The girl was reading, but put down the book as they entered and rose to her feet. Her anxious eyes questioned them. Dame Beatrice said:

'Tancred is quite well, so far as we know. Have you ever met Hubert Lestrange, a clergyman? He was to have joined the house-party, but did not turn up. We now know why.'

'He is dead?' asked Rosamund.

'Yes. By what means we do not know yet, but the police have had to be told.'

'He was killed, then.'

'The police seem to think so. They want to talk to those persons who were at Galliard Hall last week.'

'And I am one of them.'

'So am I. So are a number of other people.'

'Will the police come here, or shall you and I need to go back there?'

'They will come here.'

'I shall have nothing to tell them.'

'That, most likely, will be my case, too, so there is nothing for us to worry about, thank goodness.'

'I should never worry if you were with me.'

'Good. By the way, it is essential to be quite frank with them.' Rosamund looked scared.

'But I can be nothing else,' she insisted. 'I don't know anything about Hubert Lestrange at all. I had no idea he was dead.'

'They will ask you to account for your movements, and so forth.'

'Suppose I can't remember?'

'Tell them so.'

'But they'll bully me into trying to remember, won't they? Romilly was always bullying me and shouting at me and losing his temper.'

'The police will not behave like that, I promise you. But don't attempt to conceal anything from them, even if it is embarrassing or painful for you to admit some things which you may wish to keep to yourself. We all have our weak points and it is useless to attempt to disguise or hide them.'

Rosamund looked at the keen, black eyes and the quirky, beaky little mouth and then dropped her own eyes and said quietly:

'You are thinking of something in particular.'

'Yes,' agreed Dame Beatrice, 'I am. As I suppose you know, Hubert's body was found on Dancing Ledge.' She saw the girl flinch. 'Yes,' she went on, 'Romilly will have told the police that he saw you drown the cat and the monkey somewhere along that stretch of coast, and throw the large doll into the sea.'

'But you don't believe him, do you?'

'No, I do not, but I am anxious that you shall not deny having run away to those cliffs or that Romilly found you and brought you back – that is, if these things really happened.'

'But the police may believe I drowned things – living creatures – and they may think I'm mad, and that I pushed Hubert over the cliff.'

'Tell the truth, simply and openly. Then I can help you. And now I will tell *you* the truth about myself. My name is not Beatrice Adler. I did not correct you at the time, because it was unnecessary and, for you, perhaps, alarming. I am Beatrice Adela Lestrange Bradley, and I am attached to the Home Office in the capacity of psychiatric adviser.'

'But then – but then – ' she raised her eyes and gazed first at Dame Beatrice, who had seated herself composedly in an armchair, and then at the tall and magnificent Laura, who, like Rosamund herself, was still standing.

'Yes,' said Dame Beatrice quietly, 'failing yourself and Romilly, who is quite as infamous a man as you have always suspected, I am the heiress named in your grandfather's Will. Nevertheless, I have every intention of seeing that you get your rights. I cannot prove this to you at present. I can only ask you to believe me and to tell the police the whole truth.'

'But I – but I – "

'There's nothing else you *can* do,' interpolated Laura bluntly, 'so there's no point in raising objections. Besides, you're being cagey. You read this morning about the body on Dancing Ledge."

(2)

The police, called up by Laura and told that Dame Beatrice was at home and would be pleased to see them, turned up in the person of a friend of hers, Detective-Inspector Nicholas Kirkby, recently promoted, youngish, keen, efficient and fair-minded. He was shown into the library, where she greeted him warmly. Laura had already made his acquaintance through Dame Beatrice and her own husband, so Rosamund was introduced and the two young women went out of the room.

'So that's the young girl I've been hearing about,' said Kirkby. 'The lady who chucks things, animate and inanimate, into the sea. The theory at Galliard Hall seems to be that this dead man was one of them. What can you tell me about her, Dame Beatrice? I was told you've been staying at the house, but left before the body was discovered.'

'That is so. I was invited to go to Galliard Hall to examine and treat this girl with a view to curing her of what I was told was an obsession. In my opinion, she is perfectly normal, and the stories which have been put about are lies. I hasten to add that this is only an opinion. After all, I have only known her for about a week. In her own view, she is the centre of a conspiracy to rob her of her fortune. When she dies, after she attains the age of twenty-five, the money goes to the man who claims to be her husband.'

'Mr Romilly Lestrange? Yes, he told me she was his wife. Why, do you doubt it, Dame Beatrice?'

'Yes, I do. I believe the girl, who asserts that she is merely his ward. I think the housekeeper, Mrs Judith, may be married to him.'

'It sounds an odd sort of set-up. Reminds you of a mid-Victorian novel, doesn't it? However, all I have to find out at the moment is who killed the Reverend Hubert Lestrange, so I am trying to discover where everybody was, and what each of the household was doing, at the probable time of his death.'

'And when was that?'

'That's my chief difficulty at present. It's hard to pin the doctors down about it. The furthest they will go is to say that when they examined him he had probably been dead for five or six days, but that, as the body had been in water, it could be as long as seven or eight days. Now, just for the record, could I have an account of your own movements for the past eight days?'

'Certainly. That takes us back to yesterday (Sunday) week, does it not?' She opened a table drawer and took out her engagement book. 'Last Sunday week I was at home here and, apart from a stroll in the garden to look at the early daffodils, I did not leave the house.

'Last Monday I went to London on a routine visit to my clinic. I caught the early train – the slow one, because the fast, which comes through from Weymouth, does not stop at Brockenhurst – and reached my clinic at twelve. I lunched at half-past one at the Dorchester, where they will remember me, took a short stroll in the Park and returned to my clinic at three. I remained there until half-past four, took tea there with the resident staff, had about an hour's conversation with the doctor-in-charge, and caught the six-thirty fast train from Waterloo to Bournemouth, where my chauffeur met me with the car. I arrived home at approximately nine o'clock, dined, talked to Laura, sent her to bed and then I stayed up and read until about midnight.'

'That seems to account very nicely for Sunday and Monday.'

'On Tuesday I attended the baptism of Laura's baby daughter. We lunched at home and the ceremony was at three in the village church. After the ceremony, which was also attended by the Assistant Commissioner and his son, I told Laura that I had received an invitation to stay at Galliard Hall.'

'Oh, yes. When did you receive this invitation?'

'On the previous Thursday. Laura usually attends to my correspondence, but this envelope was marked *Personal*, so, of course, she did not open it and, as I did not make up my mind immediately whether to accept or not, I did not mention it until I had come to a decision.'

'But you *did* accept the invitation?'

'Oh, yes, after some thought, I wrote to Romilly Lestrange on the Monday, while I was at my clinic, and posted the letter at Waterloo.'

'May I ask why it took you from the Thursday until the Monday to make up your mind?'

'Certainly you may. I had never heard of Romilly Lestrange, and his claim to be my cousin by my first marriage I mentally queried. This being so, I decided that Romilly might be a scoundrel, and I thought I would add him to my collection of smooth villains. I have done so with the greatest delight.'

'That, then, brings us to Wednesday and the time you actually spent at Galliard Hall.'

Dame Beatrice gave him a detailed account of her stay, including her talks with Rosamund and the others. He did not ask any questions until she had finished. Then he said:

'So you disbelieve Mr Romilly Lestrange's description of the strange conduct of the young lady, and she, in spite of what he told you, insists she is not his wife.'

'At present I am inclined to believe the girl. I think she has been worried, thwarted and unhappy, but that is not all. I believe she has gone in fear of her life. I do not know who Romilly is, but I doubt whether he is a member of my first husband's family. There is much that I intend to find out, but, so long as the girl is safe, I am in no hurry to continue my investigations on her behalf. They can wait until you have cleared up your case. May I ask what makes you regard the Reverend Hubert's death as murder?'

'That he was murdered is only our theory. It may have been

suicide, but, considering his vocation, we are doubtful about that. However, if he hadn't been a clergyman we should have been more open-minded about suicide than we are. Our object, when we've heard what our witnesses have to tell us, is to try to find out what on earth he was doing on the cliff at all.'

'I wonder whether he had paid any previous visits to Galliard Hall? I understand that he had not.'

'That's something I hope to find out. You mean he may have been decoyed on to the cliff-top. If he didn't know the country-side, he wouldn't have realised that Dancing Ledge is not on the way to Galliard Hall. I asked Mr Romilly for a list of his guests and his household. I wonder whether you would be good enough to check it with me?'

'I can only be sure of the people who were in the house while I myself was there, of course.' She checked the list he handed over. 'That is correct, so far as I know.'

'Good. Perhaps I could talk to – I shall have to call her Mrs Lestrange, I suppose – in your presence?'

Rosamund appeared nervous. She was still wearing the clothes lent by Binnie, since there had been no time to get her fitted out, and Kirkby was confronted by a slim, fair-haired, innocent-eyed creature in an unfashionably long skirt – for she was shorter than Binnie – and a cardigan which was almost all-enveloping, since she did not possess Binnie's beautifully-moulded figure.

Dame Beatrice presented the detective-inspector, who said at once:

'I only want to ask you one or two questions which I think you will find easy enough to answer, Mrs Lestrange.'

'No, please,' she said, 'that is not my name. I am *Miss*, not Mrs Lestrange. Romilly is my guardian, not my husband. I know what he told Dame Beatrice, but it simply isn't true. I'm not married, I'm not mad, I don't drown things and I haven't had a miscarriage. I've never been pregnant. I shall inherit a fortune on May 29th and I don't ever, *ever* want to go back to Galliard Hall.'

'Well, that seems a pretty comprehensive summing-up, Miss Lestrange, but it isn't what I've come here to find out. When did you last go to Dancing Ledge?'

'I can't remember the date. It would have been quite a long time ago. I was running away from Romilly, but he chased after me and brought me back. It was after that, that he and Judith wouldn't let me have proper clothes to wear. They took all my things away and left me only fancy dress – stage armour and a Georgian costume and that sort of thing – so that I couldn't go out.'

'A Georgian costume, eh? With all the accessories, no doubt. Can you remember what you did last Sunday week?'

'Yes. I read *The Woman in White*.'

'All day long?'

'Except for meal-times, yes.'

'Then Mr Romilly was mistaken when he told us that you might have slipped out of the house. What about the next day?'

'I went on reading my book.'

'And on the Tuesday, a week ago today?'

'Romilly told me he had sent for Dame Beatrice – only he called her Professor Beatrice Adler – and he said that she was a psychiatrist and would be examining me.'

'Did that cause you alarm?'

'Yes, of course. You see, if Romilly can prove, before I am twenty-five, that I'm not fit to manage my own affairs, my fortune will go to him, provided that he gives me a home and treats me kindly.'

'I see. Well, we can go into that later, perhaps. What did you do for the remainder of the day?'

'I wrote a long letter to Dame Beatrice, telling her all about myself.'

'Did you give it to her?'

'No. I thought I would find out first what she was like and whether she would be prepared to help me. I went to her room on the Wednesday evening, when I knew the others would be downstairs, and I found – I decided – that it wouldn't be necessary to show her the letter. She would be my friend, I felt sure of that. I have the utmost trust in her.'

'And, apart from going to Swanage with Dame Beatrice, during that week you did not leave Galliard Hall until you had an outing to Shaftesbury and then came here?'

'Only to go into an enclosed bit of garden they let me use when I needed fresh air and exercise, otherwise I never went out.'

'Which of the invited guests had you known before they arrived at Galliard Hall?'

'All of them, but only very slightly.'

'I take it you also knew Hubert and Willoughby Lestrange, as they were related to you. Had you known them long?'

'I knew Willoughby, because he was my grandfather's secretary. Hubert conducted my grandfather's funeral service. I did not know him before that.'

'I thought you said you did not know him at all,' Dame Beatrice mildly interpolated.

'Well, you couldn't call that *knowing* him!' protested the girl. Dame Beatrice let it pass.

'And Willoughby?' went on Kirkby. 'What about him?'

'I don't know what's happened to him. He lived in our hotel, so I knew him quite well, but, of course, he had nothing but his salary, so he had to get another post when grandfather died, and until I heard he was invited to Galliard Hall, I had never heard of him again.'

'How did you know he had been invited?'

'I didn't, at first. I wasn't told *who* had been invited until they came. It was Tancred who told me that Hubert and Willoughby had been invited and hadn't turned up. He told me so in bed on the second night of his stay. I asked him more about it when we were both in Dame Beatrice's car on our way to Shaftesbury. He recited a lot of his poetry to me on the journey, because, of course, we couldn't do anything but talk. I don't think I love Tancred, but he was sweet and kind, and such fun.'

'How were you treated at Galliard Hall? You say Mrs Binnie Provost and Mr Tancred were kind. How did Mr Romilly treat you?'

'Quite well, in lots of ways. I mean, I had plenty to eat, and the two maids were nice, and I had lots and lots of books. I love reading. I had a radio set, too, but they took that away just before Dame Beatrice came.'

'You had freedom to move about the house?'

'I suppose so. There wasn't much point. I had my meals by myself, but I liked it better that way. When I was with *them* they always treated me like a child who wasn't right in the head. It was dreadful to fight against *that!*'

'It must have been. Let me get one thing clear. You knew Mr Hubert and Mr Willoughby when you were with your grandfather?'

'Yes – if you call it *knowing* Hubert. I only saw him once.'

'Have you ever met them at Galliard Hall?'

'No, never, and I had only met the others once before.'

'At Galliard Hall?'

'Yes. Romilly gave a house-warming and they all turned up to it.'

'Thank you, Miss Lestrange. I think that is all for the present.' He was turning to go when a thought seemed to strike him.

'Just half a minute,' he said. He went into the hall and returned carrying an unsheathed sword. 'I suppose neither of you has seen this thing before?' he asked.

'It's a rapier, isn't it?' asked Rosamund.

'Could it have come from Galliard Hall?' asked Kirkby.

'It could have done, I suppose. Romilly has a small collection of weapons, I believe, but I've never taken any interest in the things.'

'You did not wear a sword as part of your Georgian costume, then, Miss Lestrange?'

'There was nothing short enough for me, I imagine. Romilly and Judith provided the costumes, but I certainly was never given a sword.'

'Only a horse-pistol,' said Dame Beatrice.

Kirkby stood the weapon upright on its pommel, thoughtfully sparing Dame Beatrice's carpet, for the point of the sword was very sharp.

'This thing is not a rapier,' he said. 'I am told that it is a small-sword, although, as you see, the blade is of a pretty fair length. It measures, as a matter of fact, thirty-two and a half inches, and, with the hilt, another six and a quarter inches, so, as you say, it would be too long for you to wear as part of your costume, although the date of it, according to my information, would be about right for Georgian dress. You're sure you've never seen it before?'

'I'm perfectly sure. Anyway, oughtn't it to have a sheath? It looks very dangerous like that.'

'We're still in hopes of finding the sheath, but it doesn't matter if we don't.'

'I don't see why you've brought the sword here,' said Rosamund in an unusually spirited tone.

'As I said, Miss Lestrange, to find out whether you could

identify it. We're very anxious to know where it came from.'

'Why – is it – is it . . . ?'

'We don't know for certain, not yet, but Mr Romilly picked it up on the cliff-top not a long way from Dancing Ledge.'

'By the way,' said Dame Beatrice, 'who identified the body?'

'Mr Romilly Lestrange. We've questioned him about finding the poor young gentleman and he told us that his nephews Hubert and Willoughby had not turned up at Galliard Hall, so we got him to make a formal identification, which, I may add, he was unwilling to do until we pointed out there was nothing to fear.'

'Nothing to fear?' echoed Rosamund. 'When somebody has been killed, and a sword has been found with Romilly's finger-prints on it, and you're questioning everybody who was at Galliard Hall last week? How can there be nothing to fear?'

'Now, now, miss,' said Kirkby. 'Nothing to fear, and nothing to get excited about, so long as you're an innocent party. Now you seem to be in Mr Tancred's confidence to a certain extent, and you went in the car with him and Dame Beatrice to Shaftes-bury. It's not where he lives – at least, it's not his permanent address as given by Mr Romilly Lestrange – so do you know how long he intends to stay there?'

'I don't know anything about it. We left him outside a church . . . '

'St Peter's,' said Dame Beatrice, 'in Shaftesbury.'

'He didn't mention his plans, miss?'

'Not to me.'

'Right. Thank you, Miss Lestrange. I'll have to find him, of course.'

CHAPTER EIGHT

Coranto—Felix Napoleon's Fancy

'Will it please you to see the epilogue, or to hear a
Burgomask dance between two of our company?'
A Midsummer Night's Dream.

---

(1)

Tancred was tracked down without the slightest difficulty.
Accompanied by Dame Beatrice (her companionship sufficiently
accounted for on the score that she knew the people concerned),
Kirkby went straight to the police station in Shaftesbury.

'Provost?' said the desk-sergeant. 'Why, yes, sir. He's on bail,
on his own recognisances. Charged with causing a breach of the
peace – to wit, getting drunk, insisting on reciting poetry and
assaulting the landlord when requested to leave. His case comes
up tomorrow morning.'

'I'm investigating that case of the clergyman found dead on
Dancing Ledge. This man Provost may be able to help me.'

'Well, you'll find him in his caravan on Fuddy's Farm Fields,
about four miles from here. He's living there, as usual, with a
friend.' He gave concise directions. 'The friend's a female,' he
added.

'Is she also a lover of poetry?' Dame Beatrice enquired.

'She'll have to be, ma'am, with that one. He writes it. Let's
hope, for his own sake, he doesn't start reciting to the magistrates.
Sir Bentham will send him down without the option if he
does.'

'Show me on the map where this place is,' said Kirkby. The
sergeant pin-pointed Fuddy's Farm Fields on the large-scale
wall-map. 'I see. The Blandford road, and branch off at the foot
of Melbury Hill. Doesn't look much like farming country.'

'The farm itself is more than three miles away.'

'Oh, yes, I see. Thanks, Sergeant. Well, I think I can find my
way.'

'Anything else I can do, sir?'

'Might be – later on.'

(2)

The caravan was sheltered not only from the north by the noble, beacon-topped hill, but from the south-west by a small wood. They found Tancred, in a sheepskin jacket, jeans and fur-lined boots, seated on the steps of his caravan, engaged, apparently, with his Muse, for he had a large scribbling-tablet on his knees and a pencil in his hand.

'Oh, Lord!' he said, looking up, as, the car having come to a bumping halt on the wheel-rutted turf, he saw Dame Beatrice. 'So you've tracked me down, have you? Trust the blasted police to give me away!'

'*I* am the police,' said Kirkby. 'I am conducting an investigation into the death of the Reverend Hubert Lestrange, whose body was found below the cliffs on Dancing Ledge.'

'So that's who it was,' said Tancred.

'Sir?'

'Oh, I spotted it, you know, last – when would that have been? – last Tuesday. Yes, that's right. Day after I'd accepted my invitation to old Romilly's place, Galliard Hall. I wrote a ballad about it. You know – four-line stanzas with a b c b rhymes. Martha set a tune to it, and we have it as one of our fireside songs. Would you care to hear it?'

'You saw the body last Tuesday? What time would that have been, sir?'

'Let's see, now. We'd come up here from London the day before. Martha drove me to Blandford for her weekly shopping, and we got there at ten and had loaded up the boot of her car by about eleven, I suppose. We'd planned to get lunch out, but it was much too early to have it then, so I said, 'Why don't we stick old Romilly up? Save our money, and give me a chance to find out what sort of ideas he's got, because he's holding a family pow-wow and I wouldn't mind having a shot at finding out why.' Well, Martha wouldn't wear it, so I said, 'Well, it wouldn't hurt for you to have a look at the outside of it. It's crumbling a bit, but it's a fine old place. We'll have lunch in Wareham and go on from there.'

'And did you lunch in Wareham, sir?'

'Well, no – at least, not *table d'hôte*. More *à la carte*, if you know what I mean. We bought rolls and ham and cheese and apples and beer, and had an *al fresco* in the car.'

'Whereabouts, sir?'

'There's a rather jolly little parking-place on the quay. All right this time of year, but the hell of a place to get out of in the holiday season because of the two-way traffic on the Swanage road.'

'And then, sir?'

'Well, then we came out and drove over the bridge, and we were all right until we got to Langton Matravers, but it appeared we'd missed some sort of turning and had come too far south or east or something. The post-office people directed us, but it sounded so horribly complicated that, after we'd looked at the map, when we got back into the car, Martha said, "Let's pack it in, and go and have a look at the sea. The cliffs are marvellous this side of Swanage." So, of course, that's how I came to spot the body, but I hadn't a clue who it was.'

'You did not examine it, sir?'

'Good Lord, no! I'm a poet, not a blasted bloodhound! It gave me the idea for this ballad, though. That's the main thing.'

'It did not occur to you that the gentleman might not be dead, and that maybe you could help him?'

'He was dead enough! The waves were gently rolling him about.'

'And you did not report what you had seen?'

'Why should I? It never occurred to me. Martha was a bit chastened, so I piloted her to the car and comforted her, and then we drove back to Wareham and had tea in that jolly bow-window place where they have lashings of cream and always do you so well.'

'May I have the young lady's address, sir?'

'Well, for the present, she's living here. You're not going to bully her, I hope? She can't tell you any more than I can, and, anyway, at present, she's out.'

'When do you expect her back, sir?'

'God knows! She's gone in to Shaftesbury to have her hair done.'

'We'll wait, sir. Have you anywhere for Dame Beatrice to sit down?'

'Why, yes, of course. Come in, both of you. Martha cleared

up before she went, so there's plenty of room. By the way, just as a matter of interest, who says the body was Hubert's?'

'Mr Romilly Lestrange, of course, sir,' replied Kirkby, giving him a long stare.

(3)

Martha was a very pretty girl, small-boned, well-groomed, supremely mistress of herself and, in both senses, mistress of Tancred.

'Go and sit in the car,' she said to him, when Kirkby had stated his business, 'and don't come back until I tell you. If you want something to do, you can peel the potatoes. We're having Irish stew tonight.'

Having got rid of him, she turned to Kirkby and asked:

'Have you come about the court-case? Is it worse than he told me? I hope he hasn't done anything *really* silly. He never *does* behave himself in pubs. Thank goodness I wasn't with him.'

'But you were with him on the day he went to Dancing Ledge.'

'Oh, dear! Don't remind me of that! There was nothing we could do, you know. The poor man was hideously dead.'

'You could have reported finding the body.'

'I told Tancred that, but he wouldn't, and he begged me not to. He's such a baby, you know. He always runs away from anything awkward. To stifle my curiosity, do tell me whether he seduced all the women at Galliard Hall – or only one of them. There were three possibles, he told me. He always runs into trouble when I can't keep him under my eye. I suppose he takes after that naughty old great-uncle of his, don't you? You know – the one with all that lovely money. Tancred hoped the Provosts would come in for something, but it's all been left to one of the Lestrange girls. It seems he took a fancy to her and adopted her. Disappointing, don't you think?'

'I'm afraid I don't know what you're talking about.'

'Old Felix Napoleon, the old horror who's caused all this mix-up.'

'Do you refer to the death of the Reverend Hubert Lestrange, miss?'

'Not that, so much. I really meant the old Bluebeard's Will. Tancred went to bed with the heiress while he was staying at

Galliard Hall, and she seems to have told him her troubles.'

'I wonder whether his version was the same as mine?' asked Dame Beatrice. 'Did he confide it to you?'

'Yes. He's quite a tender-hearted idiot where girls are concerned – a lot *too* tender-hearted for me to dream of going steady with him – and this girl seems to have given him quite a story. Seems she's out of the frying-pan into the fire. She'd been adopted by this old rip . . . '

'Felix Napoleon Lestrange,' interpolated Dame Beatrice.

'. . . and all went merrily until the old boy introduced a chorus girl, or some such, into the ménage, and went such a bust on this female that for a long time – a couple of years, at least – the poor girl thought her inheritance was in danger, and that Felix the tom-cat would marry this buskined beauty and she would cop the kitty when he died.

'Fortunately, this didn't happen. He gave the floosie the air when he found himself sinking, and the Will, so far as it goes, is as it should be, except for one small but all-important proviso. If the heiress goes cuckoo, or if she dies, Romilly Lestrange cops the lot. Well, of course, she's bound to die sooner or later – we all are – but, naturally, she doesn't want it to be sooner and she doesn't want it to be assisted.'

'You mean she doesn't want to be murdered by Mr Romilly,' said Kirkby unemotionally. 'Anything more, miss?'

'Well, it's all a lot of boloney, *I* think,' said Martha, 'but I don't suppose this murder business is going to make her feel any better about things, and she told Tancred she isn't only afraid of this Romilly, but also of the dispossessed chorus lady, who must also be gunning for her, and was expecting a baby by old Felix Napoleon and might show up at any minute, complete with child, and create hell and demand her rights and all that kind of what-have-you.'

'The baby would be illegitimate, miss.'

'Yes, but don't they have rights or something, these days? Heirs of the body, and so forth? Anyhow, be that as it may, this Trilby, according to Tancred, is in a real old spider's-web of intrigue and is talking of cutting her throat as the best way out of it.'

'This is all very interesting, no doubt, miss, but it doesn't help me.'

D

'Are you going to find out about this baby?'

'The question does not come within the scope of my enquiry, miss. Will you give me your account of the way in which you spent last Tuesday?'

Martha's account tallied almost word for word with Tancred's. Kirkby wondered whether they had rehearsed it.

'I'll have to get confirmation of their story,' he said. 'If the Reverend Mr Lestrange was already dead on the Tuesday, there's no point in finding out what the house-party did after that.'

'The coastguard stations, according to the Ordnance Survey,' said Dame Beatrice, 'are at Peveril Point and just south of the secondary road which leaves Worth Matravers for Ranscombe Farm. From neither spot would Dancing Ledge be visible, I imagine.'

'Probably not, ma'am. Well, if you'll drop me off in Shaftesbury, I'll have another word about Mr Tancred Provost with our chaps at the station. They'll take me to Wareham, and I'll work Provost's story back from there. He's a sufficiently striking-looking lad for the people in the tea-shop to remember. I don't suppose they get crowds of people on a Tuesday at this time of year. Then I'll tackle the post-office people at Langton Matravers.'

'Is there anything I can do in the meantime?'

'I hardly think so. When I've checked Provost's story (if I'm able to), I'll go along to Galliard Hall again and have another word with Mr Romilly.'

'Mr Giles Provost was there when you called, I suppose? He'd got back from the New Forest?'

'Oh, yes, but he'd nothing to tell me. He had been out with the New Forest Hunt all right, but that (if Tancred Provost's story is true) can't do anything to help us. I'll have to tackle him from the other end – his home – and find out what he was doing before he went to Galliard Hall. According to the housekeeper – although I think she's a lot more than that – there was bad blood between the Lestrange family and the Provosts, so the murder might tie up with a sort of vendetta. It seems a bit peculiar, if such was the case, that they had all been invited to Galliard Hall at the same time.'

'Yes, Mrs Judith told me that she had advised against having members of the two families in the house together, but that Mr Romilly had overruled her. He appears to have been amusing

himself in an unkind manner at their expense. It seems that he
had promised them, falsely, certain benefits, as an inducement
to them to come and visit him.'

'What kind of benefits, ma'am? – monetary ones?'

'Well, not exactly. It seems that he promised Mr Tancred a
publisher who would pay for printing his poems, and the schoolmaster, Mr Humphrey, a much better post. I have never met the
Reverend Mr Hubert, of course, but Romilly spoke of getting
him preferment of some kind.'

'That sort of thing? I see. Been less surprising, then, if Mr
Romilly had been bumped off, instead of the Reverend Hubert,
wouldn't it?'

'I have a theory that one of those who suffered disappointment
may have gone so far as to attempt to murder him.' She told
Kirkby of the mysterious but abortive shot in the night.

'There are two other people at the Hall I want to interview,'
he said, when he had listened to the story. 'They were in Bournemouth when I visited the Hall.'

'Oh, the twin brother and sister, Corin and Corinna Lestrange.
Yes, they are appearing on stage in Bournemouth this week. I
expect they were rehearsing when you called. They, and Mr Giles,
were the persons who really *did* benefit, although only in a very
small way, from their visit.'

'Oh? How was that, then, ma'am?'

'The twins were offered free board and lodging for the period
of their theatrical engagement, and Mr Giles obtained the loan
of a horse for the hunting-field. I do not think Romilly mentioned
to you that not only the Reverend Hubert but the eighth member
of the party did not turn up?'

'Who would that be?'

'Mr Willoughby, whom Rosamund mentioned to you. He is
the Reverend Hubert's brother, and appears to be missing.'

'Yes, I've heard of it. It might be very important. I'll ask
Mr Romilly about him.'

'I certainly think you should do that.'

'One thing I've proved. The married couple, Mr and Mrs
Humphrey Provost, are in the clear. There's no doubt their alibis
are unshakeable.'

'I'm glad of that,' said Dame Beatrice. Kirkby said thoughtfully:

'One Lestrange dead – either suicide or murder – and another missing? I'll certainly look into that. Well, ma'am, I'm most grateful for your help. If I may, I'll call on you again and let you know how things are going. It will need to be soon, because of the inquest.'

(4)

'So, according to his light-of-love, Tancred runs away from anything unpleasant,' said Laura. 'By the way, Celestine tells me we had a visitor. Pity there was nobody at home. You were off on a toot with the detective-inspector and I, in accordance with your instructions, had whisked Rosamund off to Bournemouth to get her fitted out with clothes.'

'Who was the visitor?'

'He didn't leave his name or a card.'

'Romilly, I venture to suppose. Did Celestine describe him?'

'A tall, smooth-faced, dark-eyed, grey-haired gentleman of late middle-age, wearing a very good grey overcoat and a black hat. He asked to be allowed to come in and wait, but she explained that we were both out for the day and she had no idea when to expect us. He then asked to see Rosamund, whom he called "the young Mrs Lestrange, who is staying here," and was informed that she had gone out with me, but that I had not said where I was going.'

'At what time was this?'

'At about eleven this morning, Celestine said. By the way, did you have any lunch?'

'Yes, in Shaftesbury.'

'We had ours in Bournemouth. How do you like the suit Rosamund is wearing?'

'I'm most concerned about having to owe you so much money, Dame Beatrice,' said the girl, 'but I hope that, by the end of May, I shall be able to pay everything back – everything but your kindness, of course. That I can never repay.'

'Well,' said Dame Beatrice, 'we have plans for you, to keep you safely out of the way until all the problems are solved. You are going to stay with Laura's parents in Scotland. It is all arranged.'

'In Scotland? I shall feel safer there, now Romilly has been to this house. Suppose I had been alone here when he came!'

'Well, you weren't,' said Laura, 'so don't panic. I'm taking you to London tomorrow, and one of the nurses at Dame Beatrice's clinic will take you on to Glasgow, where my brother and his wife will meet you and take you to my home. There's nothing for you to worry about. It's all taken care of. There's the dressing-bell. Push off upstairs and put on that dinner-gown you chose. It's a smash-hit in any language.'

'I like your brisk and business-like tone when you speak to Rosamund,' said Dame Beatrice.

'Ah,' said Laura, squinting down her nose, 'a talented nursery-governess was lost in me. Well, we'd better go up, too, I suppose. One of these days I shall come down in jeans and a windcheater, just to see the effect it has on Celestine. It's because of her I dress for dinner, you know, not really because I want to.'

'You have been with Rosamund all day. What do you make of the child?'

'Not too sure I like her. Bit of a rabbit, I think, to let herself be given the run-around by the despicable old Romilly. After all, this *is* the third quarter of the twentieth century and she *is* twenty-four years old, although I'll admit she doesn't look it.'

'Romilly is a cunning and unscrupulous man, I fear. I will accompany you to London tomorrow and see Rosamund handed over to the care of Nurse Merrow. After that, while you suborn your husband to neglect his duties and take you to Scotland with Rosamund and Nurse Merrow, I shall lunch by myself in Soho and then visit my sister-in-law. There is nothing Selina does not know about the ramifications of the Lestrange family tree, and if I ask her to place these new relatives of mine upon the appro-priate branches she will feel that, at last, I am showing a proper interest. George will pick me up at her house and take me back to the clinic, and I will wait for you and Rosamund there. Keep dear Robert with you as long as you can. You see far too little of one another for the parents of an eight-months-old baby.'

'If we'd seen less of one another, there might not *be* an eight-months-old baby, and that wouldn't break my heart,' said Laura, grinning. 'But what's all this about the family tree?'

'I am hoping that Selina can hang Felix Napoleon on it, that is all, and Romilly, too.'

CHAPTER NINE

Bolero—Mother and Son

'Bid me discourse, I will enchant thine ear,
Or, like a fairy, trip upon the green.'

Venus and Adonis.

---

(1)

Lady Selina Lestrange had always regarded her more eccentric
relatives with suspicion and disapproval, and it was with false
cordiality that she welcomed Dame Beatrice to the ancestral
home. She was the relict of Dame Beatrice's first husband's
brother, and therefore the relationship between the two elderly
ladies was not consanguinous and they had nothing in common
except their age and sex.

'Well, Adela,' she said, 'this *is* a surprise!'

'Yes,' agreed Dame Beatrice, meekly.

'If I had known you were coming . . . '

'I am not going to stay,' Dame Beatrice assured her. 'My
business may take half-an-hour, or very little longer, at the most.
I come in search of information.'

'Not another of your odious cases of murder!'

'A by-product of one. Did you know that Hubert has been
killed?'

'Hubert? Hubert who?'

'The Reverend Hubert Lestrange.'

'I have never heard of him.'

'That is most interesting. I wonder whether you have heard,
then, of Felix Napoleon?'

'Oh, dear! Please don't mention that old reprobate!'

'Who was he?'

'He was some sort of cousin. He was descended from a pirate
or a bushranger, I believe – something disgraceful, anyway. We
have never recognised the relationship, needless to say.'

'But he had a right to his name?'

'Oh, he was a Lestrange, if that is what you mean. He was also extremely wealthy, as a result, I have always supposed, of his ill-gotten inheritance.'

'Is there any reason why he should have entertained kindly feelings towards *me*?'

'Towards *you*? Why, did he?'

'Failing his granddaughter and her next-of-kin, he seems to have left his fortune to me.'

'Oh, well, if there is a granddaughter, you are hardly likely to outlive her.'

'In the midst of life, of course – but you have failed to grasp the purport of my question. Apart from any suggestion of a legacy, why should he have thought of me at all? To my certain knowledge, I have neither met him nor corresponded with him. In fact, I am perfectly certain that I did not know of his existence until very recently.'

'If he mentioned anybody, apart from his nearest relatives, in his Will, it ought to have been Ferdinand.'

'My son Ferdinand? Why, what has Ferdinand done? Successfully defended him against a charge of some kind?'

'Exactly.'

'Then why have I not heard of it?'

'You were in America at the time, and it never became a *cause célèbre*. The unspeakable Felix Napoleon was thought to have strangled a chorus girl or a member of a *corps de ballet* or something. She had borne an illegitimate child which she was attempting to foist on him, I believe. Anyway, Ferdinand was mixed up in it somehow.'

'Oh, was there an illegitimate child?'

'Oh, yes. That was not in dispute.'

'You would not, of course, remember the baby's name?'

'Certainly not.'

'You never heard it?'

'I may have done. I should not dream of charging my memory with anything to do with such disgraceful goings-on.'

'Suppose I suggested to you the name Romilly?'

'Is it of any importance?'

'I think it may be of very great importance.'

'You mean that this Romilly may have a claim on *us*?'

'I think he may well consider himself to have a claim on his natural father's fortune. As it is, a life interest in it is left to Felix

Napoleon's granddaughter, provided that she attains her twenty-fifth birthday. At her death the money goes to this Romilly. If she does not live to be twenty-five, I am to benefit'

'What has the death of a clergyman to do with all this?'

'That is what I have to find out. It is all very mysterious at present. Hubert seems to have been on his way to Romilly's house when he met his death, and yet the spot where his body was found does not suggest that he was on the direct route to Galliard Hall. The police have the matter in hand, but I was hoping that you would be able to give me a pointer or two which might be of help to them.'

'I am sorry, but you can scarcely expect me to interest myself in the affair.'

'You have at least persuaded me that Romilly may have some right to his surname, and that is progress of a kind.'

'You have already said that you think he may be Felix Napoleon's natural son, but that gives him no right to call himself Lestrange.'

'I have never seen why a natural son should have no right to his father's name when that name is known and the claim acknowledged.'

'Opinions differ, and I must say that I think you are unwise to have mixed yourself up in the affair.'

'It is too long a story to tell you, and I doubt whether you would be interested in it, but I had no option.'

'Because of the fortune?'

'No. Because Romilly called me in in my professional capacity as a psychiatrist.'

'You mean that the man is mad?'

'No. He was hoping I would say that the heiress presumptive is incapable of managing her own affairs. If I did so, her expectations, for all practical purposes, would cease to exist.'

'It seems that, as usual, you have got yourself mixed up in villainy.'

'That is what I think. Before I go, I must try your exemplary patience a little further. Do the names Willoughby, Corin and Corinna mean anything to you?'

'Corin and Corinna are Sally's children, and therefore are my grandchildren. Their father thought it better that they did not use his name, as they are on the stage in some dubious kind of way, so, to my great annoyance, they have taken their mother's maiden name of Lestrange.'

'I thought Sally's children were named Montmorency and Clotilda. I was present at their christening, if you remember.'

'Those would scarcely be names which could be used for the kind of act which I believe they perpetrate.'

'No, I see that. Oh, well, that accounts for *them*. What about Willoughby?'

'I have never heard of him.'

'He has disappeared. As he is Hubert's brother, I am wondering whether he also has been murdered.'

'You mean that this clergyman was *murdered?*'

'The police appear to think so. I do not know yet what evidence they have. One more question, and then I will go. Do you know anything about a family named Provost?'

'Provost? Do you mean the Marshall-Provosts? They are some sort of connections of Sally's husband, John Ponsonby-Marshall, I believe, but they are rather poor and obscure and are not really recognised as relatives by John's family. Why?'

'They seem to be well known to Romilly Lestrange, that is all, but they seem to be called, simply, Provost.'

'I will ring for tea,' said Lady Selina in a tone which indicated, beyond all reasonable doubt, that this nuisance must now cease.

(2)

Armed with such information as Lady Selina had been able to supply, Dame Beatrice rang up her son on Lady Selina's telephone and was invited to dinner and asked to stay for the night.

'Well, mother,' said the eminent man, when dinner was over and he had taken her off to his study for a private chat, 'what mischief have you been getting into this time?'

'I seem to be mixed up, to some extent, in the murder of a member of the family.'

'Don't tell me that somebody has had the public spirit and general goodwill to bump off Aunt Selina!'

'No. I came here from her house and she appears to be alive and well.'

'Who's been murdered, then?'

'A young man – well, I assume that he is young, or comparatively so – named the Reverend Hubert Lestrange.'

'A parson murdered? Rather unusual, what? What did he do? Rush in where angels fear to tread, and get himself clobbered?'

'I have no idea what he *did*. I have a feeling, however, that he was killed because of something he *knew*.'

'That sounds as though he'd uncovered the family skeleton. Have we one?'

'I hoped you would be able and willing to tell *me* that. What do you know of Felix Napoleon?'

'Oh, that old rip! I got him off on a charge of fraud once, but haven't seen or heard of him for ages.'

'When was this?'

'Oh, donkey's years ago, of course. It was before I was called to the Bar, as a matter of fact. I was up at Cambridge. How the old boy had found out I was reading law I've never discovered, or even how he knew where I was, but he wrote to me and asked me to suggest a line of defence, as he trusted neither his solicitor nor the chap who was to be briefed on his behalf. He told me his side of the story, I saw a loophole, pointed it out and the result was that the case never came up for trial. The beaks threw it out, and quite right, too, on the evidence, although, personally, I wouldn't be surprised if the old reprobate was guilty.'

'How did Selina come to hear of all this?'

'The man who was to be briefed was old John Marshall-Provost, Sally's father-in-law.'

'It seems to be a family affair all round.'

'Yes, all sorts of daddies involved. Where do *you* come in, though?'

Dame Beatrice gave him an account of Romilly's letter and of what had happened, and outlined the course she had followed since she had received the letter.

'I'm afraid for the girl,' she said in conclusion. 'When I heard that she was the heiress and was made cognisant of the conditions which were attached to the inheritance, and when I realised that Romilly (who, by his virtual incarceration of her, must be a resolute and unscrupulous man) was the next in line according to Felix Napoleon's Will, I removed the child from Galliard Hall and have despatched her, with Laura's help, to a place of safety. When I learned of Hubert's death . . . '

'If I may butt in at this point, mother, I think you should keep an eye lifting on your own account, you know. Some people can't be all that pleased with your machinations, and yet——'

'I shall take precautions, particularly as I am returning to-morrow to Galliard Hall. All the same, so far as anybody is aware, I am simply keeping the girl under treatment.'

'Well, beware of how you enter the cockatrice's den, that's all. A man with his eye on a fortune is not going to be too nice about the methods he uses to get his hooks on it, you know, especially if he's old Felix Napoleon's natural son. For one thing, he may well feel that, as the first-born, and of an earlier generation than the girl, he has the prior claim, and, for another, he may now take after his father, who struck me as a plausible and blackhearted scoundrel, if ever there was one.'

'Yet you did him a very great favour.'

'Oh, no, it certainly wasn't meant as a favour. It was just a very young man's conceit. I spotted the flaw and nothing pleased me better than to point it out to him and his solicitor. It was just one of those odd things which come along when one's looking up something quite different. I was in love with my own cleverness in those days and, after all, the old villain *was* a Lestrange.'

'Exactly what I feel about Rosamund, *La famille oblige.* Selina had some story that he had murdered his mistress.'

'One of his mistresses, she meant. He was notorious for his harem, I believe. I never heard that he murdered anybody, though. I think Aunt Selina must have got the wires crossed. She probably heard of this fraud thing I mentioned, and stepped up the details.'

'Did *you* ever hear of an illegitimate son?'

'He had two, but I don't know whether they had the same mother.'

'Would you know their names?'

'Yes, of course.'

'Why "of course"?'

'Well, because I knew them both at Cambridge. Romilly was my year and happened to be on my staircase, and Caesar came up when Romilly had gone down and I was at the beginning of my fourth year. I didn't have a lot to do with them, but when I found their name was Lestrange I felt I had to be civil. It was Romilly who put his father's case before me, as a matter of fact, and asked me what I thought, as he knew my intended profession.'

'So Romilly would be about your age?'

'Just about, I suppose. Small, dark chap and wore very powerful glasses. Blind as a bat without them, he once told me, and, on another occasion, I had evidence of it.'

'Did you know anything of his life after he left the University?'

'Yes, he wrote to me twice while I was still up, once to send me five pounds he'd borrowed the previous term, and once to tell me that he was emigrating to Kenya, as his father had bought him a half-share in a coffee plantation. I never heard from him again.'

'What about the younger brother, Caesar?'

'He got himself rusticated in his second year. Started an undergraduate paper and printed some fairly actionable items about some of the dons. Was chewed up by the Dean, but persisted in his naughty ways, so Cambridge's loss became somewhere else's gain. I believe he got into Fleet Street later on, but I didn't really know him. Different faculties, and three years' difference in our ages, you see.'

'Do you remember what he was like to look at?'

'Not very clearly. The most noticeable thing about the poor chap was that he had one leg shorter than the other and had to wear a surgical boot.'

'How did you know they were illegitimate?'

'Romilly told me. He was bleating about it in a mild sort of way, and saying that he didn't suppose his old man would leave him anything worth talking about, although he'd always acknowledged him and kept him and his brother, and all that.'

'What kind of man was Romilly?'

'As I remember him, he was diffident, kindly, a bit vague, but a completely harmless chap. He was a connoisseur of pictures, I remember. Spent all his money on good copies of old masters and said he intended to collect the real things when he could afford it. My five-pound loan, I remember, went to make up the price of a very fine copy of Francesco di Giorgio's *Saint Dorothy walking with the Holy Child*. I must say that he's just about the last man I should think of as a murderer, but, of course, when it's a question of money——'

'Did you ever hear whether Felix Napoleon's legitimate union was blest with children?'

'Yes, there was a son named Harvard, some years younger than

Caesar, but he was killed in the war in 1944. I knew about *him* because he came up once or twice to see the other two, and I was invited to cocktails.'

'Would you know Romilly again, if you saw him?'

'I might, of course, but a lot of water has flowed under the bridge since my undergraduate days.'

'You knew that Felix Napoleon was dead?'

'I'd never thought about it. I don't read the obituary columns and I don't suppose his wife would have thought of inviting me to the funeral.'

'She may have pre-deceased him.'

'Yes, of course. Well, mother, I must say that your account of Romilly really does surprise me. He must have altered a very great deal since I knew him.'

'I am suffering from dear Laura's complaint, no doubt,' admitted Dame Beatrice.

'What's that?'

'A pricking of the thumbs. Besides, now that you have described *your* Romilly to me, I do not see how he could be (however much his nature may have changed) *my* Romilly.'

'Physical description doesn't fit?'

'You said that Romilly was small.'

'And dark. Of course, he's probably grey-haired by now.''

'*How* small was he?'

'Oh, almost a head shorter than I am, and I am six feet one and a half. I should say he stood about five feet four – call it five five with his shoes on.'

'And was very short-sighted?'

'So much so that, when he mislaid his glasses one day – took them off to have a bath – I had to find them for him because he usually put them in their case on the bathroom stool, but this time had left them in his room and had been groping about for them in there for ages before he heard me on the stairs and yelled for my assistance.'

'Short sight is not usually a disability which cures itself as the years roll by. The younger brother, you tell me, had a club foot.'

'Yes. I wonder whether it had warped him a bit. His writings for his unofficial rag were extremely spiteful.'

'So, if my host at Galliard Hall is not the real Romilly, neither is he likely to be Romilly's brother Caesar. I did well to go to

Selina and be referred to you. These are deeper waters than I had
suspected. However, nothing is lost by making sure. Could you
make it convenient to call at Galliard Hall at some time during
the next few days so that you can meet this pseudo-Romilly?'

'On what pretext?'

'That you have heard from me that he has some very fine
pictures, and you are wondering whether he would be willing to
part with the Raeburn, as you particularly want to give it as an
anniversary present to your wife, whose negotiations for a Raeburn
have recently broken down. You are safe enough in making this
offer. The pictures are not his to sell, as he is not the owner of
Galliard Hall.'

'I wouldn't recognise a Raeburn if you handed one to me on a
plate.'

'With watercress round it, as Laura's favourite author would
remark. The Raeburn is the first portrait you come to as you
enter the hall.'

'Very well. I can manage tomorrow afternoon, if that's all
right.'

'Do not mention, of course, that you knew Romilly at Cambridge, unless you believe that this man really *is* Romilly
Lestrange.'

'Now what do you take me for, mother!'

'I apologise.'

'Good. Let's rejoin the family, or they'll be complaining that
I keep you all to myself. You look as though you're enjoying all
this Romilly business, though. Are you?'

'The plot thickens in the most agreeable way. I am no longer
able to keep Laura's fingers out of the pie.'

'Of course, the obvious point to consider is this: if Romilly
isn't Romilly, who the devil is he?'

'If you can tell me who Felix Napoleon's lawyers were, I hope
to be able to find that out.'

'Well, I'll enquire around. I know he'd chucked the Marshall-
Provost gang – their solicitors, I mean.'

(3)

The older members of Snapp, Snapp and Bacon had preceded
their client to the grave, but, although there were no Snapps left,

a scion of the Bacons was senior partner in the firm, and had brought a son and a nephew into the business. It was the older Bacon who received Dame Beatrice.

'Upon receipt of your letter,' he said, 'I looked up the relevant facts. In 1960, on the death of his natural son Caesar, Mr Felix Napoleon Lestrange altered his Will. Up to that time the provisions were not quite as they are at present. For one thing, they made Caesar a beneficiary to the same extent as his brother. Both, as you know, were born out of wedlock, so, until 1944, when the legitimate son Harvard was killed in the war, Harvard had been in the position of sole heir in respect of his father's property, with the exception of legacies of five thousand pounds each to his half-brothers, Romilly and Caesar.

'Upon Harvard's death, however, the Will was somewhat materially changed. For one thing, at her father's death, which occurred in January, 1944, Rosamund, who, from the twenty-ninth of May next, will have a life-interest in her grandfather's wealth, irrespective of her possible marriage, was still *en ventre sa mère*. The new Will, therefore, gave her a life-interest after she had attained the age of twenty-five. Up to that time we, as Felix Napoleon's solicitors, were empowered to maintain her and her mother in the event of Felix Napoleon's dying before she reached her twenty-fifth year, but, as it happened, the mother died in giving birth, and Felix Napoleon assumed full responsibility for the baby and had her to live with him until his death, a couple of years ago.'

'Did you approve of her going to live with Romilly Lestrange after her grandfather's death?'

'We made careful enquiries, but there seemed nothing we could object to in the scheme and, in any case, as the young lady was of age, we could have acted in an advisory capacity only, which is exactly what we did. We advised against it, but she was obdurate.'

'What was the reason for your advice?'

'The fact, which we felt bound to point out to her, that Romilly Lestrange, under the terms of Felix Napoleon's last Will, had an interest in her death, once she had attained the age of twenty-five years. The money, as you probably know, Dame Beatrice, was left in trust for Miss Rosamund Lestrange. She could not touch the capital. After her death, however, or if she were proved incapable of managing her affairs, Romilly became the heir. We had to choose our words, of course, very carefully, but I think we made it clear to her that these provisions might make it highly unsatisfactory for her to become a member of Mr Romilly's household.'

'There was never any suggestion that Romilly had married her, of course?'

'My dear lady, how could there be? She is his half-brother's daughter.'

'Of course,' said Dame Beatrice meekly. 'Was your advice given to her by word of mouth?'

'No. She refused to come and see us, or to let us go and see her. The first letter we received about the new arrangement came from Romilly, and merely informed us that as he was now domiciled permanently in England, he proposed to ask Rosamund to share his home. Upon this we wrote to ask the young lady for an interview, but this she refused to grant us. There was nothing, therefore, for us to do but to send her our extremely carefully-worded warning that her uncle's plans to give her a home might not be completely altruistic, pay her her quarterly allowance, and leave it at that. I do not see how we could have taken any more definite a course. As I pointed out, she was of age and, in a sense, we were not her lawyers. By that, of course, I mean that we had no powers, except to make sure that the terms of the bequest were carried out.'

'You mentioned that Romilly wrote to say that he was now permanently domiciled in England. I understood that, soon after he left the University, Romilly emigrated to Kenya.'

'Oh, yes, he did. Mr Felix Napoleon put up the money for him to buy a half-share in a coffee plantation there.'

'Did you ever meet Romilly?'

'Before he emigrated to Kenya with his natural father's assistance, I had nothing to do with him at all, nor with his brother Caesar. I do know, however, that Caesar left two sons. One of them went into the Church, I believe, and Felix Napoleon employed the other as his secretary, but, again, I never had any occasion to meet either of them.'

'Were these sons close friends? How did they get on together?'

'I have no idea. I have read, of course, in the newspapers, of the tragic death of one of them, and I believe the other is missing.'

'Yes. In my capacity of psychiatric adviser to the Home Office, I am semi-officially engaged in helping with the police investigation into these matters, and I am most grateful to you for giving up your time to me and providing me with so much useful information.'

'Yes,' said the solicitor dubiously. 'Of course, when you came, I had no idea that it was on police business. I trust that you will not need to involve us. We have always had the reputation . . . '

'I understand that, and I see no need whatever to involve you. I needed to be certain of my facts, that is all. I wonder whether you will be kind enough to tell me one more thing. Have you any idea of Felix Napoleon's last address?'

'I have the last letter he wrote us. It was from a hotel in Carlisle, if my memory serves me.' He touched the buzzer. 'Mr Felix Napoleon Lestrange s file, Pearson, if you please . . . Yes, here we are. He wrote a vile hand, but you can probably make out the address at the top of the letter.'

CHAPTER TEN

St Vitus' Dance—Three Wise Monkeys

'One three of them, by their own report, sir, have danced before the king; and not the worst of the three but jumps twelve foot and a half . . .'

The Winter's Tale.

'Well!' exclaimed Romilly, extending both hands. 'So you have returned to the fold, my dear Beatrice!'

'Are you still in the hands of the police?' asked his visitor, ignoring those he was stretching out to her and speaking with a calculated lack of tact.

'Oh, they are occupying themselves with the concerns of Corin and Corinna, who are closeted with them now for the third time. Giles also has been questioned. Come into the library, where we can chat. The detective-inspector and his sergeant are in the drawing-room and Judith is about her duties in the stillroom, so we are not likely to be disturbed. Have you come to report upon Trilby?'

'She seems well and has settled down with us. I must return the clothes which Binnie so kindly lent her. Can you give me Humphrey's address?'

'Certainly. I will write it down for you.' He did this as soon as they reached the library. 'I take it that you are following my plan to keep Trilby within doors. It is really not safe for her to be allowed out, if there is water in the vicinity.'

'In the vicinity of the Stone House there is nothing but the shallow and narrow upper waters of the Lymington River, and a few of the New Forest ponds. There is no fresh light to be shed on Hubert's death, I suppose?'

'The police at present are baffled, I think.'

'They are often thought to be so, when the truth is that they have discovered valuable clues which it would not be in the public interest (as they put it) to reveal.'

'Do you really think they are on to something?'

'Who can say? If they are, they certainly have not confided in me. There is no news of Willoughby, I suppose?'

'I have heard none. One hesitates to wonder whether . . .'

'Does one? I have wondered it. He and Hubert are brothers, are they not?'

'You are thinking of Cain and Abel, but is that fair? There may be some utterly innocent reason for Willoughby's disappearance, or, of course (although one hardly cares to frame the words), the murderer may have made away with both the brothers.'

'I have envisaged that possibility also. In fact, I am inclined to put it more positively. I think there is a strong probability that such is the case.'

'But what would be the reason for so dastardly a deed? Neither was a wealthy man and both seemed the last types to make enemies. I should be interested to hear what you, as a psychiatrist, make of it.'

'I cannot make bricks without straw. I have never so much as met either of the young men.'

'Have you not? You would have found them charming fellows, I am sure, and I would have said that there was the closest friendship between them, a happy state of things which one does not always find where brothers are concerned.'

'How right you are. There was no question, I suppose, of there being a woman in the case? Sometimes, between even the best of friends, or between relatives with the closest family ties . . .'

'Oh, as to that, I have no information. Hubert, of course, being a priest of the English Church, would not have been bound to celibacy. I *wonder* . . .'

The library door opened and Amabel came in.

'The police gentlemen be feneshed, sir,' she announced. 'They said as how they would be glad to speak to ee afore they go. Should Oi show 'em en here, sir?'

'Yes, of course show them in here. Do you care to stay, Beatrice, and hear what they have to say?'

'No. I expect they would prefer to see you alone. I will have a little chat with Corin and Corinna, of whom I was able to see almost nothing when I was here before, and then I will take myself off. I had better say goodbye now, in case your session with the police officers is a long one.' She thought it better not to meet Kirkby in front of Romilly, in case the latter should deduce that they were old acquaintances. She met the detective-inspector in the hall, bowed and then walked straight past him. Kirkby accepted her lead, returned her bow with a slight inclination of the head, and went on to the library where Amabel was waiting to show him in. Dame Beatrice herself went to the drawing-room.

Corin and Corinna were seated on either side of the fireplace and appeared to be dejected. Giles, looking tired, was with them. All three of the young people looked towards the door when Dame Beatrice entered. Giles and Corin stood up politely, but Corinna, with an exclamation, went towards her.

'The very person!' she said. 'A very present help in time of trouble, as the psalmist said.'

'He wasn't talking about Aunt Adela,' said Corin dispiritedly.

'We may as well unload the trouble, anyway,' said his sister. 'Have a seat, Aunt Adela, and hear us our prayers.'

'It might be more to the point were I to hear your confessions,' said Dame Beatrice. 'I take it that you have news of Willoughby.'

'What on earth makes you think that?' demanded Corinna, suddenly looking agitated. 'What can have put such an idea into your head?' She ruffled the short hair on her own head until it stood almost on end. Her brother put his face between his hands and groaned.

'Now you *have* torn it!' he said. 'I knew you would!'

'No, I haven't. Somebody had to know, and Aunt Adela is much the best person, because she'll tell us what to do.'

'If you have found out anything about Willoughby, the people who need to know are the police,' said Dame Beatrice. 'As they are in the house at this very moment, there is nothing to prevent you from waylaying them as they leave and cleansing your bosoms of this perilous stuff.'

'Well, there you are,' said Corinna. 'That's what I've been saying all along.'

'But they may suspect us of killing him,' exclaimed her twin. 'I would agree if Hubert's body hadn't already been found.'

'Well, we didn't kill Hubert, *or* Willoughby, so what?"

Dame Beatrice interposed.

'Am I to be let into the secret, or am I not?' she demanded. 'Having said so much, would it not be better to tell me all?'

The twins looked at one another, and Corin shook his head. His unkempt hair fell across his brown face. He looked like Mowgli, Dame Beatrice thought, with his expression of wariness, animal shyness and a kind of innocent cunning. He was, according to the fashion of the day, a handsome, attractive boy.

'I'm not saying anything more,' he said truculently. 'Corinna, blast her, has given you a nod and a wink, so now it's up to you.'

'But she isn't a blind horse!' said Giles quietly. 'Don't you see we can't leave it like this? It would have been better to say nothing at all.'

'Which is what I wanted. You know it is! We've argued about it enough! Corinna *will* rush in and say things in a panic. Shut up, Corinna! Believe me, I know what's best.'

'Very well. I'm sorry, Aunt Adela, very sorry, but if Corin won't listen to reason, well, he won't.'

'He can't afford to,' muttered Corin. 'In a case of murder, it isn't a good thing to know too much.'

'Well, that would appear to be that,' said Dame Beatrice equably. 'You surely do not mean that Willoughby has been murdered, too, and that you have seen the body? Do you want someone else – myself, for preference – to report it?'

'Oh, no! Goodness me, no!' cried Corinna. 'It's not that at all! No, really, Aunt Adela, it's nothing as bad as that!'

'Look here,' said Giles, 'having said so much, don't you think it might be better to say the rest?'

'No, I don't! I've changed my mind. Oh, *dear!*' cried Corinna, pushing her hand through her short, fair hair. 'After all, it's not as though we've *seen* or, really, *heard* anything – anything which points to anybody's wickedness, I mean – so it would be awful of us to *say* anything. Anyway, we've got no proof.'

'No proof of who must have murdered Hubert, no,' said her cousin, 'but we can trust Great-aunt to do the best thing. I suggest we tell her, and then leave it to her.'

'We can't tell her something that I was told in confidence. I'm sorry I ever suggested we should.'

'You know,' said Giles, 'on thinking it over, I'm inclined to agree with Corinna. What she was told – in confidence, as she says – doesn't really amount to a hill of beans. It proves nothing except that people can be mistaken, or that they think they know something when, all the time, they don't. I don't think we ought to point the finger. The truth will come out at some time or another. It isn't for us to dirty our hands.'

'That's what I've been saying all along,' said Corin.

'On the other hand,' said Corinna, wavering, 'perhaps we should tell Great-aunt and leave her to see what she makes of it. After all, she's had lots of experience of these things, and we don't owe all that much to old Romilly.'

'It may not concern him,' said Giles. 'He may have had nothing to do with it. He talked as though he was as surprised as anybody.'

'He's a cagey old bird,' said Corin. 'I wouldn't trust him an inch. We really know nothing about him.'

'I myself,' admitted Dame Beatrice, 'knew nothing about him either before I was invited here.'

'Did he make *you* any promises?' asked Corin. 'Poor old Humphrey was livid about that job he was promised . . . '

'Not a job; only an interview, wasn't it?' said Giles. 'I'm not too pleased with Romilly myself.'

'He lent you a horse.'

'He promised to lend me enough to buy a share in some racing-stables.'

'Tancred isn't very pleased with him, either,' said Corinna, forgetting her agitation and beginning to giggle. 'He's terribly funny when he's cross. But you haven't given Great-aunt a chance to answer the question. Do tell us, Aunt Adela. *Did* he promise you anything?'

'Not in the sense you mean, but I feel that my visit here has been amply rewarded. I have made the acquaintance of Rosamund.'

'How delightful for you,' said Corin ironically. 'To my mind, she's just about the most fishy young female I've ever encountered. I'm pretty sure that at some time or other she's been on the stage. She's the hammiest half-baked pro who ever gave up the business to become an old man's darling. Once you've been on the stage yourself, you can't be deceived by another who has ever worn the buskins.'

'I myself have sometimes thought that Rosamund was putting on the motley for our benefit. How long have you known Romilly Lestrange?' asked Dame Beatrice, apparently changing the subject. 'You say you know nothing about him, and you are certainly not old enough to have known him before he emigrated to Kenya. I wonder whether Luke was in service with him there?'

'It's no good, Great-aunt Adela,' said Corinna, looking alarmed. 'You can't get us back to the subject of – to the subject that way. We're not going to say any more. It's my secret, and, although I've told the boys about it, they can't, in decency, give it away unless I agree, and I *don't* agree, and I'm sorry I said as much as I did. Corin's right, I am a panicky fool.'

'I myself had come to the conclusion that there is a secret,' said Dame Beatrice, 'and I have already set my wits to work. You see, perhaps there are three other wise monkeys in this house besides yourselves.' She leered benignly at Corinna, who said, nervously:

'Maybe there are, and maybe there aren't, but, if there are, I don't believe they'll be much inclined to talk, either. It isn't their business, anyway. I just got in a panic.'

'You were asking how long we'd known Uncle Romilly,' said Corin, under the impression that he was changing the subject. His sister scowled at him, but he went on: 'Not so very long, actually. We've been here once before, that's all, to what he called his house-warming. He'd just rented Galliard Hall and wanted to show it off.'

'And were all his relatives invited?'

'I suppose all the younger ones were, except for Willoughby and Hubert. At any rate they didn't turn up. Mother and father weren't asked, I do know that, because we had rather a toss-up with mother about it, and grandma sent for us and read us the riot act, and said what a scoundrel Uncle Romilly was. I asked whether he was rich, and she said that his gains, whether considerable or not, were bound to be ill-gotten. I said that wouldn't matter, provided he cut us in on them. She wasn't pleased, and Corinna and I were shown the door, and got very sticky letters from grandma later on.'

'Did you know the late Felix Napoleon Lestrange?'

'Never heard of him,' said Corin.

'Oh, I have!' exclaimed Corinna. 'Grandma once let fall a derogatory remark about him when I was about ten and she didn't know I was in the room. I had hidden behind the curtains while they were having dinner, in the hope of sneaking out and securing some of the marrons glacés and crystallised ginger and grapes and things, before the servants came in to clear the table.'

'Greedy little beast!' said Corin. 'I don't remember that you shared anything with me. Marrons glacés, indeed!'

'I didn't get what I was after. Pilbrick spotted the bulge behind the curtain and said, "Now just you come out of there, Miss Clotilda, and pop straight up to bed, else I'll tell your mamma about you, see if I don't." Pilbrick was an old beast.'

'Oh, I don't know,' said Corin. 'He lent me five pounds once, when dad had already supplemented my allowance and I dared not go to him for any more. Speak as you find is my motto. Anyway, I'd prefer Pilbrick any day to the Sweeny Todd they've got here.' As he made this statement, he winked conspiratorially at Dame Beatrice. His sister intercepted the wink and confirmed Dame Beatrice's suspicions by shouting:

'You promised! You promised! Don't you dare give me away!'

'Of course I shan't,' said Corin. '*Soit tranquille. Je suis chevalier d'honneur, moi.*'

'I've never noticed it. Oh, Lord! I wish that wretched policeman would take himself off. I want to get out of this house! We simply *must* rehearse that new number, and there isn't a piano in the place except for the one Judith plays, and she won't let us touch that.'

At this moment Kirkby knocked at the door and was invited to come in.

'If you'll give me a list of your theatrical engagements for the next few weeks, sir,' he said, addressing Corin, 'I need not keep you any longer.'

'You mean we can just simply *go?*' asked Corinna.

'That is what I mean, miss. I see no reason at present to trouble you any further, but I must know where I can find you if I want you. I may say that the same applies to you, Mr Provost. I have your address. You won't change it without letting me know, I hope.'

'Are you leaving the house, then?' asked Giles.

'For the moment, yes, sir, but my enquiries will still be centred on the neighbourhood.'

'Oh, well, of course.'

'I, too, will leave you,' said Dame Beatrice.

'You've nothing to report, I suppose?' asked Kirkby, when he and she were in the hall.

'Ask me again tomorrow. I make no promises, but there is a small matter I wish to investigate. It may lead to nothing, but I have a faint hope that it may be a little bit of help. However, it is not a thing capable of proof, so it can be nothing but a pointer, I fear.'

Hearing their voices, Romilly came into the hall.

'You are off, then, Inspector?' he said. 'Are we to expect you tomorrow?'

'Not unless anything else turns up, sir. You say you've still no news of Mr Willoughby Lestrange, so there's nothing more I can do until we trace him. You may be wanted when they resume the inquest, sir.'

'Whatever for? I have already identified the body! What more can I do?'

'The poor young gentleman was not in clerical garb, sir. What made you so certain that he was the Reverend Hubert? Did you know him very well?'

'Not to say *very* well, but well enough to know who he was,' said Romilly. 'Most young clergymen on holiday leave the dog-collar at home nowadays.'

'Oh, yes, sir, that's right, of course. They do.'

'I'll see you to your car,' said Romilly affably. Dame Beatrice waited until he and Kirkby were descending the broken steps which led to the drive, and then she made a bee-line for the kitchen, where lunch was being prepared. She was warmly greeted by Amabel.

'Well, Oi declare now, ef et eddn' Dame Beatrice! Anythen us can do, mum? Be ee stayen or goen?'

'Going, I'm afraid. This is only a flying visit. I wonder whether, when you tidied my room, you found my fountain pen? It was a particular favourite of mine, although I have others. I may have dropped it somewhere else, of course, but, as I wanted to visit Mr Romilly and let him know at first hand how Rosamund was getting on, I thought I would ask you whether you had seen it.'

'No, that Oi haven't, mum, and oi'm sure our Voilert haven't, neether, else her'd have told Oi. Can you get on with they veg,

Voilert, whoile Oi goes up to help Dame Beatrice have a search round, loike?'

'Ent no pen up there,' said Violet flatly, 'else Oi'd a-found et, wouldn't Oi? But go up and see, for your satesfaction, loike. Eddn nothen to do but they tetties.'

Arrived in the room which Dame Beatrice had occupied, she told Amabel to close the door.

'Now,' she said loudly, 'if you wouldn't mind having an extra good look round. As I say, it's quite likely I did not leave it here, but I wish to be certain. A fountain pen is such a small thing that it could slip down anywhere.'

'Very good, Dame Beatrice, mum,' said Amabel. 'Let's have the bed to bets first.'

Dame Beatrice allowed her to begin stripping the bed and then she stepped across to the shutter which blocked out the squint. As she did so, there was the slight sound of a door being very softly closed. She darted to her own door, opened it and was in time to see the back of Judith as its owner reached the main staircase. She allowed several seconds to go by, then she tip-toed to the door of the adjoining room. There had been no sound of a key, but the door, it seemed, was self-locking and she found that she could not open it. She went back to her room and said:

'Go on with what you are doing. There is something I want to ask you which I do not wish anyone to overhear. Amabel, you are hiding something from me. At least, you think you are. I am going to tell you what it is, so that, if ever the subject comes up, you will be able to say, with truth, that you did not tell me about it.'

'Oh, no, please, now, Dame Beatrice, mum! Oi don't want to get into no trouble!'

'Were you in service when Mr Romilly gave what he called his house-warming party?'

'When he first took over Galliard Hall? Why, yes, mum, me and Voilert and cook, we was all here, haven been bespoke by Messus Judeth to get the house ready for hem and Messus Trelby.'

'Do you remember who came to the party?'

'Why, the same as this toime, 'cepten for yourself, Dame Beatrice, mum.'

'I see. So the Reverend Mr Lestrange was not present?'

'No, mum. I reckon he weren't envoited.'

'Nor his brother, Mr Willoughby?'

'No, mum. It were loike Oi say.'

'Yes, I see. And the Reverend Hubert and Mr Willoughby were not invited this time, either, were they?'

'Oh, Dame Beatrice, mum, how would Oi know a theng loike that, then? Teddn no business of moine who get envoited to the house!' Her voice held a pleading tone.

'Is it Luke's business, then? Luke takes the letters down to the post-box at the gates, doesn't he?'

'That eddn nothen to do with Oi!' But Amabel looked scared.

'Look, Amabel, a man has been murdered.'

'That eddn nothen to do with Oi, neether!'

'It will be, you know, if you withhold information from the police. Luke made a remark, didn't he, before anything dreadful happened? He meant no harm by it, I'm sure. I want you to tell me what it was.'

Amabel had given up stripping the bed. She now sat down upon the mattress.

'Oi don't want nothen to do with the police,' she said sullenly. 'Oi don't know nothen, so I can't say nothen, can Oi?'

'Then I shall ask Violet.'

'Her won't say nothen, neether. Teddn no business of ourn, I tell ee. Best ee leave et alone.'

'And Luke won't admit to me what he said to you both, of course. Luke is Mr Romilly's creature. Did cook hear the remark Luke passed?'

'No, her was haven her afternoon off.'

'So Luke did pass a remark.'

'You're setten traps for me!'

'I'll tell you what Luke said, if you like. You can confirm it, or you can deny it. It will not make the slightest difference because, you see, I *know*.'

'Well,' said Amabel, 'ef ee knows, ee knows, so what call have ee to bidger-badger me loike thes here? Oi never thought, when Oi just mentioned it casual-loike to Mess Corenna——'

'I won't badger you any more, Amabel. At some time or other – it is immaterial when – Luke overheard Mr Romilly say that he could not understand why the Reverend Hubert and Mr Willoughby had neither turned up nor sent a note of explanation, but Luke remarked to you and Violet that he did not see why they should have done either, since he knew for a fact that neither of them had been sent a note of invitation to join the house-party. That is so, isn't it? He always reads the envelopes before he posts the letters, and he knew that nothing had been sent to Mr Hubert or Mr Willoughby Lestrange. Why, then, should Mr Romilly have appeared so concerned at their non-appearance when he knew perfectly well that they had not been invited? That was the substance of Luke's remark, I think, and that is what you told Miss Corinna, isn't it? Well, you've done more good than harm to Mr Romilly, so do not worry any more about it.'

CHAPTER ELEVEN

Oxdansen—Crowner's Quest

'He's for a jig, or a tale of bawdry, or he sleeps.'
Hamlet, Prince of Denmark.

---

(1)

'An odd circumstance has cropped up, Dame Beatrice,' said Kirkby. 'You remember, I suppose, that Mr Romilly Lestrange identified the body as that of Mr – or, rather, the Reverend – Hubert?'

'Indeed I do.'

'Well, it seems much more likely to have been that of his brother, Mr Willoughby.'

'Really?'

'You don't seem particularly surprised. Don't tell me you'd thought so, all along.'

'Oh, no, I certainly had not thought that. As to my not appearing to be surprised, well, when we were told that Willoughby had disappeared, I assumed that he, too, had been murdered, because, according to my reading of the case, that would have been the obvious thing to have happened. As I told you, I made it my business to find out why neither of the brothers, the sons of the illegitimate Mr Caesar Lestrange, had attended the family re-union. It seems clear that they did not go for the very obvious reason that they had not been invited.'

'You told me that that is what you thought. The interesting thing now, in view of this violent death, is to find out why they, among all the members of both families, should have been left out.'

'Exactly. And why, having been left out, one of them should have been more or less in the vicinity of Galliard Hall and should have been murdered. What makes you think that the body is that of Mr Willoughby and not that of the Reverend Hubert?'

'Because a member of his parish, which was in Buckingham-shire, has come to us with evidence that the Reverend Hubert went out to take up a position as vicar of the English church in Bella Luganti, on the Italian Riviera, where there is a flourishing community of English exiles in retirement. We've checked on this, and it's true. He's there, all right, and is greatly concerned to learn of his brother's death.'

'Is he returning to this country?'

'We shall ask him to attend the inquest and positively identify the body, as Mr Romilly seems to have been in error.'

'In that case, I hope you will promise him police protection when he comes.'

'You think that will be necessary?'

'I think it would be a wise precaution.'

'Against whom? I can see that you have somebody very much in mind, Dame Beatrice.'

'Yes, I have. In fact, I have three persons in mind, two who might be in collusion, and the third who might be unconnected with them, in so far as motive is concerned.'

'No use asking you, I suppose, who they are?'

'Well, I hesitate to name persons against whom I have no real evidence. I can merely think of a possible motive for their wishing to have the two brothers out of the way.'

'But evidence of motive would help us enormously, Dame Beatrice.'

'When I used the words I was ill-advised. Evidence of motive is too strong and exact a term. All I meant was that, if certain suppositions of mine are right, then a motive would appear to emerge, but that is as far as I ought to go. The evidence given at the inquest should make the issue clearer.'

'And with that I shall have to be satisfied, I suppose.'

'Only for the time being. I must confess, though, that, in the interests of his own safety, I wish you could have found some evidence of the identity of the corpse other than the testimony of the Reverend Hubert.'

'You don't mean he'll say it's his brother's body if it isn't, surely! You don't mean *he's* your lone wolf of a suspect? It's established that he's been on the Riviera for quite a little time, you know.'

'No, he is not my third suspect, but I fear for his safety, even if you give him police protection, should he put in an appearance at the inquest.'

'If we protect him, Dame Beatrice, he'll be all right, I assure you.'

'In England, yes. In Italy?'

'Oh, I see. But to whose advantage would it be to liquidate him?'

'I am still not prepared to mention names, but you can see that it might be to the advantage, perhaps, of the person or persons who killed his brother.'

'If it *is* his brother, as I say. The next problem is that, if Romilly Lestrange was wrong, *why* was he wrong?'

'Presumably because he did not know either of the brothers particularly well, and that is readily conceivable, especially if he had been introduced to both of them, we will say, at the same time, and a great number of years ago, perhaps. He has been living in Kenya until fairly recently, you know.'

'His story about the finding of the body is pretty fishy, don't you think?'

'I have an open mind about that. It is only fishy if he is the murderer, wouldn't you say? And, of course, suspicion must rest on him if, as the servants think likely – I will not put it more strongly than that, although, of course, *they* did – neither Hubert nor Willoughby was invited to join the house-party.'

'Could you make that a bit clearer, ma'am?'

'Yes. I mean that, if they were not invited, why should Romilly insist that they were, and make such a point of not having had a letter of explanation to account for their non-appearance? But, to return to my previous point, surely a routine enquiry will unearth somebody as capable as Mr Hubert of identifying the body?'

'I know you well enough to take as broad a hint as that, Dame Beatrice. Right! We'll scrub the Reverend Hubert and find another witness. The lawyers can do that for us, most likely.'

'I do not think you need trouble them. If it *is* Mr Willoughby, I have the witness you need in my own care.'

'Miss Rosamund Lestrange, you mean, ma'am? I'd sooner find a man. I don't think the corpse is something a young lady ought to be asked to identify. The doctors couldn't make it look exactly pretty, you know, after the bashing it got on those rocks.

No, we'll find someone, all right. We'll track down somebody on ths staff of the last hotel his grandfather stayed at. That should do the trick, I think. Mr Willoughby was Mr Felix Napoleon's secretary until the old gentleman's death, I think you said, so there will be a number of people in the Carlisle hotel who'll remember him.'

(2)

'The police don't accept Romilly's identification of the body?' said Judith. 'But why not?'

'The brothers were much alike, from what I remember of them,' said Romilly, 'and, of course, the face was in a dreadful mess. It would be easy enough to make a mistake, and, apparently, that is what I did. So Hubert is in Italy, is he? Oh, well, that settles it. Shall I still have to appear at the inquest?'

'I'm afraid so, sir,' said Kirkby. 'The jury will want to hear about your discovery of the body.'

'The jury? But this is a coroner's court! It isn't a court of justice!'

'In cases of violent death, sir, the coroner sits with a jury composed of seven to eleven persons. Their verdict need not be unanimous, but can be accepted provided that the minority does not number more than two persons. That is the law as it stands at present.'

'I don't care about this idea of a jury. It seems to me to smack of the criminal courts.'

'Well, those will have to come into it in due course, sir, won't they? This was not an accidental death.'

'Is that quite certain, though, Detective-Inspector? Those cliffs are very dangerous.'

'You will hear the medical evidence at the inquest, sir.'

'Well, Romilly,' said Dame Beatrice, when Kirkby had gone, 'it is as well that the mistake in identification was discovered in time, before the funeral took place. It is a grisly matter disinterring a corpse. What made you think it was Hubert?'

'I had not seen Caesar's boys except in the photographs he sent out to Kenya. I confused one with the other, that's all. Are they bringing Hubert over here to identify the body, do you know?'

'I doubt it,' said Dame Beatrice obliquely. 'There must be numbers of people who knew Willoughby.'

She was aware of Romilly's sigh of relief. She caught up with Kirkby. He was strolling towards the gates of Galliard Hall, outside which he had left the car which had brought him from Dorchester.

'Well?' he said. 'Any signs of guilt?'

'Nothing but signs of relief that he will not come face to face with Hubert at the inquest.'

'Oh, well, families being what they are, that's understandable, perhaps. It need not be a sign of guilt. Well, my next job is to find a reliable witness. The inquest is to be on Thursday, and it may have to be adjourned. It just depends upon what I can ferret out in the next couple of days, although I haven't much hope at present of anything new turning up in such a short time. You'll come along, I hope?'

'Most certainly. Where will it be held?'

'In the great hall of Galliard Hall itself. Mr Romilly has no objection to that, and it will be the most convenient place, as it is the only room in the neighbourhood, apart from a church hall, large enough for the purpose. I'll hope to see you at ten o'clock on Thursday morning, then.'

(3)

Kirkby's car was out of sight, and Dame Beatrice was about to enter her own, when a third car descended the long slope, a car which she recognised as that of her son Ferdinand. He was with his wife, and, with a wave of the hand to Dame Beatrice, he drove through the lodge gates and up to the house, presumably to carry out his assignment.

'Drive to the top of the hill, George,' said Dame Beatrice to her chauffeur, 'and find a place where we can park the car off the road. We will wait for Sir Ferdinand. I hope that he may have something interesting to tell me.'

George did as he was ordered, and they waited for the better part of an hour before Ferdinand's car came round the bend of the narrow road and pulled up on the grass verge just in front of them. Ferdinand got out. Dame Beatrice lowered the back-seat window.

E

'Give you lunch at Sandbanks, mother, and drop you at the Stone House afterwards,' he said, when he came up.

Dame Beatrice accepted this invitation, climbed into his car and left him to tell George to take her own car home.

'Well?' she said, when they were headed for Studland and the car ferry. 'What of Romilly?'

'Only that he isn't. There is not the very faintest resemblance. This fellow is too tall, too old and doesn't need glasses. I put my own on to look at the Raeburn, and he took a pair from its case, but put them back again and returned the case to his pocket. I received the impression that he was accustomed to produce them merely in order to demonstrate that he possessed a pair, which seems to indicate that he knows (or knew) the real Romilly.

'He doesn't know much about pictures, either. He didn't know which was the Raeburn, for one thing. To test him, I went first to another picture – you had described the position of the Raeburn and had said that it was a portrait, and it was exactly as you had told me – and began to eulogise it, and then I produced a handwritten letter of introduction cooked up, as a matter of fact, by my clerk, and asked him whether he was prepared to sell. He read it without using his glasses, and then explained that the pictures were heirlooms, so then I went over and scrutinised the Raeburn and asked him whether it was one of his ancestors. He agreed that it was. I ventured to say that it was from Reynold's best period, to which he agreed. Oh, there's no doubt about it, mother. He's an imposter all right. I wonder what's happened to the real Romilly Lestrange?'

(4)

The coroner was a solicitor and he sat with a jury of seven, two of whom were women. Kirkby had found three unbiased and reliable witnesses who, shown the body separately and being given no chance to communicate with one another until all had expressed an opinion as to the identity of the dead man, had severally asserted that it was Willoughby Lestrange. Only one of them was needed to testify in court, so Kirkby had selected the hotel manager. His evidence was clear and unchallenged. The deceased, he stated, had been a guest in his hotel in Carlisle for some years and had left it soon after the demise of Mr Felix

Napoleon Lestrange, who had employed Mr Willoughby as secretary and to whom he was distantly related. They were known at the hotel as Mr Lestrange and Mr Willoughby respectively, to avoid confusion.

The manager was succeeded by Romilly, who gave evidence of the finding of the body. Judith was also called, as she had been with him at the time, and she substantiated his account. After this came the medical evidence. Doctor Gerald Randall was called.

'You are Doctor Gerald Randall?'

'That is my name.'

'When did you see the body of the man whom you now know was Mr Willoughby Lestrange?'

'I saw it, and examined it, on the afternoon of March 4th at about six-thirty.'

'What, in your opinion, was the cause of death?'

'I found that the deceased had been stabbed through the heart.'

'Were there any other marks of violence on the body?'

'Yes, but I formed the opinion that these had been inflicted after death had taken place. The head and limbs had been battered from having been in contact, I assumed, with the rocks among which, I understand, the body was found.'

'Did you form any opinion as to the length of time the man had been dead?'

'It is an opinion only, but I should say he had been dead for at least a week. I am not prepared to be more specific than that.'

'He could not have been dead for a lesser time than that? – say, three to four days?'

'To the best of my knowledge and belief, he had been dead for not less than a week, but not as long as a fortnight. The neck and face were discoloured and swollen, and the body, I was told, had been found floating. These symptoms occur when a body has been found in water in cold weather, between five and eight days after death. I am inclined to suggest the longer period, as decomposition of the trunk, with little distension, was already apparent.'

'You conducted an autopsy?'

'I did, with the assistance of my colleague, Mr Percy Mansel, the surgeon, who agrees with my findings.'

'I do not think we need call him, although I understand that he is available. Now, Doctor, I note that you do not rule out the possibility of suicide. However, that is a matter over which I need not detain you. Call Detective-Inspector Kirkby.'

Kirkby was sworn and agreed that he was the person he represented himself to be.

'Now, Detective-Inspector, I understand that you are making some enquiries as to how Mr Willoughby Lestrange met his death. You have heard the medical evidence. Have you any comment to make, as a result of your investigations?'

'No, sir, except to say that, at first, the body was wrongly identified.'

'Wrongly identified? By whom?'

'By Mr Romilly Lestrange, sir. He was mistaken in thinking that the body was that of the deceased's brother, the Reverend Hubert Lestrange.'

'Dear me! That seems to have been a strange error. Perhaps we had better recall Mr Romilly Lestrange, so, if you would stand down for a few minutes, Detective-Inspector, we will hear you again when we have heard what Mr Romilly has to say.'

'Very good, sir.'

'Call Mr Romilly Lestrange. Now, sir, remember that you are still under oath. Can you tell us why you should have thought that the deceased was the Reverend Hubert Lestrange?'

'I can't really say. I had not seen either of my nephews, except in photographs, as I had been living abroad for some years.'

'Why, though, did you suppose the dead man to be Mr Hubert, and not Mr Willoughby?'

'I was expecting them both to visit me, and I thought it more likely, when I found the body, that an absent-minded clergyman would have taken a wrong turning to my house and fallen over the cliff, than that a business-like young man, such as a secretary, would have done so.'

'Had you any reason to think that Mr Hubert was absent-minded?'

'It is a thing one connects with scholars and clergymen.'

'You thought, then, that the deceased had missed his way and fallen over the cliff?'

'Yes, it was the obvious thing to think.'

'What did you do, after you had found the body?'

'I returned to my car and drove to the nearest coast-guard station.'

'Were you present when the body was recovered?'

'Yes, I came back with assistance, and pointed out where the body was lying.'

'Did you do anything more?'

'Oh, I knew that the doctor would see to anything that was necessary. The police sent for Dr Randall at once, of course, and he had the body moved to the infirmary, where Detective-Inspector Kirkby saw it.'

'But you still did not realise that the death was not accidental, but was caused by suicide or murder?'

'No, of course I did not realise it. There was no reason, so far as I knew, for one of my nephews to commit suicide, particularly as I was still convinced that the body was that of Hubert, to whom, with his beliefs, suicide would have been a deadly sin, and one hardly thinks of one's close relatives being murdered.'

'Suicide is indeed a "deadly" sin. I think we may agree with you there. When you heard that the body had received a stab wound, what were your reactions?'

'Until much later, I had no idea in what form death had taken place, except that I concluded it was either from the fall from the cliffs or by drowning. It was a great surprise to me, and I may say a considerable shock, when I knew that Detective-Inspector Kirkby was treating the case as one of murder. He has haunted my house continually since I reported the discovery of the body, but gave me no details as to the cause of death. I had assumed, of course, that it was accidental.'

'You have heard now that death was the result of a wound caused by stabbing.'

'Yes.'

'Did you pick up a sword which you found lying in the grass on the cliffs above the part of the coast known as Dancing Ledge?'

'Yes.'

'Did you show it to the police?'

'Yes. I thought it might be dangerous if children got hold of it.'

'Did you recognise it as being your property?'

'No, it doesn't belong to me.'

'Thank you, Mr Lestrange. Call Marlene Cobb.'

This woman was Romilly's cook. The sword was handed to her.

'Do you recognise this weapon?'

'That I do.'

'You have seen it before, then?'

'Ah, at Christmas time.'

'Under what circumstances, Mrs Cobb?'

'Beg pardon?'

'Why do you relate this sword to Christmas time?'

'Because the master cut the cake with it. Very lively and many goings-on had there been atween him and Mrs Judith, so-calling herself housekeeper, and very blaspheemious he was.'

'Indeed? What do you mean by that?'

'He told me to ice the cake with the words, "The family, God bless 'em," which I done.'

'That doesn't – that is not blasphemous, is it?'

'No, but after the goings-on – something shocking they was – he cuts the cake with this 'ere knife what you're showing me, and as he does it he gives a kind of a nasty giggle and he says, "I come not to bring peace, but a sword." Wouldn't you call *that* blaspheemious?'

'And you are certain that this is the same sword? How can you be sure?'

'Because I *be* sure. That's how.'

'Well,' said the coroner, when Marlene Cobb had been dismissed, 'I will now ask the jury to retire and consider their verdict, reminding them that this is primarily an enquiry into the cause of death. It is *not* a criminal court.'

'Might I ask a question?' said a woman juror. 'There is a point I'd like to clear up. The defendant – I mean Mr Lestrange – identified the body as that of the Reverend Hubert. Isn't it equally likely that Mr Rose, the hotel manager, is mistaken in thinking it was Mr Willoughby? I mean, it's simply one word against another, isn't it?'

'Mr Rose is not unsupported in his assumption, madam. Two members of his staff have asserted, independently of him and of one another, that the body is that of Mr Willoughby. Moreover, Mr Romilly is prepared to agree that the mistake was his,' said Kirkby.

The verdict of the jury was unanimous and was never in doubt. As he left the court, Romilly found himself touched on the shoulder by Kirkby.

'I'm sorry, sir,' said the latter, 'but I'm afraid I shall have to ask you to come with me. There will be a formal charge, and you have the right to ask for your lawyer to be present.'

CHAPTER TWELVE

Zapatos—Goody Two-Shoes

'And he that will caper with me for a thousand marks,
let him lend me the money, and have at him!'
                                            Henry IV, Part 2.

---

(1)

At the police station Romilly was formally charged and two days
later he was brought before a magistrate who, in view of the
nature of the charge, was sitting alone, and the examination was
held in private, reporters and the general public being excluded.

The charge was read, and then Kirkby said:

'If it please Your Worship, the police ask that the accused
may be remanded for two weeks pending further enquiries.'

'Remanded in custody, you mean?'

'In view of the nature of the charge, yes, Your Worship.'

'What reason have you for asking that the prisoner be remanded?'

'As I stated, Your Worship, the police wish to make further
enquiries into this case. We hope to have further evidence available at the next hearing.'

The magistrate, who was a woman, glanced across at Romilly's
solicitor, but he made no sign.

'Very well,' she said, 'but first I should wish to hear the evidence
upon which the defendant has been brought here.'

The evidence, given in the usual police-court parrot-utterance,
did not seem particularly impressive.

'You accuse him of murder, and of giving a false identification
of the dead person, do you, Detective-Inspector?'

'Yes, Your Worship, of deliberately making a misleading
statement on the second matter, with intent to defeat the ends of
justice.'

'And he was the person who discovered the body?'

'Under what we believe to be suspicious circumstances, Your
Worship. There seems to be good reason to suppose that the

accused wanted the victim out of the way, and that is the line along which we should like to acquire more evidence. Further to that, the accused has stated, in front of witnesses, that he believes his own life to be in danger. If he is right . . . '

'Why should he suppose a thing like that?'

'There is a great deal of money involved, Your Worship, and there again we need to probe into the facts.'

The magistrate turned to Romilly.

'Is there anything you wish to say?' she asked. The solicitor was the one to answer her.

'Not at this stage, Your Worship, thank you. We have no objection to a remand, and we realise that, on a charge of this nature, there can be no question of bail. We reserve our defence, both now and at the next hearing.'

'Very well. I order that the accused be remanded in custody for fourteen days, after which time he will again appear before the court to make an answer to the charge of wilful murder. The court will then decide whether the police have made out a case sufficiently strong to warrant a committal to the Assizes.'

(2)

'The next thing I've got to do,' said Kirkby to Dame Beatrice, 'is to rustle up something a lot stronger and more telling than anything I've got at present. We're batting on a very sticky wicket.'

'I am not batting at all,' said Dame Beatrice.

'I can't count on your help? I was hoping you'd turn Miss Rosamund inside out for me.'

'I will do that, if you like, but I must warn you that I think you're got the wrong murderer.'

'Oh, come now, Dame Beatrice! If Sir Ferdinand is right, and Romilly Lestrange is an imposter, surely the first thing he'd want to do is to eliminate the one person who could discredit him.'

'But Willoughby was not that one person. You yourself have already mentioned my son.'

'Ah, yes, I know. But my contention is that Romilly hasn't a clue that your son was acquainted with the real Romilly, whereas the latter would almost certainly have been acquainted with his brother's children. It seems to me that the answer lies in Kenya.'

'Lies dead in Kenya,' amended Dame Beatrice. 'The rea
Mr Romilly, I mean.'

'Murdered, you think, ma'am?'

'Not necessarily by his partner, whom I take this Mr Romilly
to have been. Either he died a natural death, or he may well have
been murdered by the adherents of Mau-Mau, in which case you
are unlikely to be able to get at all the facts.'

'Anyway, a likely review of the situation might be as follows:
the real Mr Romilly, subsidised by old Mr Felix Napoleon, his
natural father, sets up in Kenya with a partner, this man who
calls himself Romilly Lestrange. At some point – we don't know
when and, for present purposes, it doesn't much matter – the
real Mr Romilly either dies or is killed. In the early 1960's Kenya
becomes independent.'

'In the December of 1963.'

'Oh, was it? Well, perhaps at that time, or maybe earlier, or
maybe later, the surviving partner, *this* Mr Romilly, comes back
to England. Well, men in a foreign country, perhaps living
mostly among natives, with the nearest English neighbours miles
away, no doubt get to know a fair amount about one another
and about one another's business. They also get letters, we'll
say, from home, perhaps regularly, perhaps once in a while. One
of the letters, I don't mind betting, was to tell Romilly of his
brother's death. Another, written, no doubt, by Mr Willoughby
in his capacity of secretary to Mr Felix Napoleon, was to tell
him that the old gentlemen, too, had died.'

'You think, then, that this pseudo-Romilly was still in Kenya in
1966? It is quite likely, in spite of the troubles there, I suppose.'

'Whether he was still there or not, ma'am, I bet he knew his
partner had expectations under the old gentlemen's Will.'

'Yes, and very considerable expectations, if certain eventualities
came to pass.'

'Those being?'

'That if the heiress presumptive died at any time after her
twenty-fifth birthday, he, in his impersonation of Mr Romilly,
inherited the fortune.'

'Didn't you also tell me that if she could be proved incapable
of managing her own affairs, Mr Romilly would also benefit?'

'Yes, that, I think, is why he called me in in my professional
capacity. He knew that I should find her completely capable, in

spite of his own insincere insinuations to the contrary. He also
. . . ' she cackled mirthlessly . . . 'realised that I am incapable of
murdering the girl before she reaches her twenty-fifth birthday.
If she died *now*, you see, I myself would become the legatee.
Mr Romilly – we must call him that, until we know his real
name – does not want to administer the inheritance on Rosamund's behalf. He wants the money to be his entirely. For that
reason, I believe that Rosamund is in no danger from him until
after the 29th of May, so, although I believe he will make an
attempt on her life after she passes the age of twenty-five, I do not
believe he murdered Mr Willoughby. There is no evidence that
he had ever seen him.'

'Oh, but, look at it this way, ma'am. He's lived and worked
with the real Mr Romilly over a number of years. How many
years we don't know, but if, as Sir Ferdinand suggested to you,
they went out to Kenya soon after Mr Romilly left the University,
it must have been a fairly considerable number. He'd surely have
known of Mr Romilly's relatives, including his two nephews,
Mr Hubert and Mr Willoughby. Likely enough, he'd been shown
their photographs. That means he would have been in a position
to recognise *them*, whereas they wouldn't know *him* from Adam.'

'All this is nothing but surmise, you know – that he would
have seen their photographs, I mean.'

'Granted, ma'am, but it's a probable and workable hypothesis.
Besides, he *claims* he had seen photographs. Well, now, his
partner dies. All he has to do is to keep that fact dark, so far as
relatives in England are concerned – it isn't as though there were
any women to poke and pry . . . '

'Except Rosamund, of course.'

'Too young to be interested in an uncle I don't suppose she'd
ever met. I think we can leave her out of my argument. Well,
the partner comes home when he gets a letter addressed to the
dead man reporting the death of old Mr Felix Napoleon, assumes
Mr Romilly's identity, buries himself down at Galliard Hall,
adopts the heiress and knows that all will be well so long as he
can choke off Mr Hubert and Mr Willoughby, the only relatives
who might possibly realise that he wasn't their uncle. He stages
this house-party, so as to have plenty of suspects on the spot,
entices Mr Willoughby down, murders him and makes himself,
as he thinks, secure.'

'Yes,' said Dame Beatrice doubtfully, 'but we have no evidence to show that Mr Hubert and Mr Willoughby had ever met their uncle *or* seen a photograph of him. Men do not usually send photographs of themselves or their grown-up nephews to other men. We may assume, too, that both nephews were very young when Mr Romilly emigrated. They may not even have been born, in fact. Their father was younger than Romilly. I do not see why they should have been in any better position to expose the imposter than Rosamund was, and she, it is quite clear, has no idea that her guardian has no right whatever to claim kinship with her. He made a very bad slip when he told me he was married to her.'

'There's this fact that neither Mr Hubert nor Mr Willoughby was invited to join the house-party, ma'am.'

'Yes, but thereby hangs a tale. It seems that they *were* invited, but the letters did not reach them.'

'Sabotage, eh? Miss Rosamund, do you think? Well, then, I'm afraid I'll have to ask you to allow me to question her.'

'I myself would like to hear what she has to say. She is staying with Laura's family in the Highlands. When could you make it convenient to accompany me there?'

'I'd much sooner talk to her down here, ma'am.'

(3)

Laura's father worked for the North of Scotland Hydro-Electric Board, and the family occupied a pleasant, fair-sized house at Moy, about a mile beyond the point where the River Spean emerges from Loch Laggan. Laura, who had spent only a couple of days in Scotland, and had returned with Gavin and the nurse, sent word that she would be visiting the family with the object of returning to the Stone House with Rosamund, whose stay in the Highlands had never been intended to be other than temporary. She and Dame Beatrice were met on their arrival with the news that Rosamund had vanished.

'It was as though she was getting an awful fright when I told her you were coming,' explained Laura's mother, 'and this morning, when I went up to wake her, as she wasna down to her breakfast, I found her gone, and her wee kist with her.'

'Oh, if she's taken her suitcase, she must have intended to hop it for good,' said Laura. 'I suppose you've sent the bloodhounds after her?'

'Och, she'll not have gone far,' said Mrs Menzies. 'Your father and the lads are away to Spean Bridge. That's where she'll likely make for. She could get a lift from there to Fort William, or maybe even as far as Glasgow, although I dinna care to think of a young lassie stopping a stranger, ·with so many droch weans about the place.'

'Yes, and from Glasgow,' said Laura, 'she'd go to Carlisle, I don't mind betting. Anyway, I wouldn't worry about her safety. She's well able to take care of herself, if you ask me.'

'An interesting side-light on her abilities,' said Dame Beatrice, 'and an opinion with which I find myself in tentative but increasing agreement.'

'Well, I vote we make for Carlisle and wait for her to turn up. She'd hardly know of anywhere to go except the hotel there, where she lived with old Felix Napoleon,' said Laura. 'She told me quite a bit about it while we were together. Oh, I'll bet she's in Carlisle all right.'

'Your idea has much to recommend it. We can safely leave the search at this end to your father and his helpers,' said Dame Beatrice.

'Aye, you can that,' agreed Mrs Menzies. 'But I dinna ken why the thought of you, Dame Beatrice, should have given the caileag a fright.'

'No, I can't either,' said Laura. 'But she isn't such a "caileag," you know. She's nearly twenty-five. I say, mother, you won't call the police in, will you, if she doesn't turn up? I mean . . .'

'Is it the police!' exclaimed Mrs Menzies, with as much horror as if she had been born in the west of Ireland. 'Indeed I will not, then! My Cruachan! The police! Whatever next!'

'Oh, that's all right, then. Well, we'd better stay the night here, and tomorrow to fresh woods and pastures new.'

There was no very direct route to Carlisle. George, who wanted to avoid Glasgow, drove to Fort William (Laura and Dame Beatrice looking out for Rosamund the while), and then made for Stirling by way of Lochearnhead and Callander. From Stirling the road went through Airdrie and Lanark to Beattock, and thence to Lockerbie and Carlisle. The journey was one of more than two hundred miles, but they made it, with a stop for lunch at Stirling, in very good time.

Enquiry at the reception desk failed to produce any information. If Rosamund had booked in at the hotel, she had not done so under the name of Lestrange. Laura, who had undertaken the enquiries, pursued them.

'This girl lived here for some years – anyway, up to 1966 – with an old gentleman named Felix Lestrange. She is his grand-daughter.'

'Oh, I wouldn't know,' said the receptionist. 'I wasn't here then.'

'Can you find rooms for us for one night? Two singles?'

As she signed the register, Laura looked down the list of names and addresses, but there was none which indicated that Rosamund had made an entry in the book. She was given keys and the suit-cases were taken upstairs. She saw Dame Beatrice settled, and then went out to the hotel parking yard to find George. He was seated in the car.

'Had something to eat, George?'

'Yes, thank you, madam.'

'We're staying the night. Can you fix yourself up, as usual?'

'Certainly, madam. I have bespoke a room on the off-chance already, as I guessed you wouldn't be proceeding any further today. May I ask if there's any news of the young lady, madam?'

'No, George, I'm afraid there isn't. I would have betted any money that she'd come to this hotel, but, so far, there isn't a sign of her.'

'What time will you be requiring the car in the morning, madam?'

'I'm not sure. I haven't asked. Better be ready to start off at ten, anyway. I don't know what the plans are, but I should imagine we'll go straight home from here, unless we hear something about Miss Lestrange.'

Dame Beatrice was in the hotel lounge when Laura returned.

'I have spoken to the hotel manager,' she said. 'He, of course, knows Rosamund quite well. It is certain that she is not here.'

'What do we do next?'

'I have engaged our rooms for the next two nights. It is possible, if Rosamund is reduced to asking for lifts on the road, that she is still bound for Carlisle, but has not yet arrived. Your dear

mother has the name of this hotel, and will send me a telegram if
Rosamund returns to Moy.'

'You think of everything,' said Laura, tongue in cheek. She
was not surprised, however, when, at lunch-time on the following
day, Rosamund walked into the dining-room under the solicitous
escort of the head waiter and was given a corner table with her
back to the rest of the room.

'Looks a bit the worse for wear,' commented Laura, regarding
the drooping shoulders and the general air of limpness which
Rosamund displayed. 'She'll have a nasty shock when she finds
us here, I shouldn't wonder.'

They administered this shock some half-an-hour later. Outside
the dining-room swing doors was a small ante-room which, in
its turn, opened into the cocktail bar. In this ante-room Dame
Beatrice took up her position, bidding Laura to leave her there
alone. Laura sought the lounge, found a seat by the fire and a
magazine, lit a cigarette and waited upon events.

She had discarded her second magazine and was looking
through the pile for a third, when the two came in.

'Well, here we are,' said Dame Beatrice, smiling like a replete
python. 'I have asked for coffee, and now we can have a cosy
little chat.'

'Hullo, Rosamund,' said Laura, without enthusiasm. 'Where
did you spring from? We left you in Scotland with my people.
How come that you're here?'

'Oh, I was homesick, and I have to see my lawyers,' said the
girl. She was looking strained and tired. 'Please don't pester me.
I'm ill.'

'Rosamund walked from Moy to Spean Bridge, and from there
obtained a lift to Inverness,' said Dame Beatrice. 'From Inverness
she got a train to Edinburgh, but there her money ran out, so she
has alternately walked and thumbed lifts from there.'

'I threw away my suitcase,' said Rosamund. 'I got a lift as far
as Peebles, and then I began to walk, and the suitcase was just
simply too heavy. At last I got to Galashiels and a lorry-driver
took me the rest of the way.'

'Well, I should say you'd been pretty lucky,' said Laura.

'My feet are blistered, and I've lost my luggage, and I haven't
any money,' said Rosamund. 'I don't know whether you call *that*
being pretty lucky.'

'All's well that ends well,' said Laura, 'but I do think you might have let my people know you intended to sling your hook. They've been somewhat worried about you.'

'Yes, I know. I'm sorry about that. Your mother has been very kind to me. But I was afraid she wouldn't let me go, if I told her I wanted to leave.'

'Good heavens, of course she'd have let you go! You're a free agent, aren't you?'

'For the past year I haven't thought so.'

'Ah,' said Dame Beatrice, 'here comes the coffee. Speaking of the past year, my dear Rosamund, you will like to know what has happened to Romilly. He has been arrested and has been brought before the Bench and remanded in custody for a fortnight. After that, he will again appear in court, when it will be decided whether or not he is to be sent for trial.'

'Romilly?'

'Romilly.'

'Do they really think he killed Hubert?'

'It turns out not to be Hubert, but Willoughby.'

'Willoughby is dead?'

'Yes. His was the body which Romilly and Mrs Judith saw at Dancing Ledge. How well did you know Willoughby?'

'Pretty well, in a way. He was my grandfather's secretary, you know.'

'Yes, I did know that. Did you like him?'

'Oh, yes, I suppose so. At least, I didn't dislike him, But, of course, I didn't have a great deal to do with him. I was away at school a lot of the time between the ages of nine and eighteen, and in the summer holidays I was sent away to the seaside, and at Christmas time Willoughby was given a fortnight's leave of absence, and grandfather and I usually went to London.'

'That leaves the Easter vacations. Did you see much of him then?'

'No. Grandfather used to take me to Rome or Santiago. He was very devout.'

'Did the Reverend Hubert ever come to see his brother?'

'Not that I can remember, but I believe they kept in touch.'

'So you have never seen Hubert?'

'If ever I did, I was so young that I don't remember it. Oh, I forgot. Of course I saw him at grandfather's funeral.'

'So if you had been called upon to identify the body, you would not have made the mistake which Romilly seems to have done?'

'No, of course not. I should have known it was Willoughby. After all, it was only just over a year since I had seen him.'

'Quite so. Well, now, Laura and I are staying here for two nights. I propose that you do the same, and then we can all travel back to the Stone House together.'

'But it's three hundred and fifty miles! When Romilly kidnapped me, we stayed a night on the way.'

'Yes, we will spend a night in Birmingham. I have friends there. They are related to Laura through her husband. They will find us an hotel. Laura will telephone them forthwith.'

'Sure,' said Laura. 'I expect they will put us up in their own house, though.'

'But I don't want to go back to the Stone House. I'm not safe there,' protested Rosamund urgently. 'It's much too near Galliard Hall.'

'Well, I can hardly ask Mrs Menzies to take you in again at Moy, after you left her house without even the ceremony of a leave-taking,' Dame Beatrice pointed out in mild tones. 'You would not expect me to do that, I'm certain.'

'I shall stay in Carlisle. I like it here.'

'I thought you had spent all your money,' said Laura brusquely.

'I have only to telephone grandfather's lawyers. My allowance is already overdue.'

'Very well. You are of age and I have no jurisdiction in the matter,' said Dame Beatrice, 'so you must do as you please. You had better make sure of your standing with the management of the hotel, though, had you not, before you decide to stay? I fear they may expect to be paid before your allowance comes through.'

'Couldn't *you* advance me a few pounds to be going on with?'

'I could, but I do not propose to do so. If you are determined to be independent, you must not begin by living on borrowed money.'

'No, I suppose not. I see you intend to force me to come to the Stone House with you.'

'Not at all. On the other hand, I am under no obligation to support your intention of remaining here.

'I thought you were my friends.'

'Be that as it may,' said Laura, 'it wasn't very friendly on your part to cut your stick and vanish the moment you heard that we were coming to Moy. Oh, well, I'll go and telephone Gavin's brother in Birmingham.'

She went out, humming a tune. Dame Beatrice, who still had faith in many of Freud's theories, recognised it as the Esther and Abi Ofarim number, *Darling, go home.* It ended, she remembered, *What's that you said? – The Will's to be read . . . I must go weep for my poor old man.* She had realised, from the beginning, that Laura, always prone to strong and uninhibited emotions, had disliked Rosamund, but this expression of cynicism was sufficiently remarkable to be worthy of notice. As soon as Laura was out of the room, Rosamund said:

'It's Laura I'm afraid of. That's why I ran away from Moy, and that's why I didn't want to go back with you to the Stone House. Do you realise that I've almost worn out my shoes walking all those miles to escape from her? That shows you how scared I am of her. I have bad dreams about her every night – dreadful dreams.'

'These remarks,' said Dame Beatrice calmly, 'are on a par with your impersonation of Ophelia, are they not? As such, they do not impress me. To quote the classic *Campbell of Kilmhor,* I would just counsel you to be candid. Whatever you have to fear, it can scarcely be Laura, and so long as Romilly is in custody you have nothing to fear from him, either. Why do you not tell me what is really in your mind?'

'I am quite safe from Romilly until after the end of May, so I don't mind about him any longer, but Laura hates me. I suppose it's because you take an interest in me, isn't it? I suppose she's jealous. Oh, well, I can understand it, I suppose, but it doesn't make things easier.'

'My interest in you is purely professional. Go along now, and make sure of your room for tonight, and then I should lie down and rest those blistered feet, if I were you.'

'Do *you* think Romilly killed Willoughby?'

'I think it is just as likely as that any other member of the family killed him, not less and not more.'

'They don't hang people now, though, do they? – so, even if Romilly is convicted, he'll still be alive and I shall still be in danger.'

'I have a plan for dealing with the situation,' said Dame Beatrice. 'Go and get some rest.' She sent for the hotel manager when Rosamund had gone to her room.

'You recognised the young woman who booked in this morning?' she asked. The manager hesitated a moment before he replied. Then he said:

'Oh, yes, I recognised the young lady, madam, but I was under a misapprehension. This young lady was certainly here under Mr Felix Lestrange's protection, but she is not the young lady I thought you had in mind.'

Dame Beatrice nodded. Felix Napoleon's reputation had rested on solid evidence, she thought. His wild oats, self-sown, had produced another crop, even though, in his dotage, it must have been a thin one.

CHAPTER THIRTEEN

Basse Danse—Confrontation

'The prince discovered to Claudio that he loved my niece, your daughter, and meant to acknowledge it this night in a dance.'

Much Ado About Nothing.

---

(1)

Dame Beatrice had left Rosamund little choice, and so was not at all surprised when the girl indicated that she was ready and willing to return to the Stone House. In the car she sat in front, next to George, and the journey was uneventful. They were accommodated, that night, in the Birmingham, or, to be exact, the Solihull house belonging to Laura's husband's brother. The household consisted of the man and wife and their daughter, aged sixteen. This child went to a day school, and her homework occupied her for most of the evening. She had done well in her ordinary level examinations and was now halfway through the first of the two years she would spend in studying for her advanced work.

There was high tea at six, followed by supper at ten, and between these meals the girl went up to her room to study and Rosamund elected to rest. The others chatted, looked at a television programme and played a rubber of bridge. After supper, to which the two girls were called down, the schoolgirl, Kirstie, requested Laura to go up and say goodnight to her, for, although they saw little of one another, there was a strong bond of sympathy between aunt and niece.

At half-past eleven the bedtime nightcaps were drunk and, Rosamund having retired soon after Kirstie, the older members went to bed. Laura followed Dame Beatrice to her room.

'Kirstie seems a bit browned-off,' she observed. 'Rosamund doesn't appear to have left her much time for work this evening. She seems to have been unburdening herself to the kid. Wish I'd known. I'd have gone along and broken up the party.'

'Unburdening herself? Dear me! To what extent?'

148

'According to Kirstie, to some considerable extent. She has told her the whole history of the toy trumpet, the radio set, the cat, the monkey and the baby doll. Kirstie, who's a sensible, level-headed kid, as befits Gavin's niece, dismissed the revelations as a lot of boloney, but what do *you* think?

'That Rosamund, lacking the stimulus of being the mis-understood and persecuted heroine, is seeking compensation.'

'I thought you liked her, and felt sorry for her.'

'I feel sorry for anybody who is under sentence of death. As for liking her, well, as you know, I like very few people, and poor Rosamund has never been among them.'

'Well, you could have fooled *me*. In fact, you jolly well did. I thought you disapproved of my disapproval of her.'

'I have overwhelming faith in your intuition.'

'Well, be that as it may – and there's no need to pull my leg – what do we do, if anything, about these disclosures? Kirstie, far from being sworn to secrecy, was told that it had been great fun leading us up the garden and that she could jolly well tell us so. When did you begin to rumble Rosamund?'

'First, when it was clear that she had the run of Galliard Hall. Secondly, when she refused to allow me to see her room there.'

'Well, Romilly thought it was dreadfully untidy, you told me.'

'I think the real reason was that she had plenty of ordinary clothes locked away there, as well as her fancy costumes.'

'Wouldn't Romilly and Judith have known that?'

'Judith did know it. She mentioned the matter to me. At first I think they must have believed she was playing into their hands by her eccentric behaviour in the matter of dress. Later, of course, it was borne in upon Romilly that for him to inherit the fortune outright would be infinitely preferable to administering it on Rosamund's behalf if she were found incapable of managing her own affairs. At that stage I was called in for the purpose of certifying that she was of sound mind. Rosamund, whose in-telligence is not to be gainsaid, had realised that this was the plan and that, if it succeeded, her life was in danger once she attained her twenty-fifth birthday. I will now confront her with what she has told Kirstie, and see how she reacts, but I shall not do this until we are back at the Stone House.'

They left immediately after breakfast, reached Salisbury at lunch-time, visited the Cathedral, which Rosamund had not seen before, and then made uneventful progress to Ringwood and Brockenhurst, and, from there, to the village of Wandles Parva and so home.

'Did you finish giving me your reasons for thinking that Rosamund isn't the sweet, persecuted innocent she pretends to be?' asked Laura, late that night, after Rosamund had gone to bed.

'Not quite. I was unfavourably impressed by her unnecessary histrionics.'

'Oh, you mean when she took Ophelia on her. Yes, that *was* rather on the lines of gilding the lily, wasn't it. Anything else?'

'It is understandable that she confessed to your niece the very things which she denied when I talked to her.'

'Yes. What do you make of that?'

'That she was play-acting again. There are matters on which I should like more information. I may get it when I question her tomorrow.'

'What sort of things do you want to know?'

'Details of her life with Felix Napoleon and what was her relationship with Willoughby Lestrange.'

'You think Romilly may have killed Willoughby not only because he was in a position to expose him as an imposter, but because Willoughby would champion Rosamund and see that she came to no harm? Well, that's quite possible, I suppose, isn't it?'

'Decidedly possible, but not, I fancy, very probable. If that were the case, one would be justified in wondering why Willoughby had not come to the girl's rescue long ago, and removed her from Romilly's jurisdiction.'

'Well, I suppose it was difficult, if Romilly had made himself her guardian.'

'We have no proof that such was the case, you know. On the contrary, Rosamund appears to have gone with him willingly.'

'But we've always kept in mind the possibility that Romilly may have kidnapped her after Felix Napoleon's death.'

'Yes,' said Dame Beatrice doubtfully. 'Is it really so simple a matter to run off with an heiress without her consent? After all, it isn't as though Rosamund had been alone in a private house. She was staying – living, in fact – at an hotel. There was plenty of assistance at hand. An abduction, as such, was surely out of the question.'

'She may have been tricked into going off with Romilly, I suppose, without realising what she was letting herself in for.'

'Tomorrow I shall ask her to tell me all about it.'

'Do you want me to sit in on the interview and take notes?'

'I think it might answer my purpose better if you were not present. The antipathy between you and Rosamund is mutual, if I am any judge, and she is likely to speak more freely in your absence.'

'Just as you say. When do you want to have her to yourself?'

'Immediately after breakfast. At the conclusion of the meal I shall send you on some errand which will ensure your absence for at least a couple of hours. That should give me all the time I need.'

'But you do still think she is in danger from Romilly?'

'I am sure she is, and from that hazard I shall protect her.'

'She's an odd bod. Do you think she will tell you the truth about herself?'

'I know enough of it, I think, to be able to decide whether she is telling the truth or not.'

Laura, according to plan, was despatched to Bournemouth with a shopping list, and left the Stone House in her own little car at half-past ten. Rosamund was still at breakfast, and poured herself a last cup of coffee as Dame Beatrice came back into the pleasant morning-room after having seen Laura off.

'It's going to be a nice day, Dame Beatrice,' she said. 'Couldn't we go for a drive into the Forest?'

'I think I am a little tired of the car,' Dame Beatrice responded. 'I seem to have used it so much during the past week.'

'Oh, yes, I'm sorry. Of course, at your age, you must get worn out rather easily. I don't stop to think. Well, do you suppose George could take me on my own? I had such a dreadfully boring time in Scotland.'

'It is better, perhaps, to be bored than dead, although not much, I suppose. Would you like to return to Galliard Hall?'

'Return there? But I thought . . . '

'Romilly is no longer there, of course.'

'No, but Judith is.'

'Did you know Judith before Romilly took you to live there?'

'No, of course I didn't. How could I? I didn't know Romilly himself until after grandfather died.'

Dame Beatrice picked up the newspaper which was delivered from Brokenhurst each morning by a boy on a bicycle.

'Dear me! The Ides of March!' she observed, placing a thin yellow forefinger on the date at the top of the front page. Rosamund was unimpressed.

'Is it?' she said. 'Less than a month until Easter. Do you have Easter eggs?'

'No, it is not a custom I observe.'

'Why do you want me to go back to Galliard Hall?'

'I do not want you to go back to Galliard Hall. I asked whether you would like to return. I gather that you would not, neither have you chosen to remain in Scotland.'

'I don't want to stay here, either. It's Laura. I tell you I'm scared of her. I know she doesn't like me. Do you think I could go and stay with Binnie?'

'That is hardly for me to decide. It would depend on Mr Humphrey's views, would it not?'

'They're rather poor. I could pay them well.'

'Why not write to them?'

'I don't know their address.'

'I have it, but, before you put your suggestion to them, we had better find out what the legal position is.'

'The legal position? Oh, you mean consult grandfather's lawyers. Yes, I could do that, I suppose. They are the people who pay me my allowance.'

'I do not know whether that constitutes them your guardians under the terms of your grandfather's Will. Technically, of course, you are of age, but doubtless conditions will have been laid down for their guidance. That can be discussed later. As you will have guessed, I have sent Laura out on an errand, which will take her the rest of the morning to execute, so that you and I may have plenty of time for a chat.'

'What about?'

'Laura's niece told her of the conversation you had in her parents' house in Solihull.'

'Yes, I'm sorry about that. I'm afraid I interrupted her school work.'

'That is not my concern. Why did you confess to her that

Romilly's story of your having thrown various articles into the sea was a true one?'

'Oh, that? I thought it might interest her.'

'It did. Where did you obtain the monkey?'

'Oh, I didn't, of course, or the cat or the baby doll.'

'How old were you when Willoughby became Felix Napoleon's secretary?'

'How old? I don't remember. I suppose I was about fifteen. We weren't living in Carlisle then. Grandfather never stayed long in one hotel. He said the staff got used to you, and the service became unsatisfactory and they thought they wouldn't get as much in tips as they did from people coming and going.'

'How old were you when Felix Napoleon adopted you?'

'I was ten when my father died.'

'Did you ever meet Hubert, Willoughby's brother?'

'Oh, yes. I told you. He conducted grandfather's funeral service and came back to the hotel to hear the Will read.'

'Did you know that he went to Italy?'

'Italy? No, I had no idea of that. To live, do you mean? But he's a clergyman.'

'He went out to take charge of an English church.'

'Oh, so that's why he didn't come to Galliard Hall.'

'I think he did not come to Galliard Hall for an equally cogent reason. I do not think he was invited.'

'Oh, but Romilly said . . . '

'And others said something different.'

'You don't need to believe that man Luke. He's an awful creature. Anyway, Romilly may have been telling lies about Hubert, mayn't he? I expect he knew he'd gone to Italy, so, of course, he wouldn't have invited him.'

'My information is that he did not invite Willoughby, either.'

'But how can you be sure? After all, Willoughby's body wasn't all *that* far from the house when Romilly and Judith found it. You know, I've been wondering about that. Do you think they knew *where to look?*' She gave the last three words considerable and conspiratorial emphasis.

'I think it more than likely,' said Dame Beatrice, giving her a hard look. 'That does not prove that they killed him.'

'Well, one mustn't say so, I suppose. Do you know when he'll be brought to trial?'

'Romilly? It may not come to that. He is remanded in custody and will make a second appearance before the magistrates in about a week's time.'

'I don't understand these things. I thought he was in prison for killing Willoughby, and would be brought to trial. You see, it's very important to me that Romilly should be locked up for the rest of his life. It is the only thing, except his death, which would make my own life safe.'

'Yes. Your present plan, then, is to stay with Humphrey and Binnie, if they are willing to have you, and if your grandfather's lawyers agree. Have you any plans for the more distant future, in case they do not see their way to having you as a permanent guest?'

'I expect I shall marry Tancred.'

'When I saw Tancred last, he seemed very well satisfied with his present domestic arrangements.'

'You mean he's living with a girl?'

'So it seemed to me.'

'Has she any money?'

'I did not think to ask.'

'You're being sarcastic. If she hasn't any money, I shall have an advantage over her. I like Tancred. He's kind and I think he's very clever. With my money he could write as much poetry as he wanted to, and he wouldn't have to work for a living.'

'*Does* he work for a living?'

'I think he's in advertising. I think he writes rhymes for soaps and cereals and things. He told me something about it the night he slept with me at Galliard Hall.'

'Tell me about the toy trumpet.'

'The toy trumpet?'

'The one which was used at the séance.'

'Oh, *that*! How did you know about the séance? Did Romilly tell you?'

'Yes, he mentioned it. It seems that it made him very angry.'

'How could it? It was his idea, his and Judith's, and they both were present at it.'

'And the nurse?'

'What nurse?'

'The nurse who suggested that the séance should be held.'

'There wasn't any nurse. Why should there be? There was the

medium, of course, and Judith and Romilly and me. That was all.'

'I see. So Romilly and Judith suggested that the séance should be held?'

'Judith, actually. At least, I *think* it was her idea. She wanted to call up my grandfather.'

'Did this thought alarm you?'

'It didn't *alarm* me, but I didn't think it right to meddle in such matters.'

'But you attended the séance.'

'I had no choice. They made me do it. They said it wouldn't be any good without me, so I had to go.'

'What did Judith wish Felix Napoleon to tell her?'

'I don't know. The séance broke up. I broke it up. I snatched the toy trumpet out of the medium's hand and dashed out of the house and flung the trumpet and the medium's tape-recorder into the sea.'

'I thought it was a transistor radio set.'

'Oh, no, it was a tape-recorder. As soon as I saw it, I knew there was going to be trickery.'

'Indeed? What trickery did you suspect?'

'That Romilly had secretly taped some talk of grandfather's about the Will, and that I was not to have the money, but it was to be divided among Romilly, Willoughby and Hubert.'

'But a recording of such a conversation would have no significance, since Felix Napoleon had left a valid Will.'

'They wanted to prove that I had used undue influence. They intended to upset the Will, you see.'

'I think you must be mistaken. They would never have thought that such a means would be tolerated by the courts.'

'That lot would do anything for money. I think, if you'll excuse me, I'll write to Humphrey and Binnie to find out whether they will have me. You *did* say you had their address?'

'There *is* one other thing,' said Dame Beatrice. 'Who was the *other* young woman who lived with Felix Napoleon Lestrange?'

(2)

'So what was the upshot?' asked Laura.

'Nothing emerged that I did not know or had not guessed. She denied all knowledge of Felix Napoleon's young paramour.'

'A bit silly of her. Maiden modesty, just plain ignorance – no, it couldn't be either of those. On her own admission she went to bed with Tancred at Galliard Hall.'

'Yes, it seems she did,' Dame Beatrice agreed.

'I should think the best plan would be to get Hubert over here, and confront Romilly with him. Then we could at least note their reactions.'

'Yes. My good opinion of Rosamund was not enhanced by our interview.'

'I didn't think your opinion of her *was* good. Didn't you say . . .'

'Yes, I did. I think I must go and see Judith.'

'She won't tell you anything to Romilly's detriment.'

'We shall have to find that out.'

'You'll look out for yourself, won't you? They seem an odd lot at Galliard Hall. Do I go with you?'

'It depends upon whether Humphrey and Binnie agree to take Rosamund unto themselves. That is the first consideration.'

'Do you really think they will?'

'I believe I can find means to see to it that they do, on the understanding, as with your parents, that it will be no more than a temporary arrangement.'

'And meanwhile?'

'Meanwhile, I find out whether Humphrey and Binnie *are* prepared to have Rosamund to stay with them. She herself proposes to write to them, and I have furnished her with their address. Before they receive her letter, I shall have spoken to them on the telephone.'

'What do you suppose their reaction will be?'

'I am in a position, as I say, to make it almost certain that it will be favourable.'

'Bribery?'

'Let us call it by a pleasanter name. I am about to play the part of fairy godmother.'

'It comes to the same thing.'

'A cynical observation, surely? There will be (in your phrase) no strings tied to the benevolence I propose to extend. I have already bespoken a partnership in a small but flourishing preparatory school. This I shall have considerable pleasure in presenting to them.'

'In return for services rendered? I can hardly believe it of you!'

'I am sorry that my altruistic actions should be misconstrued.'

'Well, I suppose the guardianship of Rosamund will crop up in the course of your next conversation with Romilly. Shall you go to see him?'

'We shall see. I am sorry for Humphrey and Binnie. I should like to do something for them.'

There was a sound of footsteps.

'Herself, not a picture,' said Laura, as Rosamund, in dressing-gown and slippers, entered the room.

'Here's my letter to Humphrey. You may care to read it,' she said. Dame Beatrice cackled harshly, took the letter and glanced it over.

'I see,' she said, 'that you mention you were once engaged to Willoughby. That would have been before your grandfather's death, of course. Did he know of the engagement?'

'No. We kept it secret, but I think Romilly found out. That's why he killed Willoughby. As for Humphrey, he hates Romilly as much as I do, so, now that Willoughby's dead, I'm going to plot and plan. If Romilly escapes the law, he's not going to escape *me!*'

'Oh, don't be such a nit!' said Laura.

'I mean it! I mean it! Of course, you're so stupid you wouldn't understand! It's Romilly or me, I tell you! Kill or be killed! Well, I'm not going to be the one to die!'

CHAPTER FOURTEEN

Danse Champêtre—Joy in the Morning

'Make tigers tame and huge leviathans
Forsake unsounded deeps and dance on sands.'
Two Gentlemen of Verona.

---

(1)

'I suggest,' said Dame Beatrice, ignoring Rosamund's outburst, 'that you rewrite this letter, leaving out all blood-thirsty sentiments – *litera scripta manet*, do not forget – and address yourself not to Humphrey but to Binnie.'

'He bullies her. He'd never let her do what she wanted to.'

'I have good reason to believe that, in the present case, she would have the whip hand. She is kindly disposed towards you, is she not?'

'Oh, yes. If it were left to her, I'm sure she'd have me.'

'Then it will be left to her. Go back to your room, rewrite your letter in the morning, but, if you will take my advice, do not post it until I have spoken to Humphrey on the telephone.'

'You'll really persuade them to take me?'

'I can but try.'

'You want to be rid of me, don't you? I know why you sent me up to Scotland.'

She retired to bed.

'So say all of us,' observed Laura. 'Nothing like bed!' At ten on the following morning Dame Beatrice put through her call to Humphrey's semi-detached house. She was connected; Binnie answered.

'Dame Beatrice? It's sweet of you to call me. Humphrey is in school. Oh, you thought he would be? Oh, you want to speak to *me!* Would I what? I don't think I can be hearing you properly. I thought you said I was to own a share in a school. You *did?* Oh, goody! And you can make Humphrey the headmaster? I can't *believe* it! Of course I'll tell him about it. There's something else? Rosamund? Poor little Trilby? Wants to come and live

158

with us? Why, of course! I'd love to have her, if Humphrey agrees. Could she bring the baby? I love babies. Oh, didn't you know there was a baby? You ask her. She told Tancred all about it when she slept with him, and Tancred told *me*. Yes, all right, then. I'll tell Humphrey, but I expect he'll think half the school ought to be his, not partly mine. Oh, no, of course I shan't let him. It will be the first time I've had any money of my own, and I shouldn't let him take it away.'

'I wonder what else the little bird told Tancred that night,' said Laura, highly amused when Binnie's remarks were passed on to her. 'I say, I do hope the Provost couple will have her. It will be a weight off our necks, won't it?'

'Until Romilly is released.'

'You think he will be?'

'I see no reason against it, unless Detective-Inspector Kirkby has procured evidence of which I know nothing.'

'And you don't think that's very likely?'

'Who can say? He is a thoroughly painstaking officer and he firmly believes that Romilly is guilty.'

'And there's nothing in Romilly's character to make it seem unlikely, so far as we know.'

'I am not convinced of that. If we stand by our theory that Romilly intends to kill Rosamund at some time after she is twenty-five years old – and he may be in no particular hurry to do that, since, to do it too soon, might bring much stronger suspicion to bear on him than if he were to wait awhile – then surely the last thing it would be safe for him to do would be to commit another murder in the interval.'

'But if Willoughby had been in a position to expose him as an imposter, he was in a pretty sticky position so long as Willoughby was alive.'

'There are two other thoughts about that, you know. We have not yet proved that Willoughby *would* have been in a position to expose him. We may know more about that when I have introduced Hubert to him, but, on present evidence, it seems most unlikely that his nephews had ever met him.'

'I thought you were against bringing Hubert over here.'

'To identify his brother's body, yes, I was. But once we have the responsibility of Rosamund off our hands, I should like to confront Romilly with him to test my conclusions.'

'Be that as it may, what's your second point?'

'That what I took, some time ago, to be Romilly's lies appear, with regard to the most important of them, to be somewhere in sight of the truth. From Binnie's artless prattle it seems to emerge that Rosamund *did* have a baby.'

'But do you think Binnie is to be relied on? I mean, she's such an absolute pinhead that she could easily get her facts mixed up.'

'In the ordinary course of events, I would agree with you. My experience goes to show, however, that one of the things which even the stupidest of women does not get wrong is whether or not a baby has been born, and the identity of the woman who has borne it.'

'She only got the information very much at second hand. And Tancred may have been leading Binnie up the garden. He's quite capable of it. I mean – *would* Rosamund have told him such a thing about herself?'

'*In vino veritas*, child, and I think the same may very well apply to the bed. *In lecto veritas* one would say, perhaps.'

'But then, surely, if that baby is still alive . . . '

'Which Binnie seems to think likely, and which Romilly denies . . . '

'It won't help Romilly if he kills Rosamund. The baby will inherit, won't it?'

'It will be the lawyers' business to decide that, I fancy. Rosamund has only a life-interest in the estate. That being so, I should imagine that, on her death, it passes to the person named in the Will, and that is Romilly Lestrange.'

'Who, as we know, is *not* Romilly Lestrange.'

'*Who* isn't Romilly Lestrange?' demanded Rosamund, entering the room. 'Have you telephoned yet? Has Humphrey answered? Am I really going to live with him and Binnie? Oh, isn't it all exciting!'

'I am happy to have you think so,' said Dame Beatrice. 'Yes, I have telephoned, but Humphrey was out of the house. However, I think you may post your letter. Binnie will be delighted to have you. Tomorrow we will go to see her. She will have heard from you by then.'

'We hope!' muttered Laura, a confirmed critic of the post-office and its ways. 'Did anything strike you as a sort of confirmation of what you'd just been saying?' she asked, when Rosamund had gone out with her letter.

'Quite a number of things are beginning to confirm me in my opinions,' Dame Beatrice replied, 'but, in case I misinterpret your question, pray expound.'

'Well, it's obvious Rosamund hasn't a clue that Romilly is an imposter. That being so . . . '

'Exactly. But pray continue.'

'That being so, it seems to follow that you are right. Willoughby wouldn't have rumbled him either, so why did he have to be murdered? I mean, it seems that Willoughby *couldn't* have been a menace. He'd have taken this Romilly at his face value, the same as Rosamund has done.'

'Yes, I deduced as much, some little time ago.'

(2)

There was no doubt about the warmth of Binnie's welcome. Even Humphrey, enjoying his mid-week half-holiday, contrived to smile at Rosamund. Binnie, in characteristic fashion, came straight to both her points.

'Humphrey says Rosamund can stay, and what's all this about a school?'

'My dear girl, give Dame Beatrice a chance to sit down,' protested Humphrey. 'Yes,' he went on, when she had done this, 'Binnie seems to have got hold of some extraordinary idea that you've promised us a part-share in a boarding-school.'

'I find,' said Dame Beatrice mendaciously, 'that Binnie is distantly related to me through my last husband. She has inherited the blood of the Bradleys.'

Binnie squeaked excitedly. Humphrey scowled at her.

'Related to you?' he said. 'Well, I'm sure that is a great surprise to her, and – er – a pleasure, no doubt.'

'Therefore,' Dame Beatrice continued, 'I have decided, as I have many nearer relatives who will benefit under my Will, to give Binnie something from which I hope she will derive a certain amount of consolation for being left out of it. I know the owner and sleeping partner of a prosperous little preparatory school in Somerset. The headmaster is retiring at Easter. My friend would like to offer you the first refusal of the headmastership, together

F

with a one-eighth share of the profits (which, of course, would be additional to your salary), and Binnie a three-eighths share of the profits, subject to two conditions. First, that you will take Rosamund into your care for as long as she is prepared to stay with you, and secondly that Binnie, who would also receive a salary, albeit a considerably smaller one than your own, shall act as matron, a position for which I feel she is admirably suited. While you are thinking the matter over, you may care to go down and look over the school. Could you go, perhaps, this week-end, taking Rosamund with you?'

'You'll come as well, won't you?' said Binnie, anxiously.

'I should like to do so. I can introduce you to the present headmaster, and so forth.'

'And your friend will retain only a half-interest in the school?' said Humphrey. 'Well, I confess, I hardly know what to say, except that I feel somewhat overwhelmed. A headship! I can scarcely believe it!'

'You've always wanted to be a headmaster,' said Binnie, 'and if I were a shareholder it would be nice for both of us, wouldn't it? And I'd love to be matron and look after the boys and bandage them up and see to the housekeeping and the bedding and the garden and the school fête and the refreshments on Sports Day and give the new boys' mums cups of tea and . . . '

'Yes, yes, my dear. We may take all that for granted. Well, Dame Beatrice, it's very kind of you. Yes, we could manage this week-end, but, really – well, as I say, I am completely overwhelmed. What's more, it seems I owe it all to Binnie.'

Binnie turned to him and impulsively hugged him. In a sedate manner he kissed the top of her head. She began to cry. He sat down and pulled her on to his knee. Dame Beatrice leered maternally at them.

'I shall breakfast at half-past six and leave at a quarter-past seven on Saturday morning,' she said to Laura, when she had returned from her visit.

'Anyway, what *is* all this about a school? Do you really think Humphrey will make a go of it?' Laura demanded.

'I have hopes – more, I have expectations – that he will. Besides, I have an affection for Binnie, and I think she will have an affection for the children under her care.'

'But, if Humphrey bullies the boys as much as he bullies *her*,

I don't see much future for the school with him as headmaster.'

'I think you will find that nothing is further from Humphrey's thoughts. It is no longer in the interests of preparatory schools for the headmaster to bully the boys, or to permit them to bully one another. Humphrey bullies Binnie because he is a thwarted, frustrated man and therefore is easily irritated. Binnie is irritating because she has always had far too little to occupy her mind . . . '

'Such as it is!'

'Very well – such as it is – and not nearly enough money to gratify her not unreasonable requirements. She is quite a pretty woman, and it irks her that she cannot dress prettily. I think you will find that everything will work out quite well, the marriage included. Nothing fails like failure, and now Humphrey will prove that nothing succeeds like success.'

'It's your pigeon, not mine, thank goodness, but why concentrate on Humphrey and Binnie?'

'Because they can further my plans. Altruism, as such, is not a feature of my character.'

'Thank heaven for that! If there's anybody I hate and distrust, it's an indiscriminating do-gooder, and I never *did* seem to see you in such a fearsome rôle.'

'Thank you. As soon as Humphrey and Binnie have seen the school and (I hope) approved of it, I think we may place Rosamund in their charge. Then for the second hearing before the magistrates. After that, we can decide what to do for the best.'

'If the magistrates throw out the case, as you seem to think they will, it won't do for Romilly to find out where Rosamund is.'

'Part of the bargain between myself and Humphrey will deal with that question. Have no fear for Rosamund's safety. I shall have none.'

'Unless she gets some notion about running away from the school, the same as she did from my people at Moy.'

'Ah, well, whom the gods intend to destroy, they first make mad. At any rate, she will be safer with Humphrey and Binnie, in a place of which Romilly has never heard, than with us here, or even with your parents in Scotland.'

'You're so certain that the magistrates are going to dismiss the case against Romilly, aren't you? And you are equally certain that Romilly and Willoughby have never met.'

'I am not certain of it, and, as I said before, I cannot be certain until Hubert and Romilly *have* met.'

'I should say it's a foregone conclusion *they've* met. Rosamund should know. If they met nowhere else, they met at old Felix Napoleon's funeral. Ask Rosamund about it again. Didn't she say that Hubert conducted the funeral service? Willoughby, as the old man's secretary, would certainly have been present, too.'

'Ah, but we cannot show that Romilly was at the funeral, you see.'

'Oh, come, now! If he hadn't been, would Rosamund have gone off with him afterwards to Galliard Hall? She must have been pretty certain of his *bona fides* if she was willing to do that, surely?'

'There is much in what you say. However, to a subject of more immediate importance. We went to Scotland at Detective-Inspector Kirkby's request, to bring Rosamund home. He prefers, it seems, to question her on English soil.'

'Well, I hope she tells him what he wants to know, and I hope it will be the truth. She's a slippery young customer, to put it in the most charitable light, and I don't trust her an inch.'

'You make no allowance for one who knows that her life is in danger?'

'Oh, well, if you put it like that . . . All the same, I feel a violent antipathy to the wench. I suppose it makes me unfair to her, but I can't shake it off. When do you expect Kirkby?'

'I have already summoned him. He must speak to Rosamund before she takes up residence with Humphrey and Binnie.'

'For their sakes, you mean.'

'I have been told that he has already been to see them. They cannot be expected to welcome a second visit from him.'

Kirkby came that same afternoon. He talked to Rosamund in the presence of Dame Beatrice. This was at the girl's own request.

'Now, Miss Lestrange, I believe you knew Mr Willoughby Lestrange quite well,' Kirkby began.

'Well, he was my grandfather's secretary, and at one time I was engaged to be married to him.,

'Were you engaged at the time of his death?'

'Oh, no. I – we broke it off.'

'Why?'

'Look, what has that to do with Willoughby's death?'

'I don't know. I am still collecting evidence. It will help me if you will answer my questions. I am groping in the dark, you see.' He smiled reassuringly.

'Oh, well,' said Rosamund, capitulating to the smile, 'I was afraid grandfather would cut me out of his Will if he found out I was engaged to be married. He didn't approve of marriage. He liked Romilly and Caesar, his natural sons, much better than he liked my father, Harvard, who was his legitimate child.'

'I see. Were you surprised that neither Mr Willoughby nor his brother Hubert was ever invited to Galliard Hall?'

'I didn't think about it. I was glad I didn't have to meet Willoughby again. It would have been embarrassing.'

'Did you know that Hubert had been given charge of the English church in an Italian Riviera town?'

'I – no, I don't think so – that is, I may have known. I can't remember whether I knew or not.'

'That's a little strange, isn't it?'

'No, I don't think so. I've been living a strange and frightening life these last months, and, as Dame Beatrice will tell you, I'm still on the edge of a volcano.'

'I know what you mean, Miss Lestrange. Don't worry. We shall protect you. Now I have only one more thing to ask you, unless anything arises out of your answer to it. Can you remember exactly who were present at your grandfather's funeral?'

'Oh, yes, of course. I didn't go – I was too much upset by his death – and Binnie wasn't there, but otherwise all the relations went – well, I took it for granted they did.'

'*All* the relations? Dame Beatrice, for example, and her sister-in-law, Lady Selena?'

'Oh, I see. I really meant all the relations who were at Galliard Hall. I didn't know I had any others. Grandfather never mentioned any, and I was not the sort of child to ask questions.'

'And the Reverend Hubert Lestrange conducted the service?'

'So I understand. Anyway, I suppose he came back to the hotel afterwards to hear the Will read, and have something to eat and drink.'

'How did he appear to get on with his brother? What sort of feeling was there between them?'

'I don't know. I spent most of the time in my room, crying. Grandfather's death, you see, had turned my world upside down.

I didn't even listen when the Will was read. That's why I went off with Romilly. He said I had to. He said it was in the Will. Willoughby tried to interfere, and they argued, but, in the end, Willoughby gave in, and I went off with Romilly and was shut up at Galliard Hall without any proper clothes or any hope of escape. I went in fear of my life until Dame Beatrice came along and rescued me. Oh, you won't let Romilly go free, will you? Please don't let Romilly go!'

'That doesn't rest with me, miss, but, whatever happens, we'll see you come to no harm. I understand you're going to stay for a bit with Mr and Mrs Humphrey Provost.'

'Oh, yes! Won't it be fun? Binnie telephoned me. They're going to have a school of their own, and I'm going to run the drama group.'

'Very suitable,' said Laura sourly, when this remark was reported to her.

CHAPTER FIFTEEN

Country Dance—Parson's Farewell

'Say to her we have measured many miles
To tread a measure with her on this grass.'
Love's Labour's Lost.

(1)

The Reverend Hubert Lestrange was met at the airport by Dame
Beatrice two days after Rosamund had gone to stay with Binnie
and Humphrey. His resemblance to her son Ferdinand was so
striking that she had not the least difficulty in picking him out.

'It was extremely kind of you to pay my fare,' he said, when the
car was on its way to the Stone House. 'I understand that the
police need my help, but I can't think of anything I can do.
Willoughby and I have been largely out of touch for some time.
I was rather disconcerted when he entered my grandfather's
service, and then when he wrote to me and told me that an un-
married girl was to bear his child, I'm afraid my bump of
Christian charity was considerably diminished. I have seen the
English papers, of course, and I read the report of his death, but
I can tell the police nothing at all about it.'

'It is not directly with reference to your brother's death that
we want to see you,' said Dame Beatrice, 'but I will introduce you
to Detective-Inspector Kirkby, and he will tell you what he
hopes you'll be able to do.'

Kirkby had been in consultation with Dame Beatrice before
she drove to the airport, and was at the Stone House at ten on
the following morning, the day before Romilly was to appear
before the magistrates for the second time. He was introduced to
Hubert and greeted the swarthy young cleric cheerfully.

'I don't know whether Dame Beatrice has briefed you, sir,' he
said, 'but, from what she tells me, you are the one person who
may be able to help us.'

'No, I have told him nothing,' said Dame Beatrice. 'I thought
it best that everything should be discussed at official level.'

'Well,' Kirkby went on, 'tomorrow, if you'll be good enough, we'd be glad if you'd accompany us to court. We've got a man coming before the justices accused of murdering Mr Willoughby Lestrange who, we understand, was your brother. This man represents himself to be your uncle, Mr Romilly Lestrange, but Dame Beatrice has reason to believe that he is nothing of the sort, but is a fortune-hunting imposter.'

'Then what do you require of me?' asked Hubert.

'Why, to tell us whether Dame Beatrice is right,' replied Kirkby, with an air of surprise. 'That is all, sir. There is no need for anything more.'

The clergyman shook his head.

'I am afraid you have had your trouble and expense, and I my journey, for nothing,' he said. 'To the best of my knowledge, I have never seen my uncle. He went out to Kenya before I was born.'

'Family photographs,' suggested Kirkby, hopefully. Hubert shook his head again.

'I have none. I was never shown any. You yourself, Dectective-Inspector, could pass yourself off as my uncle without my being able to contradict you. I am very sorry, but there it is. I can be of no help to you at all.'

'No help to us, sir, but possibly a very great help, then, to the man we are holding in custody,' said Kirkby, disguising his disappointment. 'Just one more question. To the best of your knowledge, would your late brother be similarly placed to yourself? By that, I mean, would he also have been unable to tell us whether our man is Romilly Lestrange or someone impersonating him?'

'I cannot answer for my brother. We have seen little of one another since he became my grandfather's secretary and I entered the Church. On the other hand, I imagine that his circumstances would be similar to my own. Willoughby was younger than myself by two years. Unless he saw my uncle very recently, he would not have been in a position to recognise him. Moreover, even if Willoughby *had* met him (assuming that Romilly had returned to England), he would have had to take his word for it that he *was* our Uncle Romilly. He could not possibly have been in a position to say whether Romilly was what he claimed to be, unless he had my grandfather's word for it.'

'I do not think he had that,' said Dame Beatrice.

'That settles it, then,' said Kirkby. 'We shall have to tell the beaks we have no case. The only motive this charlatan could have for getting rid of Mr Willoughby was that the poor gentleman might have given the game away. Take away that motive, and the ground disappears from under our feet. At least, that's the way I see it.'

'The motive would still hold if Romilly *thought* that Willoughby could unmask him,' Dame Beatrice pointed out.

'Yes, ma'am, I agree, but how are we going to prove that he *did* think it? If he was (as seems pretty certain) the real Mr Romilly's partner in the coffee plantation out in Kenya, he'd know there weren't photographs sent home, I take it, and he'd know that the nephews hadn't been born when Romilly emigrated. No doubt their father sent the news, and he *may* have sent photographs of them when they were children, *but*, as the Reverend Mr Lestrange has just told us, there was no reciprocation. Anyway, it seems to me now that there was no chance whatever that Mr Willoughby could have known that his so-called uncle was an imposter. What do you say to that, ma'am?'

'Several things,' replied Dame Beatrice, 'but perhaps the time is not ripe to say them. I will go so far as to point out, however, that, although it seems more than likely that this Romilly was the real Romilly's partner out in Kenya, even *that* is not an established fact. Secondly, if this Romilly supposed (mistakenly, as it turns out) that Willoughby could expose him, why did he not suppose that some one or other, or possibly all, of the other young relatives would be in a similar powerful position?'

'Yes, I *had* thought of that, ma'am, of course, and, so far, we don't know the answer.'

'Well, I have one more question to put to you, my dear Hubert. Is it true that you officiated at your grandfather's funeral?' asked Dame Beatrice.

'I? Oh, dear me, no. I had no idea he was dead until I had a letter from Willoughby to tell me so, and to inform me that we should get our father's share of the money left him in the Will. I was, even then, in Italy, and had been there for a couple of years. My grandfather was buried long before I got Willoughby's letter.'

'Pelion on Ossa,' said Dame Beatrice. 'I understood that you had been in Italy for merely a matter of months. However, it probably makes no difference, as neither you nor your brother was invited to the house-warming at Galliard Hall.'

'Pelion on Ossa?' repeated the Reverend Hubert. 'No, I assure you! My stipend is anything but large. The money came, after probate had been granted, and I was exceedingly grateful for it.'

'That was not what I meant,' said Dame Beatrice.

'What *did* you mean, ma'am,' asked Kirkby, 'apart from what you said about the house-warming?'

'Only that, if I were Willoughby's murderer, I would be inclined to exclaim, "How all occasions do inform against me!" I am not Willoughby's murderer, but what was a theory of mine is now in a fair way of becoming susceptible of proof. Tell me, Mr Kirkby, why do people lie?'

'From fear, in the hope of gain, for social reasons or just because they're made that way,' said Kirkby.

(2)

'Of course,' said Dame Beatrice to Laura, that same evening, 'we get a different and a more interesting picture if we reverse our point of view.'

'About what?'

'About which party to believe. Led partly by your almost violent antipathy to our fosterling, I long ago examined matters afresh. Let us look at them together. For some little time I accepted Rosamund's story as being true in the main. What if Romilly and, particularly, Judith, are speaking the truth, and Rosamund has been lying?'

'You mean that she *is* Romilly's wife?'

'That is a possibility, among other things.'

'What other things?'

'Let us go back to the beginning of my acquaintance with the inmates of Galliard Hall. Almost immediately I arrived there, I was given two versions of the same thing. A bevy of relatives had been invited as members of a house-party. Judith informed me that they had been invited by Rosamund. Rosamund insisted that they were Romilly's guests.'

'Well, on that, I should be prepared to accept Rosamund's

version. It doesn't seem that she was in a position to invite hordes of relatives to the house.'

'I did accept her version, and I am inclined to continue to do so, but with certain mental reservations. She may not have issued the invitations, but I think she supplied the addresses.'

'So, on point number one, she wasn't lying.'

'On the second point, however, I think she was. She claimed to possess no modern clothes. She insisted that Romilly and Judith caused her to wear nothing but fancy dress so that she could not hope to escape from Galliard Hall without attracting so much attention that she would inevitably be traced and brought back. There is evidence, however, that she had a wardrobe filled with suitable attire which, for her own purposes, she declined to wear.'

'If so, she lied, and the score is one-all, but what makes you think she *did* lie?'

'There is the fact that I was never allowed to see Rosamund's room.'

'That was at Romilly's suggestion, though, didn't you tell me?'

'Oh, no. It was at Rosamund's own wish. Romilly merely pleaded that the room was very untidy.'

'Well, we'll keep an open mind about the clothes, then, with the balance in favuor of a lie by Rosamund, but it's all very sketchy, you know.'

'I realise that. I am not trying to blacken Rosamund's character, but nothing is lost by going over the ground in a critical spirit, and it is always interesting to see what a thing looks like from another angle. Well, then came the rather odd affair of the picture which covered the squint in my bedroom wall. It was Rosamund herself who drew my attention to it.'

'Only because she said it had not been there before you came. You thought you'd been given that particular room because the squint was there, and you deduced that anybody in the adjoining room could hear what passed between Rosamund and yourself while she was having her treatment.'

'Yes, but suppose Rosamund drew my attention to the picture because she wanted me to take it down?'

'But why should she want that?'

'I have not yet made up my mind whether that is what she

wanted, but there is something about which I have misled you. When I realised that a rifle-shot, fired through the squint, would have a fair chance of killing anybody lying in my bed, and when I discovered that the bed was clamped to the floor, so that its position could not be altered, I told you that I took the precaution of changing round the bedding, so that my head was out of range of a gunshot. My feet were in no danger, since I am considerably shorter than a full-length bed. Well, the disturbance I mentioned took place in my room.'

'Good Lord! You don't mean somebody *did* take a pop at you?' Laura looked so horrified that Dame Beatrice cackled. 'Do you know who it was?'

'No. However, I am very much obliged to you for saving my life.'

'When did I do that?'

'Well, as I said before, but for a long and fascinating study of your swashbuckling, romantic nature, I should never have envisaged the possibilities of that squint. Enough of that. Let us proceed. I realised, of course, that if Rosamund really needed psychiatric treatment, the atmosphere in a houseful of guests was the last which I would choose. I suggested to Romilly, therefore, that I should remove Rosamund to my own house and continue the treatment there. To my astonishment he consented, making no conditions and placing no obstacles in my way. I was suspicious of his attitude, I must confess. On the other hand, it hardly coincides with Rosamund's complaint that she was never allowed to leave Galliard Hall.'

'All the same, he did his best to persuade you not to take her to Swanage that first day.'

'I have thought about that, too. His concern for my safety may have been genuine.'

'But you had George with you.'

'Romilly does not know George as well as we do. Besides, a young woman who was prepared to murder *me*, would have no scruples about making sure that my chauffeur did not live to tell the tale. In the country of the blind, the one-eyed man is king. Against a determined gunman, even the most resourceful and courageous of the unarmed are at a serious disadvantage.'

'But she didn't have a gun?'

'Oh, yes, she had a gun, child, but then, you see, so had I.

The difference was that hers was an old flint-lock pistol – part of her costume, she assured me – and mine was a modern automatic.'

'So, in the country of the one-eyed, the two-eyed man was king. Well, all I can say is that, for my own sake, I'm glad I didn't know about this at the time. All the same, you can't mean that it was Rosamund who shot at you through the squint? Why should she, anyway? – not that I'm sticking up for her, of course.'

'The bullet came from a ·22 rifle, so I keep an open mind. However, I was not sorry when the time seemed ripe for me to leave Galliard Hall.'

'I should think not, indeed! Of course, Rosamund *could* have had the horse-pistol merely for show, or to protect herself against Romilly and Judith, I suppose, and an old horse-pistol isn't a rifle.'

'One does not need to exaggerate the significance, if any, of the horse-pistol, and I did not do so. The next point of interest relates to Rosamund and the child, but, so far, the evidence we have is so conflicting that perhaps this is not yet the time to consider it.'

'Do you think there *was* a child?'

'If there was, it might account for Rosamund's conduct as reported by Romilly.'

'Conduct which she denies.'

'And if there was a child, it might be important to find out the identity of the father.'

'You mean it might have been the illegitimate baby mentioned by the Reverend Hubert?'

'Well, Rosamund lived in the same hotel for some years as Willoughby did, and Willoughby has been murdered. I thought at first that it was because Willoughby would have been able to certify that Romilly was an imposter, but, now we can be reasonably certain that Willoughby could not have known this, the picture alters. We have realised that.'

'That's if Hubert was telling the truth. As he's a clergyman, we're inclined to believe him without further proof.'

'Therefore, if we believe Hubert, Romilly was in no danger from Willoughby. Why, then, was not Willoughby invited to Galliard Hall along with the others? That is still the question to which we must find the answer.'

'Perhaps he was, and decided not to go.'

'If so, why did Luke lie about the number of letters he posted? On the other hand, if we suppose (merely for the sake of argument) that Judith was telling the truth when she said that Rosamund, and not Romilly, sent out the invitations, then Rosamund may have had a very good reason for excluding Willoughby.'

'You mean he may have been the father of her baby, and she hadn't forgiven him for seducing her?'

'We might entertain that as one theory, I think, but there could be others.'

'Meaning there is something you've guesssed, and I haven't. Oh, well, that's nothing new. Are you going to tell me what it is? You don't think it was *Judith* who abstracted those two letters?'

'I know nothing now which you do not know. Did anything strike you about the remark made by the manager of the Carlisle hotel?'

'About the other girl, the little friend (as the French have it) of Felix Napoleon? What an old rip he must have been!'

'Yes, about the other girl. I wonder what has happened to her? It might be interesting to find out.'

'I suppose, when Felix Napoleon died, there was nothing for her to do but to fade out. Incidentally, what about the tale Rosamund told about Hubert's officiating at the funeral?'

'I do not suppose she envisaged the possibility of our approaching Hubert to ask whether it was true.'

'Any good confronting her with him?'

'It will not be necessary.'

'Well, what do we do now?'

'That will depend upon whether the magistrates decide in favour of Romilly (we must continue to call him that, I am afraid, although he has no right to the name) or against him. So far, the police have very little evidence for a committal.'

'There's the sword.'

'His prints would be on it in any case, since he picked it up from where it was lying in the grass.'

'That's his story – that he found it lying in the grass.'

'Judith is his witness.'

'Hopelessly biased in his favour, of course.'

'The fact that he reported having seen the body lying out on

Dancing Ledge will also be in his favour. I really see no reason why the justices should commit him.'

Kirkby, however, was obstinately hopeful of a conviction.

'The evidence offered by the weapon is significant, in my opinion, ma'am. I know he says he picked it up on the cliff-top, but the coastguards to whom he reported spotting the body didn't see him with it. It wasn't until I visited Galliard Hall that he produced it and told us this tale about finding it above Dancing Ledge. Says he concluded the death was due to an accidental fall on to the rocks and that the sword had no connection with it. Affected to be quite astounded when he heard that the deceased had died of a stab wound. Then, if his prints (and he, and other members of the household, certainly let us take as many as we liked and made no objection), if his prints, I was saying, had been superimposed on any others, we might be disposed to believe his version, but his prints are the only ones on the hilt of the sword. Of course the defence will be that the murderer had wiped the weapon clean before Mr Romilly handled it, but the prints, taken in conjunction with the fact that he may have reported finding the body as a means of putting up a sort of screen, seem to me quite enough to justify a committal. Besides, there's no real evidence to show that Mr Willoughby could not have exposed Mr Romilly for the imposter he is. The clergyman, Mr Hubert, no doubt spoke in good faith when he told you that neither he nor his brother had ever met the real Mr Romilly, but he could only speak out of his own knowledge, and that may not be sufficient. I think we shall find that the magistrates decide there is a case to answer. I shall be very much surprised if they don't. There's the cook's evidence that the sword belonged to Mr Romilly, although he denies it.'

'I noticed that, at the interview in which you produced the sword, you pressed Rosamund very hard. Do you suspect *her* of the murder?'

'No, ma'am, not to say "suspect her." It was only that, as she was accustomed to wear fancy dress, it just made me wonder whether a sword went with it.'

'Ah,' said Dame Beatrice, 'that, as Laura would say, rings a bell. The first time I met Rosamund she was in costume – that is to say, in stage armour – as Joan of Arc. She was not wearing a sword. I noticed, by the way, that at the time you entirely disregarded my remark that, sword or no sword, she certainly was in possession of an old-fashioned pistol, which she was carrying in her pocket when we went to Swanage together.'

'I didn't disregard it, ma'am. I was on a different tack, that's all. It's not as though the bullet you found came from that pistol, and I didn't want to confuse the issue, me having only a single-track mind, as Mrs Gavin would put it. Moreover, you have never made any formal complaint about that shooting. You merely told me about it in the course of conversation. Whom do you suspect of taking a pot-shot at you?'

'How can I suggest any particular person? There were nine other people in the house, apart from the servants. Of course I think it was Rosamund or Romilly. The only other likely suspect is Judith, but I doubt whether she had murderous intentions towards me. All the same, it will not do, at present, to rule out anybody. No harm was done, as it happens, so the incident has little importance.'

'You can't expect me to agree about that, ma'am. But for the precautions you took, it might have had very great importance indeed.'

(4)

The failure of Hubert Lestrange to denounce Romilly as an imposter deprived the police of their principal weapon. He had briefed an efficient Counsel, and although the prosecution pressed home the incontrovertible evidence that his fingerprints, and his only, had been found on the hilt of the sword, his statement that he had done no more than pick up the weapon and hand it over to the police was accepted by the magistrates, particularly as he also claimed that as soon as he had seen the body lying out on Dancing Ledge he had immediately reported a drowning fatality (as he thought) to the authorities.

The medical evidence, which had been given at the inquest and repeated at the first hearing before the justices, had established that the sword could have been the means by which Willoughby had been killed, but the defence produced expert witnesses who questioned this. The upshot was that the magistrates, accepting Romilly's mistaken identification of the body as an error pardonable under the circumstances, and bearing in mind the absence of motive and that there was no evidence of opportunity, refused to commit him and dismissed the case.

'We'll get him later, on a charge of fraudulent misrepresentation, and see how we go from there,' said Kirkby grimly. He waylaid the Reverend Hubert as that mild cleric was about to step into Dame Beatrice's car to spend his last day and night at the Stone House before he returned to Italy. 'Might I have another word with you, sir? How can you be certain that your brother did not know Mr Romilly Lestrange?'

'Oh, I can't be certain. I can only speak to the best of my knowledge. I don't see how poor Willoughby *could* have known Uncle Romilly.'

'If both were present at your grandfather's funeral, sir?'

'I suppose they could have met like that, if Uncle Romilly had attended the funeral, but Dame Beatrice tells me that she is certain he did not. Lies have been told that I conducted the funeral service – *why*, I do not know.'

'As the so-called liar was not present at that ceremony, it was perhaps not so much a lie as a simple mistake,' said Dame Beatrice.

'You don't believe that, do you?' asked Laura, later.

'Not any more than I believe that this Romilly and Willoughby met at the funeral,' said Dame Beatrice cheerfully. 'Romilly could not *possibly* have attended that funeral. He did not even know that Felix Napoleon was dead until the lawyers sent out the news to him (or, rather, as they thought, to the real Romilly) in Africa, and *that* would have been after probate was granted.'

'Was it by accident or design that Rosamund went to live with Humphrey and Binnie before she had a chance to meet Hubert?'

'It would make no difference whether she met him or not. I am certain she does not know him,' said Dame Beatrice.

'She knew his brother Willoughby, and a bit too well, by all accounts.'

'That is a different story, and is the one which estranged the brothers, if you remember.'

G

CHAPTER SIXTEEN

Calushari Dance—Evil Spirits

'And though the devil lead the measure, such are to
be followed.'

All's Well That Ends Well.

'Surely you're not tailing me again?' said Romilly. The silvery,
romantic portrait of a fashionable lady by Sir Peter Lely gazed
down upon the scene with an equanimity at odds with Romilly's
flushed and apprehensive countenance, Dame Beatrice's interested
leer and Kirkby's massive masculinity. 'I've been acquitted.
You've nothing on me now.'

'Just a continuation of my enquiries into the death of Mr
Willoughby Lestrange, sir, together with a little matter of false
pretences,' said Kirkby.

'You'd better come into the library,' said Romilly. 'Does
Beatrice have to be present?'

'Yes, I do,' said Dame Beatrice. 'I can bring witnesses to prove
that you are not what you represent yourself to be; that you are
no relation of mine; that you have assumed the identity and have
inherited the effects of a man you know to be dead. What do
you say to all that?'

'Witnesses? What do you mean – witnesses?'

'It was very rash of you to bring me here before you had found
out that my son knew the real Romilly Lestrange, and somewhat
foolish to suppose that a man of your age could pass himself off
as one who was at least twenty years younger than you are.
Furthermore, I have noticed that you never wear, although you
appear to possess, spectacles, whereas Romilly Lestrange was
almost blind. Then, again, I doubt very much whether you can
tell me the name of the sitter in a single one of the portraits in
this house – and there are a dozen or more – or the name of the
artist, unless the portrait is signed. Romilly Lestrange was a
connoisseur of paintings. Apart from all this . . . '

'All right,' said Romilly, 'that's enough. I'll tell you everything. I've done nothing against the law. I haven't inherited anything except the ten thousand the lawyers sent me. That's in the bank, and, if you'll drop the matter, I'll pay it all back.'

'False pretences is a serious offence, sir,' said Kirkby. 'It isn't only the money you've taken out of the estate of the late Mr Felix Napoleon Lestrange which is involved. We believe that you have also been engaged in a conspiracy to kidnap the principal beneficiary and that you held her prisoner here until Dame Beatrice came along and rescued her. If you would care to make a statement – that is, if you have any explanation to offer . . . '

'May I write it in my own words? I give in. I think you've got me, but I'm not as much involved as you make out. If I could tell the story in my own words I think you'll see that I haven't done anything wrong except to pass myself off as poor old Romilly when, of course, as you say, I'm *not* Romilly. There's no law to say I can't *call* myself Romilly if I want to, is there?'

'Definitely, if fraudulent representation is involved, sir.'

'But it isn't. Give me a couple of hours or so, and I'll let you have the whole works.'

'Very well. My sergeant will sit in with you.'

'Oh, I shan't attempt to make a bolt for it, or kill myself, or anything of that sort.'

'I'll just fetch my sergeant, all the same, sir, but, before we leave you to it, perhaps you would answer a question Dame Beatrice wants to put to you.'

'I wonder that you believe I shall answer it truthfully!'

'It might very well be in your own interests to do so,' said Dame Beatrice. 'Besides – if I may anticipate my question a little – as Willoughby Lestrange was killed some days before your house-party guests arrived, a truthful answer, as you will perceive, can scarcely harm you. When I thought that you might have killed Willoughby because he was in a position to expose you, I could not believe that you would have drawn attention (as you did) to the fact that he had not turned up. Then I perceived a flaw in this reasoning. Suppose that Willoughby (as I now know to be the case) was *not* in a position to recognise that you were an imposter? I examined the facts, and discovered that it was more than probable that you and he had never met. In that case, you would have no more to fear from him than from any other of the young people you had invited to your house. My question, therefore, is – *was* Willoughby invited, or was he not?'

'Look,' said Romilly, 'you've got me in a cleft stick. I'll admit that, but, simply because of that, you'll have to believe what I say. I have no idea whether Willoughby was invited or not. I certainly thought he was, and his brother, too, but (as you've just pointed out) I wasn't related to the brothers, so I had to ask Trilby for their addresses because she knew them and I didn't. She wouldn't have them at the housewarming, but on this second occasion I insisted, and I thought—— '

'Let's have that statement,' said Kirkby. He went to the door and summoned the sergeant.

'On second thoughts,' said Romilly, 'if the sergeant writes shorthand I may as well dictate it. It will save a lot of my time.'

'Far better, from my point of view,' said Kirkby. 'I can chip in if I want anything enlarged upon or explained. I note you haven't asked for your lawyer to be present.'

'No need. Now you know I'm not Romilly Lestrange I've nothing to hide. Here goes, then.'

'One moment,' said Dame Beatrice. 'As you have nothing to hide, we should like to know your name.'

'Groot de Maas. I'm Cape Dutch. That's one reason why I was able to stay in Africa until 1966. I joined forces with Romilly Lestrange as soon as he first came out to Kenya. He'd bought a half-share in my estate, so we were partners. Later on came the war. It was an odd sort of time, although, of course, the colony had always netted a mixed lot of fish. You'd find English, Poles, Scandinavians and South Africans, especially in Nairobi. The South Africans were mostly farmers. Lestrange and I were partners in a coffee plantation, but we went into town for stores or when we wanted some fun.

'The colony wasn't actively involved in the war. Some of the younger Englishmen volunteered, but, by and large, things didn't alter much until the war was over. When the end came, we seemed to become a dump for high-ranking officers who saw no future for themselves in Britain, I suppose, but had the chance of a good life with us. They weren't the only immigrants. So long as they had the necessary capital to be allowed in, we got other ex-servicemen who became traders, technicians and farm managers – neither fish, flesh nor good red-herring, you might say – and the old snobberies which had always obtained, and which had developed into a sort of feudal relationship between ourselves and our native servants and workers, were gradually overwhelmed. Now, to my mind, snobbery isn't always such a bad thing. It acted in Kenya much as I imagine it does among the so-called County families in England. That's to say, it involves people in a certain code of behaviour and lays certain responsibilities on them.

'Well, those soon went by the board. These newcomers had no feeling for the country as such; they had simply come out to grab what they could. They didn't dispossess us old hands, of course, but they embittered the relations between the whites and the blacks. Most of our work-people – Lestrange's and mine – were Masai, a peaceable, pastoral people, no trouble at all, but the dominant tribe were the Kikuyu, a very different sort of animal, and a lot of the newcomers, not being the best type of white man, put their backs up more than a little, and made them fighting fit.

'The tensions weren't improved by the Indians. There were a good many of these. Some were pedlars who used to go up-country and trade with the natives, but others were money-lenders, very extortionate and bitterly hated and resented. But you probably know all this.

'Well, so far as the blacks were concerned, things went from bad to worse. They were exploited and underpaid in the towns, and they got a pretty dirty deal over land-holding. I'm not saying they were good farmers – they were not. All the same, scientific methods were improving their stock, and health measures were increasing the population, and what they wanted was more land. It hadn't been so bad for the tribes in the old days, because they were partly nomadic and could follow the pasture around. But with these new whites also needing land, the tribes became legally bound to tribal territory, and as much as a quarter of the arable land, as distinct from pasture, was in the hands of Europeans.

'Well, that was the set-up when the Kikuyu got really restive, and the result, as everybody knows, was the emergence of Mau Mau. That came about in 1950, and we were in a right mess, I can tell you. Oaths were taken, all kinds of violence broke out and neither life nor property was safe. Every sort of bestiality was practised, cattle were stolen or killed, and not only Europeans, but fellow-Africans who didn't belong to Mau Mau, were butchered.

'Our own boys, being Masai, were not involved, but that didn't keep us out of trouble. Three times the plantation was overrun, and the third time Lestrange was killed and I was very lucky to escape before the evil business began to die down. Well, after a time, the thing was brought more or less under control. However, to us who knew the country, it was easy enough to see what was going to happen. African nationalism was up on its hind-legs, and by 1960 the political initiative was with the Africans. You'll have read or heard about all this, so I needn't elaborate. It's ancient history now.

'The next thing we feared was a new Mau Mau rising. Some of us sold up and went to Southern Rhodesia or South Africa. As I told you (I think), I was one of them. I settled in Natal. I came to England in 1966 when I heard that Felix Napoleon Lestrange, Romilly's father, had died, and the rest you know.'

'Now let's have the details,' said Kirkby. 'No doubt you have given us a very interesting potted version of the history of Kenya from 1938 to 1960 or so, but we are far more interested in the history of your dealings with Romilly Lestrange and his family during that time.'

'I'm coming to all that, but you had to get the set-up clearly in your mind. I wouldn't want you to think that I was responsible for Lestrange's death. I liked him. We got on well together.'

'Be that as it may – and it's not my purpose to enquire into it at present – what gave you the idea of impersonating him after he was dead?' asked Kirkby. 'We can see you did it to benefit yourself, but how did it begin? Let's have the whole story, shall we?'

'Oh, yes, if you wish it. You seem to know how bad Romilly's sight was. Well, on one occasion, he broke one pair of glasses and had mislaid the other pair, so he asked me to read his mail for him. It was rare enough for either of us to get letters. We didn't talk about the past, either. I knew he had a brother, and the letters I read on that first occasion came from the lawyers and from Lestrange's grandfather. Both were to tell him that his brother had died.'

'Did he seem distressed?' asked Dame Beatrice.

'No. He said, "Poor old Caesar," but that was about all.

Oh, he added that he supposed he was now the only one left. He told me he was illegitimate, but had always got on well with his father. The legitimate son had been killed in the war, and old Felix Napoleon had gone on to say that he was acting as guardian to this son's daughter, a charge that would devolve on Romilly later.'

'And the lawyer's letter was to confirm this, I suppose,' said Kirkby. 'All clear so far. Then what happened?'

'Nothing, until Romilly got killed. We'd been overrun, as I said, but Lestrange and I had never had anything to do with politics, and Mau Mau was basically a political movement, although its bestialities had nothing to do with the government or the majority of Africans. Lestrange had been in Nairobi for two or three days. He and his party were ambushed and slaughtered on their way home. It wasn't Lestrange himself they were after. He simply happened to be there. Almost immediately after. this particular "incident" – to use the cant phrase – troops were drafted in, and Mau Mau went under cover.

'Well, when I knew what had happened, I went through Lestrange's papers and began to pack up his personal belongings with a view to sending them to his relatives. Among the letters I found an old one from his brother Caesar in which he said that "the old man" was not going to forget the two of them in his Will, and, now that Harvard was dead, he thought it might be something substantial.

'Well, I knew who Harvard was, and I was tempted. I thought things over. I knew that Caesar himself was dead by that time, so I decided not to report Romilly's death to the relatives, but to hang on and see what transpired. Once the old man himself was dead – and that was the time for the benefits to be shared out – it seemed to me that, if I chose to represent myself as Romilly Lestrange, there wouldn't, most likely, be anybody to gainsay it.

'Well, as I told you, things didn't go any too well, and I cleared out of Kenya and went to Natal. I took care, when I got there, to let the lawyers know where I was. I knew that Lestrange had never communicated with them direct, so that there was no chance they'd recognise a forged signature. You can work out the rest for yourselves.'

'We'd rather hear it from you,' said Kirkby. 'Do go on. You chose to pretend that you were Romilly Lestrange.'

'Yes, well,' said the pretender, 'I couldn't see that it would do anybody any harm, and I thought it might do me quite a lot of good, if I could pass myself off as Romilly. Then came the business of the girl Trilby – Rosamund to you – who turned out to be the heiress. By the time I heard from her I'd bought a small property in Yorkshire (with my own money, I might tell you) and had decided to stay in England and settle down. I'd given the lawyers my address at their request, and they, it seems, had passed it on.'

'Miss Lestrange wrote to you, then?'

'She did. She pointed out that, with the exception of some cousins whom she didn't know, I was her only surviving relative, and she asked whether she could come and visit me. Naturally, I was a bit flummoxed by this, but, as I thought it might look suspicious if I refused to see her, I wrote back to say that she would be welcome, and she came along.'

'Was Judith living with you at the time?' Dame Beatrice asked.

'Yes. I met her and Luke, my servant, in South Africa. We're not married, neither is she anything more than my housekeeper, no matter what you may think. I suppose Trilby has told you something different, but that is the truth. Well, Trilby came to see us, but Judith didn't like the Yorkshire house, so when Galliard Hall came on to the market for rent, not purchase, we came down here, and Trilby came along with us. That was just over a year ago.'

'For rent?' repeated Dame Beatrice. 'Did that include the furniture and the fittings?'

'Yes. Why do you ask? It included everything. The lawyers gave me excellent references, especially as Trilby was with me.'

'It would account for the pictures which the real Romilly Lestrange would have recognised, although you did not. What made the owners leave such valuable paintings in the house?'

'They are travelling abroad, and are spending time with relatives in America and Australia. I have the house on a three-year lease and everything in it is fully insured, or so the owners told me. I've never bothered to check.'

'Clear, so far,' said Kirkby. 'Please go on.'

'I don't know what more there is to tell you.'

'Oh, surely!' protested Dame Beatrice. 'The mysterious letter summoning my assistance in treating Rosamund, the mysterious shot at me through the bedroom squint, the mysterious business of the death of Willoughby, the question as to whether he and his brother were or not invited to join the house-party, the mysterious assertion that Rosamund had formed the habit of drowning things . . . '

'Oh, well, as to all that,' said Romilly, 'I have no explanation to offer, except that I was in a pretty desperate strait when I sent for you. Trilby had already tried twice to kill me. That girl is utterly depraved and evil.'

'Tried to kill you, sir? Why haven't we heard anything about this before?' demanded Kirkby.

'Don't be a fool!' said Romilly roughly. 'How could I bring the police in on my affairs? Now that you know all the rest about me, I can tell you about the devilish girl, but I didn't want the police poking about while I was passing myself off as Romilly Lestrange. I knew he had relatives all over the place, and I thought the less publicity my affairs had, the better it would be for me.'

'Chapter and verse might be desirable, Mr de Maas. Will you tell us about the times when Miss Rosamund tried to kill you?'

'Once when she enticed me to bathe with her and then deliberately tried to drown me . . . '

'Do not tell me that *you* were the life-sized baby doll!' said Dame Beatrice. 'It seems a wildly inaccurate description, except for the first adjective.'

'And the other time was when she fired at Dame Beatrice, thinking it was at me,' went on Romilly. Then, perceiving his error, for he remembered that Rosamund had known perfectly well that his original room had been allocated to Dame Beatrice during her stay and that Rosamund had visited her there for the so-called treatment, he amended his statement hastily. 'No, I'm getting mixed up. Not that time. At an earlier date. That's why I hung the picture in front of the aperture. It could not be dislodged from behind, from the other side of the hole, you see.'

'You indicated to me that you knew nothing about the squint,' said Dame Beatrice mildly.

'I know, I know. One had to do some quick thinking.'

'I found the bullet. It came from a ·22. How would Rosamund gain possession of a sporting gun?'

'How should *I* know? She's as cunning as a monkey. I searched her room, of course, and found nothing, but there are several guns in the smoking-room and she had the run of the house.'

'I wonder you risked allowing her another opportunity, sir, by filling the house with a number of her relatives, any one of whom might have been suspected.'

'What could I do? Besides, the more the family got to know me as their uncle, the safer my position became, I thought. In any case, on this second occasion, I took the best precaution I could. In fact, I was determined to bring matters to a head. I intended to have an experienced, unbiased witness present.'

'Oh, really, sir? Who was that?'

'On my own responsibility, and without reference to Trilby, I invited Dame Beatrice to join us. I knew that if anybody could put a spoke in Trilby's wheel, *she* could. Of course, I had to find some reason for inviting her, a reason I knew she would accept, so I told her Trilby needed psychiatric treatment, which, in my opinion, she does. The wretched girl must have seen through my little ruse, and took a pot-shot at Dame Beatrice through the hole in the wall. How did you manage to escape?' he asked, breaking off his narrative to ask the question.

'By a slight re-distribution of the effects of the bedroom,' she replied, 'that is all.'

'Well,' said Romilly, turning again to Kirkby, 'what are you going to charge me with this time?'

'Nothing, sir, if you pay back to the lawyers the sum which you say that they paid to you under the terms of Mr Felix Napoleon's Will, and which you state is lying untouched at your bank. My assignment at present is to find the murderer of Mr Willoughby, not to prosecute you for false pretences. That can come later, if need be.'

CHAPTER SEVENTEEN

Country Dance—Mage on a Cree

'He at Philippi kept
His sword e'en like a dancer.'

King Henry V.

---

(1)

'And how much of *that* tale do we believe?' asked Laura, when Dame Beatrice had described the interview.

'Time will tell us that, child. There are two things to be done at present, as I see it. The first is to talk to the man Luke.'

'But I thought you indicated that he is Romilly's tool. That being so, can we believe what he says?'

'In this instance I think we may.'

'You want to find out about the letters of invitation, I suppose?'

'Yes. It is not clear to me why he should have mentioned to the two maidservants that, so far as he knew, Hubert and Willoughby had not been invited.'

'You mean he must have had some reason for actually mentioning them by name? I expect it was because they were the two who hadn't been invited on the only other occasion when there had been a family gathering at Galliard Hall. He would have realised that those were the names on envelopes which must have disappeared.'

'I agree, and that raises an interesting point which I should like to have cleared up. We have enough to do without having minor mysteries cluttering up our path.'

'Do I go with you to Galliard Hall?'

'I see no reason why not, and I shall be glad of a verbatim report of what Luke says in answer to my questions.'

'The only thing is, won't he turn rather coy at the sight of a shorthand writer with a notebook?'

'That we shall need to find out. My impression is that the man, in this particular instance, can have nothing to hide, or he would

187

not have spoken out as he did in the presence of Amabel and Violet.'

'By the way, do you attach any importance to the fact that none of the servants heard that pot-shot which somebody took at you through the squint in your bedroom wall?'

'As George did not hear· it, any more than did the others, I attach no importance whatever to the fact. The Hall is solidly built, my room was on the first floor, and the servants sleep at the top of the house and in another wing.'

'Oh, well, that's that, then. I suppose you'll have to let Romilly (I still call him that) know that you want to talk to Luke?'

'I can hardly do anything else, but I cannot think that he will raise the slightest objection. Why should he? He knows that Luke will say nothing to his disadvantage. The man, although surly, is faithful. In fact, I want to talk to Romilly himself before I tackle Luke.'

(2)

Dame Beatrice had not announced their coming, but it came as somewhat of a surprise to find Galliard Hall deserted except for a caretaker, his wife and his two daughters. The latter turned out to be Amabel and Violet, who received Dame Beatrice and Laura with acclamation and carried them off for a cup of tea in the kitchen.

They were informed that Romilly, whom the servants still referred to as Mr Lestrange, since they had not been told his real name, had left Galliard Hall and did not propose to return. As the rent had been paid in advance and the maids had been given a month's wages in lieu of notice, nobody appeared to object to his sudden departure, and he had left a forwarding address.

'Not sorry, us beant, to see the back of hem and Messus Judeth,' Amabel confided to Dame Beatrice, 'what weth the police and all. And as for that there old Luke, fair gev ee the creeps, he ded.'

'As a matter of fact, it was Luke I came to see,' said Dame Beatrice, seizing upon the opening, 'but I daresay you and Violet will do just as well.'

'About they envitation letters?'

'Yes.'

'Oi dedd'n ought to have let on to Mess Corenna. Oi know that. But you know how 'tes. Mouth opens and sommat comes out as you never entended.'

Dame Beatrice, whose own beaky little mouth did not play her this disconcerting trick, responded sympathetically and then added:

'But that's all over now, and no harm done, as I told you. What *exactly* did Luke say about the letters? Can you remember?'

Violet and Amabel could. They had the unspoilt verbal memories of those who have never had occasion for taking written notes to aid their natural faculties. Corroborating one another without difficulty, they told the artless but highly important story.

'Luke, he blamed us, you see, for tamperen, which us surely never ded. "Oi counted they letters as they laid there on hall table," he says to we. "What have you two gals been a-playen at? Report ee to Mester, Oi well," he says, "ef they letters ant put roight back be the toim Oi goes down to the postbox to catch the post," he says.'

'What did he mean, do you suppose?'

'Oh, he went all on about et, he ded. "There be two on 'em messen," he says. "Oi counted 'em careful as Oi laid 'em down. Eight there was, and sex there es," he says. "Who's been playen the fool, then?" he says.'

'He couldn't have made a mistake in his counting, I suppose?' suggested Laura.

'Hem? He used to fenger the letters loike as ef he couldn't hardly bear not to tear 'em open and read 'em. Oh, no, he wouldn't make no mestake, not old Luke wouldn't. And the job us had to convence un, then, ee'd never believe. Good as told us we'd penched 'em to foind out whether there was postal orders ensoide, ef ever you heard the loike!'

'Do you know whether he reported to Mr Romilly that two of the letters were missing?' Dame Beatrice enquired.

'For certain sure he ded not,' said Violet. 'Hem put hesself in the wrong? Not old Luke, no fear! What he ded say to us, when Mr Romelly was belly-achen about getten no answer from two of his relations, was as how he dedden see how Mester Romelly could expect to get answers to letters that hadden never been sent.'

'Was he still of the opinion that you had impounded the missing letters?'

'Oh, no. Us swore our Bible oath, so then he says, "Then et's that wecked Messus Trelby," he says. "Woulden put nothen past *her*, I woulden," he says.'

'Did you agree with him, I wonder?'

'Could have been Messus Trelby or Messus Judeth, I suppose, or even Mester Romelly hesself, come to that, as took 'em off hall table.'

'Yes, I suppose it could,' Dame Beatrice agreed. 'Can you give me his present address?'

Amabel applied to her father, who produced the piece of paper which Romilly had left with him.

'He told us you moight be comen,' he said. 'He said as how you moight care to see Messus Trelby's room. The gals could show ee whech one et were.'

Rosamund's room was on the second floor.

'Something a bit like Bluebeard's chamber about all this,' muttered Laura, as they traversed the gallery and followed their guide up the second flight of stairs. 'Of course, anything we find in the room could have been planted there since Rosamund left, I suppose.'

'What do you expect to find?' Dame Beatrice enquired. Laura laughed.

'The ·22 rifle and a selection of modern clothes, perhaps,' she said.

'By the way, Amabel,' said Dame Beatrice, as the maid halted at a door on the second-floor landing, 'did Luke realise which particular letters were missing? Did he mention that they were those addressed to the Reverend Hubert and Mr Willoughby Lestrange?'

'I coulden say. He never mentioned any special names, Dame Beatrice, mum. He just said how could Mester Romelly expect eight to come when only sex had had the envoite.'

'What has happened to the cook?'

'Her wented home. Weren't no sense in her stoppen. Nothen for her to do weth our mam here.'

'I suppose it did not occur to Luke, or to either of you, that *she* might have purloined the letters?'

'What for would her do a theng loike that, then?'

'I cannot imagine. Well, let us take a look at Miss Rosamund's room. This is it, I assume?'

The room was large and gloomy. It was panelled in oak from the floor to within a foot or so of the ceiling, the woodwork topped by a plaster frieze. The ceiling itself was plain, unlike the heavily-decorated ceilings of the first-floor and ground-floor rooms. The furnishings consisted of a modern three-foot bed, a bedside cabinet, an enormous wooden chest, an armchair, a dressing-table with a low stool, a bookcase and a double wardrobe.

'Be locked, I daresay,' observed Amabel, as Dame Beatrice went towards the massive piece of furniture. This proved to be so. 'Don't ee fret, then,' the maid continued. 'There's the twen to thes un en Mester Romelly's room. Oi'll breng ee the key.'

Romilly's key fitted, and they soon had the wardrobe open. It contained a fair selection of dresses and suits and a couple of long coats. On the shelf above these were two or three hats.

'Can you date these garments?' Dame Beatrice asked Laura.

'Not the newest fashions, obviously,' Laura replied, 'but quite wearable if you shortened the skirts a bit, I suppose. The hats – well, they didn't come out of the ark.'

'You mean that anyone appearing in these garments in public at the present day would not cause hurtful comment?'

'Oh, no, of course not. You'd easily pass in a crowd if you went out in them.'

Dame Beatrice was looking for maker's tabs. There were none, but there was blood on one of the coats.

'Amabel,' she said, 'when you and your sister first came here, the family, I believe you once told me, were not already in the house.'

'That's roight, Dame Beatrice, mum. Our vecar, he come to our cottage and told our mam as he'd had a letter to say Galliard Hall was let at last, and there was a place for two maids, and he was be-en asked ded he know of any loikely young women, so he gev us first go, knowen us respectable, loike, and be-en chrestened in church and all that.'

'Were you out of a job at the time, then?' asked Laura.

'No, but us dedden loike et where us was, and me and Voilert, us allus wanted to be together, so both of us gev notece and vecar had been sent key of the house, so us went along and cleaned up and aired out, and our mam helped and so ded our dad.'

'You and Violet were here to receive the incoming tenants, then?' asked Dame Beatrice. 'Do you remember how Miss Rosamund was dressed?'

'Oh, yes, of course Oi do.' She touched a tweed costume and indicated a coarse straw hat. 'They there was what her had on.'

'What impression did you get of her?'

'Oh, quiet loike – nothen much to say. Her brought a rare lot of luggage, though – trunks and suitcases and packen cases – took our dad and Luke all their toime to get et all up the stairs.'

'Packing-cases?'

'Ah, too and all. What the fancy dresses come en, Oi daresay.'

'I suppose they are in that large chest.' They went over to it and Laura lifted the lid, for the chest had no lock. 'Did Miss Rosamund ever refer to these?' Dame Beatrice continued, indicating the theatrical costumes which lay neatly stowed away, with Joan of Arc's mimic armour on top.

'Oh, yes, her said her loiked to take part, but her dedden suppose there'd be much chance down in these parts.'

'She didn't say whether she had been on the professional stage, I suppose?'

'No. Come to thenk of et, her covered up a lettle bet, Oi reckon. When Oi was helpen her onpack and that, her says, "Fancy dress dances, Oi mean," her says. "London an't loike this old hole," her says. "Us be gay and happy, and there be noight loife, and all of that koind of theng," her says. "You don't lev down here; you be more loike cabbages," her says. "Oi don't thenk Oi'll be able to steck et," her says.'

Dame Beatrice closed the lid of the chest.

'Was she an untidy young woman?' she asked.

'Ontoidy? Oh, no, Dame Beatrice, mum, her wasn't ontoidy. Made her own bed, put away her thengs . . . '

'When did you first receive the impression that she was not quite like other people?'

'Not tell her started wearen they fancy dresses. That was after her cut and run, and Mester Romelly, he had to go after her to fetch her back, loike.'

'Oh, that actually happened, did it? Do you remember when it was?'

'Shan't never forget et. Upsoide down, the house was. Et was after her and Mester Romelly had their holleren match.'

'They quarrelled, did they?'

'Oi never heard the roights and wrongs. You can't hear all that much through these here old doors and walls. All us heard was Mester Romelly shouten out. Well, next theng us knowed, Luke had to get the car out, and they brought Messus Trelby back. Her had run away, so et seems, on account her coulden get her own way. Well, nothen else come about tell the toime you knows on. Mester Romelly wroites the letters and two of 'em gets lost off hall table, and then you come, and the relations come, and sence then there haven't been a menute's peace in the place. And now they've all gone, and you've come back, and what's to do now Oi *don't* know!'

(3)

'Well,' said Laura, as they drove back to the Stone House, 'that wasn't particularly helpful, was it – except to confirm that Rosamund had plenty of ordinary clothes if she chose to wear them. I mean, even if Romilly *had* locked the wardrobe and taken the key, she could easily have busted the lock if she'd really wanted to. I notice you didn't ask any questions concerning the attempts that Romilly claims Rosamund made on his life.'

'There was no need, child. For one thing, I doubt whether the servants knew anything about them. The attempt to drown him – if there was one – came to nothing, and if, as he alleges, she had already made an attempt to shoot at him through the bedroom squint, we have evidence to show that the servants would not have heard the shot.'

'If it was Romilly who shot at *you*, what motive could he have had? You weren't a menace to him at that time.'

'I think now that it was Judith who shot at me. Romilly's interests were hers, and she was always suspicious of my sessions with Rosamund. I think she feared lest Rosamund might let fall something which might suggest to me that Romilly was not what he represented himself to be. She and, at that time, she and Luke alone, knew that Romilly was, in actual fact, Groot de Maas.'

'I had an idea you thought it was Rosamund who took that pot-shot at you.'

'I did think so, for a time, and, of course, it may be so. Whoever was responsible for inviting the other guests, there can be no doubt that Romilly invited *me*, and that without the knowledge of either Judith or Rosamund, I feel sure. Rosamund may have seen me as an enemy, but, as she had other eliminations to plan, I hardly think, now that I have a more complete understanding of events than I had when I first went to Galliard Hall, that she would have risked killing me. To have done so might have put an end, not only to me, but to her more important schemes.'

'Well, what's the next move?'

'Since we now know that neither Willoughby nor his brother Hubert could have offered any threat to Romilly, the question still before us is the reason for Willoughby's death. I think our next assignment must be another interview with the manager of the Carlisle hotel, who, you will remember, not only gave evidence in court, but who made a most illuminating and helpful remark.'

'About old Felix Napoleon's little friend, you mean? Yes, we agreed we'd have to find her before we could tie up all the loose ends. When do we go?'

'Immediately. We must act before Rosamund leaves the care of Humphrey and Binnie.'

'You think she'll slip her collar and make off?'

'She still intends to kill Romilly Lestrange.'

'But now it's proved he *isn't* Romilly Lestrange, she's got nothing to fear from him. Why don't you tell her? He can't possibly inherit under Felix Napoleon's will, so there's no sense in *either* of them killing the other one, is there?'

'What you say is true, and very much to the point. Nevertheless, I have a fancy to go to Carlisle while Humphrey's zeal in keeping a sharp eye on Rosamund is still at boiling point. There will be plenty of time to talk to Rosamund when we come south again next week.'

(4)

'I particularly want you to accompany us,' said Dame Beatrice to Kirkby. 'To obtain the information which we must have if you are to make out a case against the murderer of Willoughby Lestrange, an official approach is indicated.'

'Just as you say, ma'am. Certainly, from what we've heard, there is no longer any occasion to suspect Mr de Maas of murder, and, now that he's paid back the legacy in full to the lawyers, there's not much point in charging him with false pretences. Merely to assume someone else's name, so long as he didn't benefit fraudulently, isn't such an offence as any magistrate would look at twice.'

'I hope, too – in fact, I confidently expect – that our visit to Carlisle will end in a peaceful settlement all round and put an end to all murderous plots and family disagreements.'

'You wouldn't care to confide in me, ma'am?'

'I think we should manoeuvre without prejudice. You will be fully enlightened, I trust, when we have spoken with the manager of the hotel.'

The manager remembered Dame Beatrice and Laura. Kirkby produced his credentials and asked for the privilege of a few words in private. The manager's apartment was on the first floor, to which he preceded them and, after offering them chairs, he closed the door and went over to the sideboard for drinks.

'I hope nothing wrong with the hotel,' he said, offering beer to Kirkby, sherry to Dame Beatrice and whisky to Laura.

'Nothing at all,' said Kirkby cheerfully, looking at the froth on his beer with a connoisseur's eye. 'Far from it, so far as I know. Actually, I'm here with what you might call a watching brief. I've come at Dame Beatrice's invitation. She wants to ask you some questions about a gentleman who was resident here up to the day of his death.'

'Mr Felix Lestrange, I take it,' said the manager. 'A lively old gentleman, if I may say so, but a generous guest. Lived here for years and became a law unto himself, as they will, you know, old people, especially when they're financially independent and in a position to pay for their fancies.'

'And Felix Napoleon's fancies lay in the direction of young women, I believe,' said Dame Beatrice.

'Oh, well,' said the manager, returning to his chair with a glass which contained a finger of whisky and a great deal of soda-water, 'I never believed the story that one was his granddaughter, and the other his great-niece, you know. Still, they all had separate rooms and I've no doubt he squared the chambermaids when necessary, and I will say that all three of them were very discreet. It was the secretary, who also claimed to be some sort of a nephew to the old gentleman, who was the cause of the upset, I imagine.'

'A granddaughter and a great-niece?' said Dame Beatrice. 'Yes, you appeared to mention two girls when we were here before. The trouble is, you see, that there is some confusion about the terms of the late Felix Napoleon's will. I am here to try to establish which of the two girls my late cousin intended should be his heiress, and which was to remain without benefit. I am hoping that you can help me.'

'Then why the detective-inspector?' asked the manager.

'I'm investigating a case of murder which may tie up in some way with Dame Beatrice's enquiry,' Kirkby replied. 'Oh, nothing whatever to do with you. This happened in Dorset, so it could hardly be further away from your hotel. Don't give it a thought.'

'I wish you to describe these girls,' said Dame Beatrice, 'and then to tell us what you meant by your reference to Willoughby Lestrange, the secretary.'

'Oh, if that's all – that's the young man who was murdered in mistake for his brother, or some such, isn't it? The head waiter drew my attention to a piece in the paper about it, but I can't say I took much notice. The two girls? Well, the one he brought with him – she was not much more than a child at the time – this would have been some years ago, of course – was a slightly-built, dark-haired, dark-eyed young thing, quite pretty and very shy. The two of them, she and Mr Lestrange, lived on terms of close relationship, and the girl, of course, was at boarding-school. It was during term-time that the old gentleman entertained his other ladies. As I said, he was very discreet. There was never any open scandal, and, until the granddaughter blotted her copybook with the secretary, there had never been any other ladies of her grandfather's fancy about the hotel when she came home for the holidays. Of course, the business with the secretary came long after she had left school.

'Well, she left school when she was, I should guess, seventeen or eighteen years of age, by which time Mr Lestrange had been resident here for some years. Then he took her travelling abroad for the best part of a couple of years and, when they came back, the party numbered four – the old gentleman, as lively and genial as ever, the secretary, the dark young lady, whose name was Rosamund, and a fair young lady of about the same age, who didn't sign the book because the old gentleman signed for the whole party, so we never found out who she was, except that he claimed she was his great-niece.'

'But you heard her name?' suggested Dame Beatrice.

'The old gentleman called her Trilby, but I think that was by way of being a joke between them, because the granddaughter and the secretary both called her Dora. Well, it was pretty clear that Mr Lestrange had picked her up somewhere on his travels. Mind you, she was a lady, if you understand me. She wasn't gutter-trash. She was polite and very correct in public, but there were rumours among the staff that I had to deal with pretty drastically, because the old gentleman, what with his regular payments, his drinks and his cigars, was a valuable guest and the last thing I wanted was to lose him.

'Well, there was no open scandal – never was, so far as the old gentleman was concerned – until it became pretty clear that there was something very wrong with the granddaughter. To begin with, the old gentleman neglected her in favour of the other girl, and she was thrown far too much into the society of the secretary. The parties would all go out together, but, after a time, they did not come home together. It was always Miss Rosamund with the secretary, whose name was Mr Willoughby Lestrange, and Miss Dora with the old gentleman. The secretary and Miss Rosamund were always back well before the other two, and reckoned to go up to the old gentleman's suite, but rumours began to circulate that they really went into the secretary's bedroom, because the desk had orders to put a call through to Number Thirty-six as soon as Mr Felix and Miss Dora arrived at the front door.

'The next thing we knew was that there had been a terrible row and that Miss Rosamund had been sent packing. Miss Dora and Mr Willoughby stayed on, although Mr Willoughby looked pretty hang-dog for the next few weeks. However, a letter came for him one day with an Italian stamp on it, and that seemed to cheer him up no end.

'Well, as you know, in 1966 the old gentleman died. The funeral took place from here, and, when it was over, Mr Willough-by left, but Miss Dora stayed on until after probate was granted. What expectations she had I don't know, but she was in high feather until a gentleman turned up here, signing in as Mr Romilly Lestrange. He said he'd heard of the old gentleman's death, had been sent a copy of the Will, and had flown over from

South Africa to see whether he could be of any help to his niece. The upshot was that he and Miss Dora went off together, and that's as much as I know.'

'You never believed that Dora *was* his niece, I suppose?' suggested Dame Beatrice.

'I was pretty certain she wasn't, but what was I to do? The new gentleman's name was Lestrange, and Mr Felix had always claimed that Miss Dora was his great-niece, so it wasn't up to me to say anything. None of it affected the good name of the hotel, and it was none of my business, anyway.'

'You never discovered what had become of Rosamund, of course?'

The manager shrugged.

'It was none of my business,' he repeated.

CHAPTER EIGHTEEN

Hornpipe—The Boat Comes Home

'Tell him there is measure in everything, and so dance
out the answer.'

Much Ado About Nothing.

---

(1)

'But how did you tumble to it, ma'am?' asked Kirkby, when they
were on their way home, having dined and spent the night at the
hotel. 'It's very rich, I must say – almost Gilbertian, in fact – both
Mr Romilly and Miss Lestrange being impostors and each taking
the other for the genuine article. What put you on the trail?'

'Laura's unaccountable dislike of Rosamund, whom, I suppose,
we had better call Dora or Trilby, the girl's own posing and play-
acting, and, above all, the murder of Willoughby.'

'You mean *she* murdered him?'

'Well, someone did, and, so far as we know, she was the only
person with a motive.'

'I see that now, ma'am, but you seem to have seen it all along.'

'By no means. It did not dawn on me until it was clear that Mr
de Maas could not be Romilly Lestrange. When, however, I
realised that not one of my younger relatives was able to expose
him for the impostor that he was, I began to wonder why, on the
two occasions on which he held a house-party, the same two young
men were not invited. Hubert, of course, on both occasions, must
have been abroad, but that did not apply to Willoughby.

'At the house-warming I understand that Dora made an issue
of it, and insisted that neither brother was to be invited. The maid
Amabel told me that there had been a quarrel and that the girl had
tried to run away. On the second occasion Romilly seems to have
put his foot down, obtained their addresses from her, and added
them to his list of guests. He wanted to be sure that *all* the
younger members regarded him as their uncle. As, of course,
Willoughby would have been in a position to expose Dora as soon
as he saw her, she abstracted the two letters from the pile before

199

Luke took them down to the post-box, not realising that he had already counted the envelopes and read their superscriptions.

'Well, with Dora it was in for a penny, in for a pound, I suppose. She wrote her own letter to Willoughby, and arranged to meet him. What she said in it we shall probably never know for certain (although I can guess) but, whatever it was, it was sufficiently threatening or persuasive to bring him to this part of the world. Realising that so long as he was alive her impersonation of Rosamund was a source of danger to herself, she met him, treacherously stabbed him to death and rolled the body down the cliff at or near Dancing Ledge.'

'We'll have a job proving it, ma'am.'

'I know, but I found bloodstains on her coat, and she would have known of the sword which was found. It had been used to cut the cake. I accept the cook's evidence as to that. She purloined it . . .'

'How did she manage to stab him with it, though? He was a tall young fellow and she's only a slip of a thing.'

'I think she stood at the foot of the steepest and most tricky part of the descent – you will know the bit I mean – called to him, and then, as he came bounding and sliding, in the usual careless, young-man sort of fashion, down the sharp and awkward slope, she picked up the sword from where she had hidden it in the grass, and spitted him on it,' said Laura. 'That's what I should have done.'

'Taking a big chance, Mrs Gavin,' said Kirkby critically. 'Suppose it had only grazed him, or bounced off a rib or something?'

'Well, the plain fact is that it didn't,' said Laura. 'Then, I suppose, she put her foot on the corpse – he'd have fallen backwards, most likely, if that's the way it was done, because of the force with which he was careering downhill – pulled out the sword, wiped it clean, got the corpse to the edge of the cliff and tumbled it over, leaving the sword in the grass, where Romilly (de Maas) found it.'

'Yes,' said Kirkby doubtfully, 'but we spoke to the people at the farm and they had seen nobody.'

'The chances are that there was nobody to see, because you can reach Dancing Ledge without going through the farmyard at all, so long as you don't mind a long cast round. You can reach the coast by various tracks over those hills,' argued Laura. Kirkby turned to Dame Beatrice.

'What I'd really like to know, ma'am, is what took Mr de Maas and Miss Judith there, the day they found the sword,' he said.

'Maybe nothing but chance, you know,' said Dame Beatrice. 'And, in spite of Laura's dramatic reconstruction of the event, I doubt very much whether it was the *sword* which killed Willoughby. I think he would have seen a thing that size in time to avoid it. I think Dora left it there as a blind, knowing perfectly well that if it was traced to anybody it would be traced to de Maas, as, of course, it was. Besides, although I greatly admire Laura's spirited picture of Willoughby galloping down the hill and spitting himself on the sword, I cannot help realising that, from the spot Laura means, to get to the edge of the cliff would involve a considerable effort if one were burdened with the corpse of a man considerably taller and heavier than oneself.'

'What is your theory, then, ma'am? I see the difficulty of accepting Mrs Gavin's reconstruction. What is yours?'

'Oh, I feel certain that they met on the cliff-top itself. No other theory is half as likely.'

'But what argument could she have used to persuade him to meet her there? It's a wild and desolate spot in mid-February.'

'He may not have known that until he got there. I think she probably wrote him to the effect that she was in durance vile and in fear of her life, and that old Felix Napoleon had given her a considerable sum of money before he died instead of mentioning her in his will. I think she may have told him that she was willing to share her gains with him in return for his help in getting free from Romilly, as she would have called him. She does not know, even now, that he is Groot de Maas.'

'Do you think that, when she wrote, she claimed to be Rosamund?' asked Laura.

'No, because I have an idea that she thought Willoughby knew quite well where Rosamund had gone when her grandfather turned her adrift, and that it was not to Galliard Hall. Of course, Dora could not meet Willoughby there, where she was masquerading successfully as Rosamund, but it was safe enough to assume her own identity at an assignation during which she knew she was going to kill him. As she saw it, so long as he was alive, he was a threat to her safety.'

'If he wasn't killed with that sword, Dame Beatrice, we shall have to find the weapon she used. Have you any theories about it?'

'Only that it was something short and handy. A fairly broad-bladed kitchen knife is the likeliest thing, unless she could get hold of a dagger. She denied ever having had a weapon as part of a fancy dress, but that assertion may well be disregarded, I think. I know that an eighteenth-century horse-pistol was in her possession, and we both know that there was at least one sword in the house. I think we may venture to say that you will trace the weapon in time, unless she flung it far out to sea, as well she may have done.'

'I can see why she decided to kill Willoughby,' said Laura. 'She was safe only so long as he never came to Galliard Hall. But she need not have given de Maas Willoughby's address. How did she know it, anyway.'

'I'll ask her,' said Kirkby. 'It's clear they must have kept in touch after the old gentleman's death.'

'She probably got it from the lawyers,' said Dame Beatrice. 'Willoughby is almost certain to have kept in touch with them in the hope that Felix Napoleon had left him some money.'

'Could he expect *that*, when he had caused so much trouble for his cousin, the real Rosamund?' asked Laura.

'Well, Felix Napoleon kept him on as his secretary after he had turned the girl out.'

'Yes, but that seems so unaccountable.'

'Not if you allow for Felix Napoleon's mentality. A pregnant unmarried granddaughter was one thing - a problem and an acute embarrassment, no doubt. A young man on whom he had grown to depend and who had done no more than take a leaf out of his own book, was quite another. However, we shall know more about all this when I have made contact again with the Reverend Hubert.'

'If Felix Napoleon had turned the real Rosamund adrift, you'd think he would have cut her out of his will,' said Laura.

'May have meant to do it, but never got around to it,' said Kirkby. 'People do tend to put things off.'

'It is another point to which Hubert may be able to furnish an answer,' said Dame Beatrice. 'However, we have at least made sure that the scoundrelly de Maas will not carry out his former plan of murdering Dora after the twenty-ninth of May.'

'You'd better put her wise,' said Laura. 'So far, as you say, she hasn't a clue that de Maas isn't Romilly.'

'I'll be the one to let her know, ma'am,' said Kirkby. 'In view of what Dame Beatrice has told me, I have some awkward questions to put to that young lady.'

At this moment the telephone rang. Laura answered it, and came back almost at once.

'She's hopped it,' she said. 'That call was from Binnie. She wanted to say a lot more, but I cut her off. Dora's bed hadn't been slept in last night, and there's no sign of her or any message left. Binnie is naturally somewhat agitated.'

'I'll get along there at once, if you'll give me the address, ma'am,' said Kirkby. 'I don't want her to slip through my fingers, although I'm bound to say that the evidence I've got against her so far isn't going to get her convicted of murder.'

'There's blood on that coat,' said Laura.

'Meanwhile, I shall get on the track of the missing heiress,' said Dame Beatrice. 'She probably does not realise her good fortune. But first for Mr Hubert.'

(2)

The Riviera town just inside the Italian border was sheltered on the north by hills and even at the end of March was pleasantly warm. There was no difficulty in finding the English church, and the near-by vicarage proved to be a small, white villa set in a garden which overlooked the sea.

The door was opened by a smiling Italian maid to whom Dame Beatrice presented her card. They were invited to wait while the girl conveyed the card to her mistress. They were not kept more than a couple of minutes before the maid reappeared and ushered Dame Beatrice and Laura into a spacious room which seemed to combine the properties of drawing-room and study, for, in addition to deep armchairs, ornaments and vases of spring flowers, there was a roll-top desk in the window and shelves of books against the wall.

A tall, dark-haired girl almost ran to meet them, holding out both hands.

'Hubert got your letter,' she said. 'He's told me all about you.

I *am* so glad to see you. Have you anywhere to stay? If not, I can find you beds.'

'Thank you, but we are off again almost at once, my dear Rosamund,' said Dame Beatrice. 'We are putting up at the *Splendide* for a day or two, but my work does not permit me to make a longer stay.'

'Well, do sit down, and I'll get Lucia to bring us some tea. We keep English customs here. I'll go and wake Hubert. I make him take a *siesta*. He works very hard, and needs the rest. I won't wake the baby, but after tea I'll take you up to have a peep at him. I'm going to have another one in October – Hubert's baby this time.'

(3)

'So you guessed all the time that Hubert had married Rosamund,' said Laura, as they made their way back to their hotel. 'He didn't tell you so, when he came over to England, did he?'

'No, he did not. I think he believes in doing good by stealth, and probably would be among the first to blush when he found it fame. Having learned of his brother's importunity and Rosamund's plight, he felt he must come to her rescue.'

'And Rosamund, armed with her birth certificate and other proofs of identity is coming back with us to England to see the lawyers and claim her rights.'

'Together with Hubert and the baby, yes. She will want to have him with her, and, of course, he may be needed as a witness.'

'But if he married Rosamund after Felix Napoleon turned her out, why didn't you get *him* to denounce Dora? She was in as much danger from him as from Willoughby, wasn't she? After all, who would know better than Hubert that she was an impostor?'

'Yes, but I was not sure of that at the time. Besides, I should have been unwilling to expose him to danger, and Dora is an extremely dangerous person.'

'Wonder where she is? Did you expect her to leave Humphrey's house?'

'Well, certainly not quite so soon. Romilly must have got in touch with her and told her that I had unmasked him, so that she had no need to fear him any longer. I wonder where she has gone?'

'Oh, Kirkby will find her and charge her, I suppose.'

'With the murder of Willoughby, you mean?'

'Well, I know he needs more evidence than he has at present, but it can only be a question of time before he collects it. There are the bloodstains, and now we know she had proper clothes to wear, she could have slipped out of the house at any time.'

'I am not at all sanguine as to the outcome of his enquiries. As you know, proof of motive is not nearly as important in a criminal court as proof of means and opportunity.'

'Well, as I say, those won't be difficult to establish, surely? To go on to another point, why was Willoughby against marrying Rosamund himself? Why leave his brother to hold the baby? After all, it was his child. He wrote to Hubert to confess that he was the father. That's what estranged the two brothers.'

'I should not be at all surprised to find that Willoughby was already secretly married.'

'To Dora?'

'Yes. It would explain, better than anything else I can think of, why he was willing to meet her at such an out-of-the-way spot as Dancing Ledge.'

'I don't suppose we can ever prove that they were married, though. He could have used a false name.'

'I see no need to prove it. I am concerned only to see that Rosamund gets her rights. I confess, though, that I should like to know where Dora is.'

'Do you want her to get a life-sentence, then? Personally, I should think that a rotter like Willoughby, married to one girl and getting another one into trouble, is better out of the way.'

'The law would hardly agree with you.'

'Willoughby seems to have been his great-uncle all over again. How much of a villain *was* old Felix Napoleon, do you suppose?'

'We have only my sister-in-law's word for it that he was a villain at all.'

'I think it was terrible to turn Rosamund away at a time when she needed all the help she could get. Apart from that, though, didn't you tell me that he was lucky to escape a charge of fraudulent conversion or something?'

'Ah, yes, of course. And Ferdinand connived at this piece of immorality by showing him a loophole in the law.'

'You said just now that you hadn't expected Dora to run away from Humphrey and Binnie *quite so soon*. You did expect she would leave them, then?'

'Oh, yes, I knew she would, once she had received my letter.'

'What letter?'

'I wrote to her just before we left England to inform her that on the day she received my letter we should be on the boat-train for the Continent to pay a visit to Hubert *and his wife*.'

'You think she knew that Hubert had married Rosamund? I thought you said . . .'

'Oh, my letter to Dora was a shot in the dark – or, let us say, in the half-light – but there does not seem any doubt that it found its mark.'

(4)

The last word, in a sense, was with de Maas. Some months later Hamish was at home for the school summer holiday. Kirkby had not found Dora, neither had he uncovered any real evidence against her except bloodstains whose origin he could not check. When the post came one morning, Hamish, accompanied by his Irish wolfhound and his Yorkshire terrier, picked up his baby sister and went dashing out of the room to collect the letters from Celestine. He came bounding into the breakfast room, the baby gurgling, the terrier barking, the dignified wolfhound at his heels, put down his sister, took the letters from between his teeth and handed them over to Laura, whose job it was to sort them.

'Hullo,' she said, 'there's one from the Argentine.'

'Yes, for Mrs Dame. I saw there was. Please may I have the stamp?' asked Hamish. The letter was from the erstwhile Romilly. It read: *If you can't murder 'em, marry 'em. Love from Groot and Dora de Maas, Judith and Luke.*

'Well!' said Laura. 'Back to Square One with a vengeance! How on earth did he get her to marry him? She was always scared stiff of him, I thought.'

'Like most actresses, she is a realist,' said Dame Beatrice. 'There was no need any longer for her to fear de Maas, and she was penniless, with all her plans gone awry. Besides, she knew that Kirkby would be on her track. It is notoriously difficult to extradite criminals from South America, and contrary to legal practice to obtain evidence from a husband against his wife.'

'I see another of your letters is postmarked Duncastle,' said Laura. 'Is it from . . .?'

'Yes.' Dame Beatrice opened it. 'It is from Binnie. The school is flourishing, Humphrey is nice to her, and they are expecting their first baby in December.'

'I suppose you're asked to be godmother.'

'Well,' said Dame Beatrice, 'practice makes perfect, they say, and by now I have lost count of the number of my god-children.'

'In *The Merchant of Venice*,' said Hamish, 'Gratiano wished Shylock's godfathers were jurymen.

' "Had I been judge, thou shouldst have had ten more,

' "To bring thee to the gallows, not the font." '

'Mamma, are you glad or sorry they've done away with hanging people?'

'It depends on the people,' replied Laura. 'In this particular case, the question doesn't appear to arise, I'm pleased to say.'

MORE VINTAGE MURDER MYSTERIES

EDMUND CRISPIN

Buried for Pleasure
The Case of the Gilded Fly
Holy Disorders
Love Lies Bleeding
The Moving Toyshop
Swan Song

A. A. MILNE

The Red House Mystery

GLADYS MITCHELL

Speedy Death
The Mystery of a Butcher's Shop
The Longer Bodies
The Saltmarsh Murders
Death and the Opera
The Devil at Saxon Wall
Dead Men's Morris
Come Away, Death
St Peter's Finger
Brazen Tongue
Hangman's Curfew
When Last I Died
Laurels Are Poison
Here Comes a Chopper
Death and the Maiden
Tom Brown's Body
Groaning Spinney
The Devil's Elbow
The Echoing Strangers
Watson's Choice
The Twenty-Third Man
Spotted Hemlock
My Bones Will Keep
Three Quick and Five Dead
Dance to Your Daddy
A Hearse on May-Day
Late, Late in the Evening
Fault in the Structure
Nest of Vipers

MARGERY ALLINGHAM

Mystery Mile
Police at the Funeral
Sweet Danger
Flowers for the Judge
The Case of the Late Pig
The Fashion in Shrouds
Traitor's Purse
Coroner's Pidgin
More Work for the Undertaker
The Tiger in the Smoke
The Beckoning Lady
Hide My Eyes
The China Governess
The Mind Readers
Cargo of Eagles

E. F. BENSON

The Blotting Book
The Luck of the Vails

NICHOLAS BLAKE

A Question of Proof
Thou Shell of Death
There's Trouble Brewing
The Beast Must Die
The Smiler With the Knife
Malice in Wonderland
The Case of the Abominable Snowman
Minute for Murder
Head of a Traveller
The Dreadful Hollow
The Whisper in the Gloom
End of Chapter
The Widow's Cruise
The Worm of Death
The Sad Variety
The Morning After Death